CHASING OBLIVION

CHASING OBLIVION

EVAN GRINDE

QUANTUM RUSH
LITERATURE COLLECTION

Published in the United States by Quantum Rush Literature Collection, an imprint of Quantum Rush, Virginia.

www.quantumrush.com

QUANTUM RUSH and the Quantum Rush colophon are trademarks of Quantum Rush

ISBN 978-1492869818

ASIN B00ED6K1CE

Printed in the United States of America

Cover design by Evan Grinde

Cover photography by Claire Chewning

First Edition

To those who inspired me

and made this journey possible

I have come to believe that the whole world is an enigma, a harmless enigma that is made terrible by our own mad attempt to interpret it as though it had an underlying truth.

– Umberto Eco

CONTENTS

Began: April 2012

Finished: August 2013

Created and Written by:

Evan Grinde

CHASING OBLIVION

PROLOGUE

11 JANUARY, 2009

A low rumbling broke the silence that had previously held captive the lonely African countryside. A wanderer traveling along the dusty dirt road turned a weather-beaten face to identify the source of the noise. He raised a tanned arm to shield from his eyes the midday summer sun.

Rising above the distant horizon was a convoy of vehicles that appeared to be headed the wanderer's way. The man squinted his green eyes to get a better view. A moment later, a series of rifle shots sounded, rolling through the verdant hills. Youthful whooping followed.

The traveler turned away at once and leapt into the dense brush bordering the road. He crawled away through the jungle vegetation as swiftly as he could, lugging along his large bag at his side the whole while.

When at last it sounded as if the growling engines were right behind him, he stopped and took cover behind a thick-trunked tree. His breathing remained calm and steady. He turned to peek around the tree, expecting to watch the trucks pass. The four LRA vehicles came to a sudden halt instead.

The wanderer's Bantu — the native dialect of this region of Uganda — was rusty, though he was able to understand most of what the rebel boys were saying nonetheless.

"Here, here!" one of them exclaimed excitedly before jumping off the back of the lead truck. He was a native child of no more than ten. The muzzle of the AK-47 slung across his shoulder grazed the crooks of his knees.

The eight other boys, each of whom looked to be the child's senior, remained sitting in the back of the vehicle. Several boys in the rears of the three other vehicles stood up to begin shouting and brandishing their rifles.

A man donning a crimson beret stepped out from the passenger seat of the lead vehicle and slowly approached the child. He set his hands on his hips — his fingers brushing against the handle of a pistol strapped to his waist. With an unimpressed scowl, he stared the child up and down before sweeping his gaze around in all directions. Seemingly dissatisfied, he turned his gaze back on the child.

"No white man," the man wearing the beret said definitively. "Idiot boy. White man don't come here."

"But I saw him!" the child argued. "Wait. I find him," he claimed before raising his AK and firing it uncontrollably into the brush.

The rounds tore through the jungle vegetation and buried themselves into the tree trunks like a hard rain on dry sand, each snapping like a firecracker as it made impact. One bullet whizzed by an exceptionally thick trunk to graze the fleshy surface of the wanderer's forehead. The man in hiding jerked his head back in pain and gritted his teeth, but was careful to make no noise.

After the magazine clip of the child's weapon had been emptied, the other boys began to scoff. "See? No white man," they jeered.

The wanderer, pressing the palm of his hand against his

new wound, turned to peek around the tree once more. He turned away again immediately, though, when the bereted man took the pistol from his holster and seemed to aim it directly at him. A single shot fired a moment later.

:-:

Not even a mile away, a disheveled, middle-aged woman crawled out on all fours from beneath a hollow in a tree as the shot rang out. Her clothes were in tatters. Her light brown hair was filthy and frayed. Her blue eyes — wild and fearful.

"They're coming," she muttered frantically to herself while stumbling towards the adjacent river. "They're coming. Must stay safe. Must stay— They're *coming!*" she snapped savagely, stopping in mid-stride to face a tree that had strayed too close for her comfort. She stared at it blankly for a moment before slowly tilting her head away. She once again began to stagger towards the water. "They're coming... They're coming..." She whispered over and over.

:-:

The wanderer slowly slid a hand into his bag and, after several long moments had passed, discreetly turned his head to look around the tree-trunk.

The boys in the rears of the trucks were laughing. The man donning the beret had resumed his seat in the lead vehicle. With a holler and a flick of his wrist for all to see, the vehicles' engines were reignited and the procession began again.

The child lay facedown dead in the dirt, stripped of his gun, of his shoes, and of his makeshift uniform.

The traveler shut his eyes and let out a deep sigh of relief. After tearing a strip of cloth from his shirt to wrap around his bleeding head, he checked his watch and pursed his lips in satisfaction. Though the plan was not going exactly as anticipated, the trucks had at least passed by on schedule. He must be close. When the rumbling began to fade away, he got to his feet and took off through the jungle.

:-:

"Come! Come, my dear. They've found us! We must... We must find... They're coming. They're coming!" the woman rambled feverishly as she approached the bank of the river. A week-old corpse lay headfirst and facedown in the passing waters — the toes of its feet buried in the sands of the shore. "That's enough drinking for now. No more! We must leave. They're coming. They've found us! We must find safety. They're coming..." She grabbed the body by the ankles and dragged it up the riverbank towards her shelter. Buzzing insects swarming the body flew into her mouth and eyes, but she paid them no attention. "They're coming..."

:-:

The wanderer sped down the mountain slope, dodging the jungle brush with practiced agility. His seeping wound and the large black bag strapped tightly to his back made running more difficult, but he didn't have too much further to go. He already knew he was very close.

:-:

The bedraggled woman stopped in her tracks again and dropped the ankles of the corpse to the jungle floor. The stiff feet planted themselves in the mud with a resolute *splosh*. The woman tensed her shoulders, widened her eyes as wide as humanly possible, and whipped her head around in all directions.

"Who's there?" she whispered in terror. Her arms trembled. "Who's there?" she repeated, raising her voice.

She began to weep uncontrollably.

:-:

The wounded wanderer had halted his descent down the mountainside a kilometer away from the raving woman. He could hear her, but he couldn't see her clearly enough through the abundant vegetation. Regardless, he had found her at last. He had found them both. He crouched down and began digging through his bag.

:-:

"Who—" the woman began before silencing herself. She stooped over the body and pried its ankles away from the clutches of the thick mire. The frenzied insects had seemed to multiply. Once more, she began dragging the corpse to her tree hollow. The toes of her bare feet dug deep into the mud as she tugged with all her might. Twice, she slipped and fell. She pressed on with her task nevertheless. Between her hysterical wailing, she mumbled incoherently to herself and to the lifeless body.

:-:

Peering through the scope of his M21 Sniper Rifle, the wanderer was able to look more closely upon the woman and her counterpart. But upon sighting the corpse, he cursed and looked away, baring his teeth in outrage. He licked his lips and wiped the multiplying beads of sweat from the dome of his bald head before they could spill into his still-bleeding gash. He swallowed hard, but could not rid himself of the unnerving lump in his throat.

With a renewed resolve, he resumed his composure and reset his sight on the remaining loose end, positioning the crosshairs on the back of her head. Without a moment's hesitation, he squeezed the trigger. The shot echoed through the valley. The woman dropped dead a second later.

PART I
COLLIDE

ONE

30 MAY, 2012

Preikestolen. Pulpit Rock. Preacher's Pulpit. This two thousand foot tall Norwegian wall of granite harbored many names. Colton Anders was two-thirds of the way to its peak, but he was climbing slower than he would prefer. The vertical face of the cliff had few crevices and outcrops large enough for his fingers and feet. Furthermore, this rock was dangerously unstable and inconveniently moist. Three times, already, his feet had accidentally broken off small outcrops that, on any other wall, would have held his weight. He had yet to slip a finger hold, though, and he hoped he wouldn't. After all, it was just him, the rock, and brutally unforgiving gravity — his career-long nemesis.

As he neared the three-quarter mark, he paused a moment to cast a wary glance above him. The vertical face he was climbing now would transform into a hundred-plus degree angle in a dozen or so feet. Knowing that he would have to conquer the menacing overhang momentarily, he inhaled as deep a breath as the thin air would allow.

Composure and control were the two most important mentalities to maintain on a cliff face; panic was the quickest route to death, and fighting for breath at such an elevation was not an effective way of calming nerves. To make matters worse, he was beginning to run low on chalk powder for his hands. As he looked around to spot the next hold, he could feel his muscles starting to ache. A single rain droplet fell from the heavens and crashed into his upturned forehead.

Eyes locked on target, he swung his right arm up to meet the first crevice of the sharply angled overhang. Alarmingly, however, his fingers lost hold of the granite as soon as they made contact. As his right arm fell back down, his legs swung away from the cliff face as his feet, too, lost their holdings. He felt a shock of pain traverse his left arm as his fingers caught the entire amount of stress that gravity inflicted upon his body.

He dangled there — from a crevice in the bottom of the overhang, nearly two thousand feet off the ground — held only by the four long fingers of his left hand. He gritted his teeth as a secondary wave of pain came and went.

A loud pounding suddenly buffeted his eardrums, though he could not determine whether it came from an external source nearby or from somewhere within his head. Doing his best to block it out and regain composure, he set his mind on figuring out why he had just slipped. He quickly realized that the majority of the crevices beneath the granite overhang would be extra damp — even if the sun had revealed its rays today, the overhang would have provided cool shade, not allowing for the evaporation of any moisture that had accumulated in its clefts.

While his right arm hung at his side, he figured it a good moment to replenish his palm and fingers with the little bit of powder that remained — he would need all the dry traction he could get. After dusting his hand, he swung his arm back up, aiming for the very crack that had just betrayed him. His fingers met their mark and maintained their hold. Immediately, he felt the relief in his left arm. As his feet found subtle ripples in the granite as footholds, he grinned and let out a hearty laugh. This was the thrill of the ascent that he lived for. No other sensation in the world could match the intensity of any given moment on the face of a cliff while free-solo-climbing. With that brief slip-up behind him, he pushed onward with extra caution and focus on each move he made.

Overall, however, he was making remarkable time — surely better time than that of the rope-and-harness-using amateurs with whom he loved to compete. The pounding he had heard moments ago had subsided slightly, though he could still pick up its distinct *thump-thump-thump* from not too far off in the distance. He had guessed what it was by now but did not want to turn his head to look and break his focus.

He heaved his body upward to the next fissure, able to make out the detail in the granite at the apex of the overhang by now. Climbing with his stomach facing skyward, every single muscle in his body felt as if it were on fire. The veins in his fingers and arms bulged with unprecedented fury. He feared that if his pectorals flexed any harder, they just might burst. Despite the cool, high-altitude air, he could feel a few annoying beads of sweat begin to form on his brow. He exhaled and inhaled short breaths, struggling to fill his lungs with as much air as he could gather. His muscles needed oxygen now more than ever. If he so much as cramped, he would anticlimactically fall to his death.

Utilizing the last reserves of his energy, he carefully maneuvered up the last of the cliff. He swung his hand up to grasp the rim of the plateau that sat atop the overhang. Gritting his teeth, sweat stinging his eyes and blurring his vision, veins on his arms, fingers, and forehead swelling, Colton pulled his body up over the edge.

He had made it.

He immediately rolled himself away from the ridge and towards the center of the plateau. For several long moments, he lay prostrate on his back, gasping for air. After a brief respite, he brought his calloused hands to his face and began grinning proudly, oblivious of the crowd forming around him. Even on an overcast day like today, the plateau — a popular hiking destination — teemed with about fifty other people. Not all of them were mere hikers, though.

As Colton's mind spun back to reality, he was quickly overwhelmed by his surroundings. The pounding noise he had heard before had returned. He was reluctant to open his eyes, but when he finally did he saw a helicopter fly low overhead; he had guessed correctly as to the source of the blood-pumping *thump-thump-thump*. As it swooped a little further away to land, he also became aware of the multitudes of shouting people obnoxiously hovering over him.

"Mr. Anders, how does it feel to be the first man to free-solo-climb the treacherous Preikestolen Cliff?"

"Can you tell us what prompted you to scale this wall on a day with such poor conditions?"

Are you suicidal? Are you on drugs? Where are you going next? How does it feel to conquer certain death over and over again? Do your hands hurt? Why are you sweating? Are you tired? How long have you been growing your beard? Are you afraid of death? We would like to offer you a sponsorship from...

All the questions and voices began to blend together into one head-spinning uproar. Colton decided he would rather be dangling from the bottom of the overhang again and briefly contemplated retreating back over the edge of the cliff. Unfortunately, his muscles had locked up and he was currently unable to move. When he closed his eyes and began muttering angrily to himself, the crowd began to hush.

"Shhhh! He's speaking!"

"Hey, you, that camera better be rolling!"

All was quiet. Then, a patient, hardly audible: "one at a time."

At first, the commotion came back, roaring even louder than before. In an instant, however, Colton, with his eyes still closed, raised his veiny right arm from the granite plateau and pointed randomly at the stranger hovering over his feet. Silence fell again, and all eyes but Colton's turned to the man being pointed to. When no one spoke, Colton raised his head ever so slightly and peered one eye open to mentally sum up the man he was pointing to. *Fair-skinned. Light-haired. Six-foot-two. Weathered façade. Minimalist hiking gear. Desperately in need of new shoes,* Colton thought to himself. *Hasn't spoken yet, and doesn't quite know how to respond. He's a native. Not here for me.* He let his arm fall back down to the plateau.

"You're the trail guide, aren't you?" Colton said as more of a statement than a question. He closed his eye and set his head back down on his not-so-comfortable granite bed.

"Yes, yes!" the Norwegian exclaimed, wild-eyed and nodding ferociously. "That was amazing!"

Unsure of whether the man was referring to Colton's recent accomplishment or his uncanny deductive abilities, Colton randomly pointed straight up to the person hovering over his head.

"Mr. Anders," a woman began in a professional tone.

Colton didn't even have to open his eyes to recognize the voice of this reporter; he knew it well. Scarlet Sinclair was sure to turn up after just about every ascent he completed, whether it be on the peak or at the base. She wasn't with the news, though. Instead, she free-lanced her services to various extreme sports gear-manufacturing companies. Blogging was all the rage these days, apparently, and although Colton didn't directly participate, he knew the brands that were sponsoring him featured every ascent of his on their websites. Scarlet, with her own camera crew and helicopter, always got the footage, the photos, and the story to Colton's sponsors.

"Ah, Scar... Just the woman I wanted to talk to." Colton smiled, closing his eyes harder as the mid-day sun made its first appearance through a tiny gap in the ominous clouds.

"Yes, me," Scarlet returned. "So, obvious questions first, how do you feel?"

"I'm high on life."

"Why did you not use proper climbing rope and a harness?"

"Would you be here if I did?"

"Today is the first day it hasn't rained in a week. Why didn't you wait a few more days to make your ascent?"

"For dramatic effect, I suppose," Colton suggested. "And I was itching to climb again. Being cooped up indoors was suffocating."

"What are you going to do next?"

"Probably hike back down. Eat something. Take a nap."

"I meant your next trip."

"I don't know. Haven't thought past my nap yet."

"You've climbed hundreds of death-defying cliffs, most without any rope—"

"I climb everything at least once with rope to learn my course, then I always go back and do it without any gear."

"Except this one."

"Yes, except for this one."

"Why didn't you do a test climb?"

"I didn't know how long the weather conditions would last."

"The hazardous conditions... Another storm is rapidly moving in. It'll start pouring within minutes."

Colton didn't say anything. He had felt a little bit of a drizzle while he was climbing the rock earlier, but it had ceased for the last part of his ascent. Seemingly on queue, however, droplets now began to fall from the sky.

"Many think you're getting more and more daring. Too daring, perhaps. You've only been at this career for three years."

"I have to keep pushing myself. Besides, I've made dozens of ascents higher than this one. Why are you all here?"

"Because you just free-soloed the most difficult route up a dangerously unstable two thousand foot wall of rock without a test-climb under the imminent possibility of a torrential downpour... No one even climbs this cliff under normal conditions."

"So what?"

"What if you push yourself too hard? What if you endeavor something before you're ready?"

"I'm ready for anything."

"Hypothetically, then."

"Then, I die." Colton laughed. "Hypothetically, of course."

"Do you fear death?"

"No."

"Why not?"

"I'm doing what I love. I have nothing to lose. I'm going to die eventually anyway. What's there to be afraid of?"

"Most people would say the dying part."

"I'm not most people."

"No, Colton, you're not." She smiled faintly but didn't ask anything further.

"Any more questions?" Colton asked his audience.

The uproar sounded once more, albeit slightly less boisterously than before. Questions whizzed through the air, but Colton was prepared this time. After a few loud seconds, he raised his hand, signaling for silence once more. The crowd, of course, hushed themselves immediately.

"I'm adventurous, not suicidal — there's a difference. Never taken any drugs. Yes, my hands hurt. I'm sweating because it's my body's natural method of cooling my skin; it happens when you exert physical energy — you should try that sometime. Yes, I suppose I'm quite tired. My beard is a month or so old. I kind of like it, don't you? I've already answered the death question, weren't you listening? I'm not currently seeking any more sponsors. I've got all I'll ever need and they're just fantastic. My hands are a little too tired to sign autographs. No, I can't cure your daughter's cold. No, I'm not seeing anyone right now. And yes, I suppose I am technically homeless. Anything else? No? Marvelous," Colton finished, slowly turning over to his hands and knees. He paused a moment. "Would it concern you all too greatly to give me some space?" Colton gradually rose to his feet as the crowd began to disperse. A few people cast him inquiring glances, but no more questions were sent his way.

All at once, the sky ripped itself apart with a blinding bolt of lightning. The deafening thunder sounded a fraction of an instant later to herald the arrival of the long-anticipated deluge. The firmament opened up, and rain poured down from the heavens to lay siege to the great Norwegian mountain. Colton decided then, in that moment, where his next international venture would take him — he would return to the United States for the first time in three years.

TWO

4 JUNE 2012

Emma Payton jolted upright as a sudden, loud noise awoke her from her peaceful slumber. In an instant, however, she realized it was just the telephone ringing. She rubbed her eyes before glancing over at the time. Exactly six o'clock — way too early for anyone reasonable to be calling. It had to be her mother. She closed her eyes, shook her head, and let out a sigh. It was always her mother. Emma let the phone on the nightstand ring for a long while, contemplating whether or not she was going to answer. *Well, I'm already awake*, she figured. She picked it up just before the answering machine took over.

"Hello?"

"Emilia, dearest, it's your mother. I wanted to talk to you about your flight back to the Hamptons. I booked it for this coming Saturday morning—"

"Mom, no," Emma grumbled, already frustrated. This was not the way she wanted to start her Monday. She immediately began to mentally prepare herself for the all-too-familiar diatribe she was about to hear for the nth time since her arrival several days ago. "We've discussed this already. I'm staying here all summer."

"Oh, *did* we, now? I don't believe you flying out there as soon as university let out without even asking for your parents' permission was anything we ever discussed. No. I was *informed* that you randomly decided to spend your last summer break *alone* in the wilderness," Winona Payton countered on the other end of the phone. "I honestly don't understand where or how you learned to behave so impulsively. It's not proper. It's not Payton."

Emma rolled her eyes upon hearing her mother's favorite idiom. "I'm not a kid anymore though, Mom. I'm a twenty-four year old, independent woman. And we talked about it after I got here. I needed to get away from D.C. and didn't want to spend another summer at home. I want my last summer break to be different. And besides, I called Daddy yesterday. He thought this was an excellent idea." Emma smiled to herself; this would halt her mother's tirade. She loved using the 'Daddy-said-so' card to trump her mother. Sure enough, her mother didn't say anything for a moment.

"I just love you, darling. And I miss you terribly when you aren't around."

Emma rolled her eyes again. Talking with her mother was like playing a game, and now her mother was strategically trying to guilt her. "I know. I know, Mom. I love you, too. But if you really love me, you'll let me do what's best for me."

Winona paused for a moment, considering her daughter's words. "Fine."

Emma was pleased with herself by successfully placating her mother — for now at least. Emma knew she would call again within a few days and the argument would repeat itself. When her mother seemed oddly silent, Emma knew she should exploit the opportunity to change the subject. "I'm running a summer camp."

"Oh?" her mother questioned, the surprise in her tone evident. "Why?"

"Kids are interesting. They always have something to teach you... if you can learn to be patient enough." Emma doubted her mother would catch on to her underlying message.

"Oh, so is this some sort of research venture for your PhD?"

"Yes," Emma lied, not wishing to infuriate her mother again.

"Well, why didn't you tell me this earlier, Emilia?"

"You never asked."

"You just don't talk to me like you used to..." Her mother sighed. "Never mind that. Lance is coming home tonight."

"Oh, is he?" Emma pretended to be curious, but she didn't want to talk about her brother — not after her last encounter with him.

"Yes. We're celebrating his graduation. Your father is planning on surprising him with a job offer at the firm."

"I'm sure he won't see that coming," Emma said sarcastically. When her mother didn't respond for several moments, seeming to sense the conversation wasn't going anywhere, Emma continued. "Well, I suppose I should start getting ready. Today's my first day on the job, and I have plenty to do to prepare."

"Yes, of course. Good luck, dear," Winona said before hanging up abruptly.

Emma threw the phone back onto the bed before burying her face in her hands. *Mom sure is a piece of work*, she thought. But she had always known that. She stood up and began her morning routine.

THREE

Winona Payton set the phone back in its base and clasped her hands together as she sat at the marble counter in her luxurious kitchen. Still musing over her conversation with her daughter, she recoiled as her husband walked up behind her and touched her on the shoulder. He bent down and kissed her on the cheek. Winona smiled.

"Good morning, dear," she said, turning to face him.

"Morning," Harvey Payton returned. He was already fully dressed in what he affectionately called his 'million-dollar suit' — although its actual worth was not quite so steep. His full head of gray hair was already styled perfectly. "Coffee in the pot?"

"Yes, but Thelma only put it in a few minutes ago," Winona answered, referring to their beloved housekeeper. Winona ran her fingers through her shoulder-length, dyed-blonde hair. "What's going to happen at the market today?"

"Can't say yet," Harvey lied. On trained impulse, numbers and charts about the stocks he had been watching began buzzing through his mind. It was easier to lie. He knew Winona didn't understand, nor did she really care. To her, money was money; it didn't matter where it came from as long as it kept coming. Much to Harvey's annoyance, she didn't appreciate the thrill of winning that he lived and breathed for.

"You never can," Winona replied. "But there's no denying you know what you're doing anyway."

Harvey didn't respond. He walked over to check on the coffee. Dissatisfied, he stuck his hands in his pockets and turned to gaze out the nearest window. The morning sun reflected brilliantly across the surface of the rolling ocean. A lone sailboat drifted along on the horizon. An elderly couple holding hands walked their dog along the beach as the surf gently surged outwards to lick the worn heels and wrinkled toes of their bare feet. Harvey watched the water methodically recede, surge, and recede again. Winona suddenly broke his trance.

"Are you prepared for Lance tonight?" she inquired halfheartedly, examining her pristinely polished fingernails.

Harvey blinked, a neutral look on his face. He turned to check on the coffee once more. Pleased, he took out the pot and filled two mugs. After taking one in each hand, he approached the counter where his wife sat still scrutinizing her nails. He set one mug in front of her.

"Yes, of course I am," he finally answered. "I think he'll be delighted."

"He should," Winona responded. "That boy has only got everything he's ever wanted."

"He works hard," Harvey countered. "If you work hard, you get what you want."

"I suppose he's a lot like you," Winona raised her head to meet Harvey's gaze. She smiled, her soft, brown eyes flashing.

Harvey suddenly found himself besieged by his wife's charm. Moments like these reminded him of when they first met over thirty years ago. They reminded him that he still loved her.

"Speaking of our children... was that Emma you were on the phone with before I walked in?"

"Yes. She's doing some research for her PhD while she stays in Maine, or at least that's what I was just told. She also mentioned she talked to you yesterday."

"Briefly," Harvey began, pausing to try a sip of his steaming coffee. "She called to tell me she had arrived safe and sound and was already making herself at home in the villa."

"She said you endorsed the idea of her being out there alone."

"Well, I never explicitly said that I *did,* but I also never explicitly said that I didn't. To tell the truth, I do think it's a good idea. It's exactly what she needs before entering the real world. Her life up to this point has just been that of an ultimately carefree, perpetual student. If she wants to be responsible for herself this summer, I welcome it," Harvey said, shrugging. He took another sip of his coffee before glancing at his watch.

"So, she assumed what *you* were thinking... and she played *me,*" Winona muttered, unhappy with being fooled so easily.

"She has always known how to get what she wants. Our children are winners. If the only way Emma could do what was ultimately right for her was by embellishing the truth a little, then so be it. I welcome that, too."

"Yes, of course. Whatever it takes to win," Winona said sarcastically, repeating what her husband always said when justifying his sometimes-controversial actions and decisions.

"Exactly," Harvey stated matter-of-factly, not sensing his wife's slight hint of mockery. He took another sip of his coffee, but noticed Winona hadn't touched hers. "Are you going to drink that before it gets cold?"

Winona lifted the mug gently to her mouth and took a small sip to appease her husband, although she wasn't thirsty.

:-:

Harvey Payton opened the rear door to his charcoal Bentley Mulsanne and sat down on the plush leather seat. He set his locked briefcase beside him. After shutting his door, he looked ahead to the rearview mirror to make eye contact with his personal chauffeur.

The piercing emerald-green eyes that stared back at him belonged to a bald-headed man of about forty. A three-inch scar traversed the left side of his forehead and temple. His squared jawbone was clearly defined, and a set of thin lips sat motionless upon a stern countenance that didn't betray the faintest trace of emotion.

Harvey nodded to the man. At once, the automobile's engine roared to life. The Mulsanne gently began rolling forwards, beginning its long journey down the estate's driveway. Harvey, as he did every morning, watched his grandiose home gradually shrink from sight through the car's rearview mirror.

The moment it disappeared, his expression hardened. The good-natured facade he had worn before had transformed into one that matched his chauffeur, albeit even more intimidating. His previously vibrant grey eyes suddenly became unreadable, swirling voids.

"Did your most recent expedition prove any more fruitful?" Harvey inquired, raising an eyebrow slightly and inhaling deeply. He took his briefcase and sat it on his lap. He gently set his thick, well-groomed fingers palm-down upon the case's top. He kept his gaze low.

"No." Even in admitting failure, the dignified voice of the chauffeur maintained a tone of authority. No excuses. No apologies. Just the fundamental truth. His gaze never wavered from the road, and his expression still appeared unperturbed.

Harvey's fingers balled up into fists as scorn curled his lips and burned in his eyes. As soon as it happened, however, stern composure regained control. His fists relaxed and resumed their previous position guarding the case. He sighed and shook his head slightly. "He's causing us more trouble now than he was while he was living. We underestimated him, and now we're paying for it."

"No, we're not," the chauffeur countered. "The photos are either lost or have been destroyed. Perhaps they never even existed in the first place. After all these years, no one that I've encountered has had any knowledge of them."

"You don't know that for sure, Vincent. I know about your overly eager trigger finger. You didn't question all the loose ends before tying them up."

"Well, it's a moot point now, then, isn't it? You can torture them to death, but you can't torture the dead. By the time I was done with the larger loose ends, I knew of every dark secret they'd ever kept; none had anything to say relatively related to any complicit photos of either of us. It was mercy rather than impatience that delivered a swift death to those who had no information to share. Don't let your spies tell you otherwise. Nevertheless, that leaves one remaining loose end. We can't afford to ignore him any longer. He must be dealt with sooner or later, and better sooner than later."

"I sometimes fear it's too late already."

"We would know if it was, sir. It's not. Not yet. But time is of the essence."

"Do you know where he is?" Harvey muttered, looking out the window as they began nearing the city.

"I do, sir."

Harvey contemplated for a moment. "Just follow him. Do not betray yourself to him. Blend in. Be invisible. If he has seen the photos and he recognizes you, then this situation could very quickly unravel and the worst will come. If he is truly the final loose end, then it is of utmost importance that you find out everything he knows before you terminate him. Patience is your priority with this target." Harvey paused briefly. "And Vincent..."

"Sir?"

"I cannot stress to you enough the discretion that this operation deserves. You know what awaits you if you mishandle any part of it."

"Yes, sir."

"You will leave today."

"Right away, sir."

After several more minutes, the vehicle entered a parking garage behind a towering skyscraper. The chauffeur drove to the top floor and parked.

"Leave the car here, I'll need it to drive home. Take a cab to the hangar. I'll call Royce momentarily and tell him to fly you wherever you tell him," Harvey ordered before opening his door. He grasped the handle to his briefcase and exited. Vincent turned the Mulsanne off and exited as well, handing the Bentley's keys over to Harvey. Without further ado, the two turned in their respective directions and parted.

FOUR

"No, Bradley, don't put that in your mouth!" Emma hollered as she ran as fast as she could over to a three-year-old sitting cross-legged in the grass chewing on a red felt marker.

"I'm not Bradley! I'm a dinosaur!" the boy whined, gnashing his teeth and fighting Emma as she tried to pull the colored marker from his little fingers. "Dinosaur! Dinosaur! Dinosaur!"

"Well, dinosaurs didn't eat markers, so I don't think you should, either," Emma said, setting her hands on her hips and tilting her head to the side. She waited to see how Bradley would react. Sure enough, the boy paused as well, making a funny face as he seemed to ponder Emma's words.

"Really?" he drawled, staring up at her with eyes widened and mouth agape.

"Yes," Emma responded. "What kind of dinosaur are you?"

"I'm a long-neck!" The toddler giggled. "I'm super tall!"

"Oh, my!" Emma exclaimed, feigning amazement. "You must be really hungry! Do you know what the long-necks ate?"

"Hmmm..." Bradley contorted his face, puzzled. "Nope!"

"Berries! Would you like some?"

"Yay! Berries!" Bradley shouted, clapping his hands.

"Okay, then," Emma began, offering her hand. "Come along

with me." Bradley took her hand and she helped him up. She brushed his long, blonde hair out of his eyes and tried to wipe the red ink off his mouth and cheeks, but only managed to smear the streaks. Emma made a face. "We'll get you washed up first. Oh, my! Look at your hands, they're all red, too!"

Bradley looked down and held his small hands palm-up before him. He laughed aloud briefly and tried shoving them into Emma's face. She pulled away just before he could touch her.

"Okay, come on," Emma said as she led Bradley away.

The rest of the children, about twelve in all, ranging from ages three to six, were also supposed to be attempting to draw. Each had his or her own large sheet of white paper set up on an easel. Some were doing better than others. The campground was stationed beside the ocean, so most drawings were of the waves. Besides from the popular ocean sketches, one of the older girls was drawing the nearby cabin, a boy was drawing one of the girls, and a few select other younglings were rendering what could only be considered abstract art.

Adam Lane, the teenage 'volunteer,' was masterfully sketching a killer whale submerged below the surface of the ocean. He had watched carefully, though not too obviously, as Emma dealt with the child.

Emma was now walking back from the cabin hand-in-hand with Bradley. With his other hand, the toddler was stuffing blueberries into his mouth. As Emma approached Adam, she whispered something to Bradley, letting go of his hand. He ran back towards his art easel and began coloring with his markers. Adam sensed her approaching, but pretended to ignore her.

She took hold of a nearby stool and positioned herself beside him. She narrowed her eyes and cocked her head, examining his illustration. "That's fantastic," she breathed, the wonder in her voice evident.

"Oh," Adam began sheepishly. "You really think so?" He shrugged and turned to meet her gaze.

"Yes! Adam..." She seemed to forget her words. She shook her head in bewilderment, eyes still opened wide in shock.

The silence was too awkward for him, causing him to blush in embarrassment.

"Where did you learn to do this?" she finally asked.

"It's just a hobby I've always had an affinity for," he responded, slowly regaining a bit of confidence. "I have lots others... Drawings, I mean... I can show you sometime. I draw all kinds of stuff. I think you would like them," he offered, smiling an unpracticed grin.

Emma nodded and smiled in return. "Yes, I would."

The silence returned. Adam felt the blood rush to his face and the tips of his ears began to tingle. "So, uh, Emma, how are you? What's up? What's new? Wait... Sorry about that," he stuttered nervously. His eyes darted around, sensing Emma's watching him. He could feel his heart beating rapidly in his chest. He knew he was about to embarrass himself, but his unbridled emotions were far beyond restraint at this point. "I mean nothing is up with me, I guess. I don't know." He paused awkwardly, wondering what to say. "My life is like a person wearing a clown costume to a wedding. It's out of place. Doesn't fit in. A stark antithesis to the others wearing tuxedos and dresses... Not that I would ever wear a dress, I mean," he added with reassuringly widened eyes. "Everybody else is throwing red rose petals and all I have are a few plastic daisies from the local convenient store. People around me are sitting together drinking from crystal wine glasses, and I'm the outcast drinking apple juice from a sippy cup. People are giving gifts like refrigerators and coffee makers, and all I brought was a coupon to Wal-Mart clipped out of the morning newspaper." Adam paused a moment to catch his breath, then continued, despite wondering to himself how he could make such a fool of himself in front of Emma like this. "The way I fit in with my surroundings could be compared to sketchy rap music played at a senior home's Bingo Night. My life, simply put, is that problematic moment when you answer the phone after taking an unreasonably large bite of freshly baked muffin." He sighed. "I've considered going to church just so I can hold someone's hand during the 'Our Father.' I feel inclined to carry around a box of donuts just to see how many people ask me for one. I could walk around downtown with a sign on my back that says, 'Make plans to sell your home' and nothing would feel out of the ordinary. I'm not even as successful as that person who writes songs for people that play the oboe. When I'm alone, sometimes I consider spilling my milk just so I'll have an excuse to cry." Adam shook his head and hunched over, looking to the ground, clasping his hands together. After a moment, he raised his head to look Emma in the eyes. "You know what I mean?"

Emma narrowed her eyes again. Though surprised and, quite frankly, left speechless from his rant, she decided she was glad he was volunteering here with her. He was just as interesting as the younger children. An artist in every sense of the word. Multi-dimensional. Profound. Better yet, Emma felt she had only scratched the surface of his unique character. "Yes, I suppose I do," she responded empathetically after a moment, smiling widely with lustrous, white teeth. She watched as his face lit up upon hearing that his monologue was well received. "You know, it's funny you mention the oboe..."

"Why?" Adam smirked. "Do you play the oboe?"

"No," Emma chuckled. "I don't even know what it is. I was just messing with you."

Adam's slight smile broke into an ear-to-ear grin. As he watched her soft hazel eyes dance in the warm rays of the sun, he suddenly felt perfectly content. After a moment of shared laughs, they both turned content faces towards the ocean.

"It's like a mask," Adam began.

Emma turned to give him a curious glance. She noticed his eyes, still fixated on the rolling surf, had suddenly turned cold and hard. "What do you mean?"

Adam didn't respond for a moment. His facial expression had become inscrutable. His wispy black hair tickled his forehead as a salty breeze swept by. "What we see of the ocean is just its mask. It hides what lies beneath."

"Is that another metaphor?" Emma asked without hesitation, still focused on Adam's expression.

Adam shrugged. "Perhaps."

Emma didn't say anything, but she could guess at his thoughts.

"Did they tell you why I'm really here?" Adam asked.

"Vaguely. I was told it was community service."

Adam turned away to hide a smirk. "I'm not dangerous."

"I figured," Emma started, turning her head towards the children. She was surprised to find they all still appeared to be very engaged in their drawings. "I didn't think they would stick you with a bunch of little kids if you were."

Adam nodded. "They thought it would be a good punishment for me."

"Is it?" Emma inquired, turning back to Adam.

"Not sure yet," Adam turned to face Emma without hiding a deliberately playful smirk. "It seems possible that the initial despair I felt may have been unwarranted."

"Meaning," Emma began, narrowing her eyes. "You like it

better than you expected?"

"Like I said," Adam started, turning to focus his attention back to his illustration of the surfacing whale. "I'm not sure yet."

When he picked up his pencil and started sketching again, Emma silently took her leave.

FIVE

"Thirty-one minutes and forty-two seconds!" Colton shouted. He was standing at the base of a hundred foot cliff and conversing with a man who had just scaled to the very top.

The climber let out a shout of joy from the cliff top. "Personal best! I think that's the record for this slab too!" the man shouted back at Colton. "Beat *that*!"

Colton grinned and shook his head as he began to wind up the rope Jeremy had just thrown back down. He tilted his head back up towards the peak of the cliff, squinting his eyes to block the midday rays of the sun. "All right, Jeremy! Challenge accepted!"

Colton had been hiking through the woods earlier that morning when he happened upon Jeremy's slipshod camp. Colton had attempted to pass by unnoticed, but to no avail. A man who appeared to be in his late thirties had scrambled out of his little tent to stop Colton in his tracks. Colton identified the man as a climber the moment he set his eyes on him. The unkempt five o'clock shadow, the calloused, veiny hands, the fit, fatless body, the wild look in his eyes, living in a minimalist camp surviving on canned beans and water — all telltale signs of a man whose mind could only ever be occupied by one thing. The man, who had almost immediately identified himself as Jeremy Wilde, seemed to recognize Colton as a climber as well.

"You ready?" Colton hollered up at Jeremy. Colton had situated himself beside the rock and was already planning his path up the cliff-face. His expertly decided moves came naturally to him. Rarely did he have to reconsider a decision when it came to climbing.

"Yeah, man, yeah! Go, already! The second-hand is ticking away!" Jeremy shouted back, but before he had even finished his sentence, Colton had already leapt up onto the crag and begun his rapid ascent.

Coming from Preikestolen, this was like a walk in the park for Colton. Because it sat nestled against the Atlantic Ocean, though, the rough rock was a little moist; he reminded himself to not be too careless. Even on a more amateur climb such as this, an overconfident attitude could be just as dangerous as a hesitant attitude could be on a more extreme ascent. *One cocky move, and gravity will punish me*, he thought to himself as he flew up the face.

Climbing was second nature to him — especially on an incline climb. Reacting automatically, his thoughts turned to his new companion. Jeremy was talented — maybe not a pro, but certainly not a novice. Colton had watched his technique and finesse with a critical eye, but Jeremy's skill continuously surprised and impressed him. Jeremy had told Colton little about his past, but Colton respected Jeremy's privacy as much as Jeremy respected Colton's own. Jeremy had recognized Colton as a climber, but he betrayed no sign of recognizing who Colton was. No problem with that; Colton was here pursuing anonymity — even if it may only be ephemeral.

Colton was reaching the halfway mark, and he was neither out of breath nor sweating. The air was brisk and invigorating. It seemed to urge him onward rather than drag him down. As a mighty wave swelled up from the ocean and battered the crag, frigid droplets of saltwater went flying skyward to lick his bare arms and legs. A chill traversed his spine and caused the little hairs on his arms to stand straight up. The eerie sensation, for some unknown reason, reminded him of Yosemite. A nostalgic sensation coursed through his veins as he neared the top of the cliff.

He doubted that it could have been more than twenty minutes since he had left the base. Many of his habits and abilities harmonized together to account for his breakneck speed when it came to climbing. There was, for instance, his superhuman twenty-ten vision, allowing him to easily recognize the slightest ripples and gradients in the rock as possible temporary hand- or feet-holds. There was his lightning-quick mind fed by expert intuition; he took less than half as long deciding his subsequent moves in comparison to other climbers; he planned every detailed motion so far in advance that he could say precisely where the fingers of his left hand would be in fifteen feet. There was his unique mentality constructed from years of hardship that allowed him to overcome the fear of the seemingly impossible. This mentality required a certain amount of apathy towards living, of course. But by keeping his mind free of fears of death, he could devote one hundred percent of his focus on accomplishing his next goal. Then, there was, of course, his virtually zero-fat, perfectly toned body, fully equipped with rippling muscles that allowed him to do with only two fingers what the average person would need both arms to do.

Colton reached up to the edge of the precipice with the fingers of his right hand and pulled himself up over the ridge. He clambered to his feet and rested his hands on his hips. He took a deep breath and looked around. He spotted Jeremy a few feet away with a stupefied look on his face.

"Well I'll be," Jeremy drawled.

"How'd I do?"

"You put me to shame. That's how you did."

"Not gonna share my time with me?" Colton smirked.

"Nah, you don't need to know. If your head gets too big you might lose your balance and fall off this bluff."

"Someone's being a sore loser."

"No way, man! I happily concede defeat to you! I saw it in you before, but I certainly didn't expect you to be that fast. What do you say we hike back down and find something to eat?"

Colton didn't answer. Instead, he walked over to the edge of the precipice and peered down below. The base of the crag stood resolute as waves wildly buffeted its jagged rock.

"Let's jump," he finally said, turning back around. The wild look in his eyes made Jeremy flinch.

"You're joking, right?"

"If I jump, will you tell me my time?"

"No! I'll tell you now if you promise not to jump!"

Colton shook his head. Jeremy could see an indescribable frenzy dancing in the young man's eyes.

"You'll kill yourself! There are too many rocks down there! Even if you manage to miss one of them, the current will sweep you into the crag and batter you to pieces!"

"The current's not that powerful. I'm strong enough to resist it," Colton said carelessly, looking down the cliff again. "And the water's breaking — no surface tension to worry about."

"Rocks to worry about! Look, you already conquered this bluff and annihilated my record. I think that's enough limit-pushing for one day. Come on, now. Back away. I don't like this."

Colton began backing away.

"Yes, that's it. Let's get out of here. Come on."

"Tell me my time after you see me surface, okay?" Colton said. He took his shirt off and flung it towards Jeremy.

"What? No! Colton, stop! You won't make it!"

Colton bounced on the balls of his feet and exhaled deeply, closing his eyes. "You should have just told me my time when I asked!" he breathed. He opened his eyes and began a sprint towards cliff's edge.

"All right, I'll tell you now! Your time was twenty—" Jeremy started to say, but Colton had already leapt.

Jeremy cursed and ran to the edge to watch helplessly as Colton plummeted headfirst towards the sea; the lunatic had jumped into a dive — arms outstretched, hands interlocked, and already prepared to brace the force of impact. Impact with stone or with sea, though? He gritted his teeth and feared for the worst. His breath caught in his throat. He saw and heard the sudden impact simultaneously. It didn't register in his brain until a moment later.

In a brief moment of relief, Jeremy managed to take a meager breath of air as he watched Colton plunge through the vivacious waves. The lucky fool had missed a jagged, protruding rock seemingly by inches. But did more ragged rocks lie in hidden wait just beneath the swelling ocean's surface?

He held his breath in terrified anticipation, detesting every seemingly eternal second of his helpless waiting. His nervous bite cut into his lip and drew warm blood. He ignored the mild pain that followed. His opal eyes frantically scanned the thrashing waves for any sign of Colton.

But no sign came.

:-:

Colton had laughed aloud just before the plunge. He tucked his chin against his chest. He flexed his fingers. He twisted his body ever so slightly to avoid grazing a dangerously sharp rock. He closed his eyes. He held his breath. Impact.

He broke through the crest of a peaking wave and tore through the water below. He narrowly opened his eyes only for them to be immediately sieged by stinging salt. Nevertheless, he could faintly make out blurry shapes. He continued his descent. Ahead, he could suddenly see what appeared to be a jagged rock flying straight towards his face. In one graceful motion, he swiftly spread out his arms and legs, flattening himself out and effectively slowing down. He exhaled a few nervous bubbles as he tried to twist away from the stone pike that continued to close in on him.

:-:

For Jeremy, time seemed as if it was somehow simultaneously standing still while also rapidly ticking away. The more it passed by, the quicker Colton's chances of survival dropped. Though eager anticipation still bound him motionless, save for his ever-flicking gaze, he slowly began to settle on the conclusion that he would see no more of his new companion. The savage sea, it seemed, had claimed him once and for all.

And then, when all seemed lost, his heart leapt.

:-:

Colton burst through the tempestuous surface. He whipped his head backwards as he gasped for air. He blinked rapidly, desperately trying to expel the sea from his eyes. His bloodshot, salt-ridden, ocean eyes opened wide in arrant fear when he suddenly noticed a surging current projecting him towards the serrated face of the crag. He turned heels and swam as hard in the opposite direction as his sinewy muscles would allow.

:-:

Jeremy had shouted aloud in fear as he saw the wave swiftly carry Colton towards the rocks, and he had gasped as he watched Colton begin to attempt to swim away.

At first, it seemed as though the irrepressible ocean would

easily overwhelm him. After a moment of struggle, though, he stalled in the water, neither moving towards the crag nor away. Then, he began to actually swim away from the crag, albeit very slowly.

:-:

With ferocious strength, Colton fought and fought and threw himself against tenacious waves. They sieged him. They battered him. Once. Then twice. Then a third time, the violent waves forced him under the sweeping current. He continued on, though, trying as best he could to resist total panic. Saltwater forced itself down his throat, but he kept pushing. At last, he grabbed onto a rock that lay to his left flank and pulled his weary body towards it. He hugged it and began coughing, spitting out the angry water.

After a moment of uneasy rest, he reached towards another rock. The fingers of his left hand scratched for a hold. They found it, and he let go of the first rock with his right hand. The powerful current caught him off-guard, though, and once again tried to overtake him — it seemed his quick respite had made him briefly forget the forces working against him. The fingers of this left hand were just about to lose their hold when he gave a last-ditch effort to fling his right arm forward to get a better grip before losing himself to the raging current.

He mentally prepared himself before the next attempt and successfully moved to the next rock. And then the next one. And then one more. He looked around wildly to find himself beside the stone of the mainland. He reached as high as he could to grab hold of its rough edge. His fingers found their grip. He flung his other arm up and pulled himself up onto the granite.

He rolled away from the edge. Saltwater sprayed his face and body as a fierce wave, angrily trying to reclaim him, crashed against the mainland. For several long moments, he lay prostrate on his back, eyes closed, gasping for air. He thought he could hear Jeremy shouting from the peak of the cliff, but he couldn't make out any words. His world spun before his eyes. His heart was thumping so hard he thought it might beat out of his chest. He continued to take deep, effortful breaths. He blinked rapidly. Fatigue overwhelmed his entire body. A wave seemed to sweep over him. His mind succumbed to the beckoning shadows.

The blackout triggered a lucid flashback. A memory from many years ago suddenly flooded Colton's subconscious in vivid detail. A memory that couldn't be more of a stark difference than the experience he now found himself in. Before he could wonder why his psyche had recalled it, he found himself completely consumed by it.

Japan...

He was six years old when his father had been transferred to Japan. Colton and his mother had followed. They always followed. The Kadena Air Force Base in Okinawa was the fourth place he had lived. The fourth country. The third continent.

The simplicity of the memory stood out to him as he looked back on it now. No troubles. No problems. It was just him and his father out on a casual fishing excursion one quiet afternoon. They had borrowed a small rowboat from the base and taken it out on an adjacent bay.

The two eventually found themselves surrounded by vegetation. They floated down a narrow river that fed into the ocean. Young and old trees alike drooped hanging branches over the shallow waters, providing cool shade for the creatures below. A young and curious Colton peered over the rim of the boat, trying to see what swam beneath the murky water's surface.

George Anders, satisfied with their location, stored the oar away on the floor of the boat. As he opened up his tackle box and began to rig his line with the proper bait, a six-year-old Colton questioned him about each and every little thing he did. George remained patient while he satisfied his son's unceasing curiosity. At last, the indulgent father finished rigging his line and drew a gentle finger before his closed mouth, signaling for silence. Colton hushed himself immediately, patiently awaiting what would happen next.

The boy watched in awe as his father masterfully cast his line with an effortless flick of the wrist. His little ears perked as they picked up the distinct *plop* of the spinner striking the water's glassy surface thirty feet away. With his mouth agape, he stared with curious, blue eyes as his father slowly reeled in the line. The bait shot ripples in either direction as it swam back towards the boat. Once it returned, George lifted it out of the water and prepared to cast it again.

Colton cocked his head slightly as he watched his father take aim under the boughs of a low-hanging tree. In one fluid, practiced motion, he cast the line. The bait struck the water at the desired location. Several short seconds passed, each seeming like an eternity to the young boy. He shuddered from the anticipation. His father remained motionless, letting the bait settle just beneath the surface. Colton let loose a shallow gasp as he watched the tip of the rod bounce ever so slightly. George had seen it, too. Colton looked at his father, trying to read his thoughts.

The next part happened so fast; the child struggled to follow along. A fish took the bait and immediately swam off. His previously statue-like father had not hesitated in the slightest before taking action. George knew what to do. For a few minutes, he fought with the fish, struggling to bring it in. When George finally won, Colton grabbed the net to finish the job, dunking it into the river to capture the non-cooperative creature below. George grabbed the handle of the net to help his son lift the restless animal into the boat. Colton laughed as it flopped around on the deck. George smiled as he carefully picked up the flailing creature. He showed his son how to remove the hook without causing too much damage. Next, he held the fish in place while Colton measured it. Approximately seventeen inches. Then, they weighed it. Almost six pounds.

The child asked to hold it, so George gently set in his son's outstretched arms. Colton admired it for a moment, but was unprepared when it suddenly thrashed violently. He accidentally threw the fish back into the water.

Aghast at first, the boy lightened up when he realized his father was laughing. He offered a wide smile in return, and then joined his father in laughter.

After a moment of merriment, George informed Colton it was his turn. He handed his son a spare pole and showed him how to tie on a lure. George grabbed his own rod and began casting once more. Colton tried to mimic him, casting his line right beside his father's. Although it didn't go quite as far, and he nearly hooked his father during the less-than-graceful process, he considered his cast successful enough.

When his father remained motionless, so did Colton. When his father began slowly reeling in his line, so did Colton. The six-year-old boy was meticulously careful to spin his reel's handle at the exact speed his father spun his own. They stood side by side, gently rocking the boat in the tranquil waters as they reeled in their lines together. The two watched each other from the corner of their eyes. George let out a playful sigh. A moment later, he heard his young son let out a sigh as well. George paused to wipe his forehead with the back of his reeling hand. A moment afterwards, he watched his young son do the same. George Anders smiled.

All at once, reality washed away the memory and Colton found himself lying on a block of granite, surrounded by a raging ocean. Madly disoriented, he slowly raised his body from the rock. He stood and looked around, blinking rapidly to expel the salty mist from his eyes. His vision cleared for a split second, allowing him to recognize a figure climbing down the cliff face he had scaled only minutes ago. Still exceptionally dizzy, Colton summoned all reserves of his energy to awkwardly stumble in the direction of the crag.

SIX

The loose end was a drifter — just like his stepfather; just like his real father. Vincent the "chauffeur" pondered the parallels to himself as he sat in his rental car outside of a coffee shop in Bar Harbor, Maine.

The boy had been difficult to track. He always had been. He never stayed in any one place longer than two weeks. He was a loner; his social life with the real world was nearly non-existent and the only people he associated himself with were those who actively sought him out. Wherever he went, he almost always camped, resorting on hotels or motels only in the direst of circumstances. As a result, his digital footprint was minimal. He didn't own a cellphone, nor did he own a computer. Just as well, he rarely used his credit card.

Rarely, however, happened more often than *never*, and for that, Vincent was thankful. Because for the first time in several months, the loose end had used his only credit card at an ATM machine outside of this particular café. And that had happened only the day before yesterday.

Vincent knew his window of opportunity was narrow, but he felt fortunate for being given this lead, meager as it may be. Whether or not the loose end knew that he was being following, he nevertheless portrayed all of the characteristics of a person plagued with rampant paranoia.

The chauffeur guessed he had approximately five or six days

to hone in on the boy's location. After that, the loose end would most likely slip away. Then, Vincent could do nothing but sit around and wait until another lead showed up. And if a man's history was the best predictor of his future, Vincent knew that it could be months before that might happen.

No, he had to find the loose end now. He had orders to follow, and he knew that Harvey would not approve of such a delay.

Where to start? Process of elimination was a quick way to gain ground, especially with the type of person his target was — entirely too focused and recklessly passionate. Vincent knew without a doubt where the boy would not be found: civilization.

The chauffeur, donning black sunglasses, got out of a mediocre rental sedan and walked towards the glass entry of the café. He stepped inside and glanced around, hoping that the uncomfortably crowded shop happened to conveniently sell what he needed.

Maps. He found them on a wooden cabinet amid other souvenir items in the back corner of the room. He casually sauntered over and began glancing through, searching for a geographical depiction of the local area. He scanned the map, dedicating the surrounding area to his photographic memory, and discovered just what he expected he would find: Acadia National Park. The boy had to be in there somewhere.

Vincent was shocked to see just how massive the park was. His confidence immediately shrank. Finding the loose end in the massive expanse of the wilderness could be much more difficult than he had previously expected.

He had no choice, though. He would do whatever it took. He set the map back on its shelf and casually left the café.

SEVEN

It was five o'clock: time for pickup. Bradley's parents were the first to arrive. Emma exchanged greetings with the happy couple, explaining what a pleasure it had been to meet the toddler and how excited she was about spending the next two weeks getting to know him even better.

One by one, the other families arrived to pick up their children. Similar meet-and-greets ensued and, soon enough, all the kids had been picked up. As the last car drove away, Emma rested her hands on her hips and let out a content sigh.

She was pleased with herself. Her first day, from her perspective, had been a total success. Everything had gone better than she had expected — much better, in fact. She felt very fortunate to have such a well-behaved group of children and reflected on her day as she began walking towards the cabin. Just as she opened the side door, someone called her name from behind, causing her to jump.

"Emma!" the voice called again.

As she spun around, Emma identified Adam as the source. Utter confusion seemed to suddenly besiege her mind. She had not even known he was still here. An eerie feeling about whatever was happening or about to happen began to gnaw away at her confidence.

"Emma! What are you doing? Come, quick!"

Emma now noticed that Adam was running towards the edge of the forest. Whatever he had discovered must be of paramount importance; she had not seen him move from his art easel all day long — not even to eat lunch. Without further ado, she began a jog towards the woods, more afraid than curious. The edge in Adam's voice had struck her very core. What could he have seen to stir him so?

When she reached a certain distance, she stopped dead in her tracks. Her heart drummed violently against the walls of her chest. No matter how hard she breathed, she couldn't seem to get enough air into her lungs. A sudden, blood-curdling shout from Adam shot a frigid chill down Emma's spine. A renewed sense of urgency shook her from her trance. She broke into a sprint in his direction.

Once she had arrived within close proximity, a surge of relief swept over her when she saw that Adam was unharmed. Instantaneously, though, a surge of terror, more potent than any before, petrified her.

Before her lay two men crumpled on the ground. She knew not whether they were dead or merely unconscious. There was so much blood.

One of the men had a long gash traversing the left side of his forehead, but otherwise appeared unharmed.

The other fellow was much worse off. The entire right side of his body was badly bruised — his right arm mangled; his right leg completely torn up. Wrapped around his head was a blood-soaked t-shirt. Emma had never seen a face so pale. She trembled.

"I was just drawing. I don't know what made me look... but I did, and I saw him," Adam began, raising a quivering finger aimed at the less-injured man. "He was carrying him," Adam added, slowly redirecting his trembling finger to the mortally injured man. "He seemed to look in my direction." Adam redirected his finger again once more, now aimed back at the man with the gash on his forehead. "I could feel his stare. There's no way he could have seen me or known I was there, but somehow... somehow he did..." Adam trailed off.

Emma didn't respond. She just stared wide-eyed, alternating glances from one man to the other.

Finally, Adam spoke again. "After he saw me, he just... collapsed. Then I called for you and ran over here." He looked at Emma. The evident terror in her eyes made him flinch. "What do we do?"

Emma's head was spinning. She had never encountered anything remotely like this before. She didn't even watch movies or read books that included situations like this. Reality, she then concluded, was never as predictable as fantasy.

"Emma? What do we do?"

"Call nine-one-one," she whispered weakly.

"I don't have a cellphone."

"Use mine," Emma said, tossing hers to Adam.

Adam looked at it. "No signal. I'll use the landline," he decided, about to take off towards the cabin.

"Doesn't work," Emma breathed, shaking her head.

"We have to do something!" Adam shouted, clearly beginning to panic. He paced back and forth rapidly.

"Go get the medical kit and some towels. Med kit's in the cabinet by the fridge. Towels are under the sink in the bathroom. Run fast," Emma said, seeming to have regained some of her composure. Adam took off towards the cabin without another word.

Emma approached the heavily wounded man and knelt at his

side. She checked for a pulse on his neck. Faint, though it was, at least he had one. Slow, strenuous breathing could just barely be heard coming from his mouth. He was alive. Emma let out a sigh of relief without actually feeling very relieved. Although the right side of his face was purple, swollen, and cut up, she absentmindedly took notice of his underlying handsomeness.

Because of his lesser injuries, Emma had no doubt the other man was still alive. Nevertheless, she wanted to be sure. He was not conscious, after all. She walked around to him and knelt down at his side. She buried two fingers in his shallow beard to feel his neck. She kept them there for several long moments.

He had no pulse. Emma frowned and tried a different spot.

Still... no pulse. Emma's eyes widened with renewed fear.

She prodded around with her fingers, feeling underneath his jawbone, but could still feel no signs of life. Beginning to panic, she bent her head over him until her ear hung just above his mouth.

He wasn't breathing.

EIGHT

Colton's world disappeared. Memories flooded and took shape. All experiences he had ever had now returned all at once, completely arresting him. A deluge of indescribable, nameless emotions, thoughts, sights, and sounds filled his swirling mind. His entire life flashed before the eye of his subconscious. He felt it all. He relived every single individual moment all at once. Each sensation and memory had such meaning — so much more now than before.

Then, without warning, it all ended. Everything. Gone. Only an emptiness remained in the void that his life had previously occupied. All memories had faded to oblivion. All but one — the one Colton now found himself physically reliving. It felt so real. He wondered if, perhaps, it wasn't merely a memory at all...

"Why are we here, Colton?" George Anders asked his ten-year-old son. The two sat together, dangling their legs off the edge of a cliff in the Dolomite mountain range of Northern Italy.

That warm July day, George had taught Colton all about the backcountry: how to make a fire, how to build a shelter, how to fish... the names of trees, bugs, and animals... how to climb a wall of rock... His son, George noticed with great pleasure, had intuitively and immediately connected with the natural world.

"Why am I here?" Colton wondered aloud, misunderstanding the question.

George and Colton watched from their lofty seats as a scarlet hue engulfed the valley far below. Scattered shadows drifted leisurely across the faces of the towering mountains. The flowing river at the canyon's base glittered vigorously, set ablaze by the radiant rays of the setting sun.

"No," George whispered patiently in response. "Why are *we* here?" He gently repeated.

Colton felt diminutive as he looked over the expanse of the canyon. He could feel the mighty mountains' indifference crushing him. He decided that there was absolutely nothing he could do that would affect this mountain in the slightest. He was utterly powerless.

The child picked up a small rock and tossed it over the edge. He listened as its echoes resounded against the luminous canyon walls. He wondered about the world. He yearned to learn its secrets. He desired to see all it had to offer. The enormity of it all served to strengthen his feeling of tininess.

His thoughts grew. He began to contemplate the universe; he felt a sudden, newfound curiosity towards it all. A sense of awe and wonder rushed over him as he thought of how much else could be out there. He continued to shrink as his thoughts grew.

Why are we here? The question repeated itself in his mind. Colton guessed intuitively at answers, but none satisfied him.

"I don't know yet," he answered, completely mystified.

A shadowy blanket was gradually drawn over the valley. Colton shivered as a sudden coldness nipped at his being.

The touch of his father's hand on his shoulder, however, sent warmth resonating through his core. A perfect serenity captivated him. He stared straight into the brilliance of the red sun.

Without warning, a sudden, powerful, invisible force struck his chest. The infinitely wide horizon flashed brightly. He watched as the floor of the valley fell away beneath his dangling feet.

Once more, the unseen force buffeted his chest. It was stronger this time. Once more, the horizon flashed brightly. He watched, tormented by a flood of mixed emotions, as his father faded away before his very eyes.

A sudden rushing wind befell Colton's lonely world and gracefully swept away everything in sight. The canyon walls, the clouds, the rising moon — all disappeared in the sourceless gust.

As quick as it had arrived, however, the mysterious wind subsided. Colton found himself sitting alone atop the dolomite cliff, staring anxiously into the white oblivion.

Then, after a moment of empty silence, the wind returned to fill the white void. Colton breathed in deeply, allowing the air to rush into his lungs. The surreal feelings faded away. Everything turned black. And in the darkness, he found reality.

NINE

Emma leapt backwards when the man suddenly jolted upright. He gasped for air with widened eyes. Fresh blood spilled from the wound on his forehead. After a moment, he began to look around wildly. His gaze glanced off Jeremy before finally settling on Emma. As he worked to fill his lungs with air, he cocked his head and narrowed his eyes.

Colton tried to summon the words to speak, but his throat had locked up. He could see that a woman was speaking to him, but he could not hear her words.

"Are you alright?" Emma asked again, bewildered.

A shrill ringing noise hammered at his eardrums. He winced uncomfortably, trying to block it out. It began to fade away after several moments, and eventually he was able to elucidate her speech in mid-sentence.

"—to the cabin to get some—"

"Is he alive?" Colton interrupted, inclining his head towards the man who lay crumpled beside him.

Only a heavy silence responded. Emma opened her mouth, but she forgot her words the moment they came to mind. Something had taken hold of her, effectively distracting her from the pressing situation at hand. She stared intently into the swirling depths of the man's cerulean blue eyes. They had drawn her in and locked her in some kind of detached stupor. She had never seen anything quite like them before. She felt transparent as they stared back at her.

Without wasting any further time, Colton tore his gaze from the confounded woman and went to Jeremy's aid. He was relieved to discover that his friend did, in fact, have a pulse. Colton gently wrapped his arms around a battered and bloody Jeremy and slowly picked him up. "I have to get him some help," he muttered as he slowly stood up. He ached, but refrained from betraying any sign of it.

Emma widened her eyes when she suddenly realized Colton was shirtless. As inopportune as the thought was, she could not restrain herself from considering his finely sculpted chest and bulging arms the most perfect she had ever seen. She tried to refocus her wits, but everything about this mysterious man seemed to captivate her. His tender yet unmistakably authoritative voice alone would have been enough to enthrall her. Add in his ocean eyes and godlike physique, though, and she considered herself a complete and total victim of his natural charm.

"Would you mind if I take him to that cabin over there?" he asked calmly, though his patience was wearing thin.

Emma took a moment to orient herself. "By all means," she began. "Do whatever it takes."

With his plan approved, Colton headed in the direction of the cabin. He dared not run nor even jog out of fear of bringing further harm to Jeremy. Instead, he walked swiftly.

To Emma, he appeared to glide across the field. His movements were so graceful and fluid. The more she studied him, the less human he seemed.

Emma followed close behind. She found it odd that she had seen no sign of Adam yet. "I'm going to run ahead and get some things prepared for your friend," she said, beginning to run past

Colton. He nodded in affirmation. For the split second that they made eye contact again, Emma once more felt besieged by his otherworldly allure. She managed to tear herself away from his gaze before too long, however, and took off in a sprint towards the cabin.

When she arrived, she burst through the side door to find Adam collapsed in a heap on the kitchen floor. She let out a quick, frightened shout and rapidly made her way over to him. He was unconscious and appeared very pale.

"Adam?" she asked deliriously, taking hold of him. His eyes gradually flickered open after a moment.

"Sorry," he murmured softly. "Blood freaks me out."

"Hush, hush." Emma offered a shadow of a smile. She moved his dark hair away from his forehead, noticing blood underneath. "You must have hit your head when you fainted."

Adam winced and drew a hand to his forehead to feel the bleeding bruise. "How bad?"

"Not very," Emma answered gently. "I think you'll live."

"What about the others?"

"They're coming."

"I never did get the med kit and towels. I think I fainted as soon as I walked inside."

"It's all right," Emma said. She got up and walked to the cabinet where the medical kit was stored. "Are you well enough to care for yourself?"

"I think so."

"Wash away the blood and pad the cut with some paper towels. Then take some ice from the fridge, bag it, and hold it over the bruise," Emma instructed. Adam got up slowly and began to do as he was told. Emma laid out the medical kit on the kitchen counter and opened it up, examining its contents. Satisfied enough, she ran to the bathroom to grab the towels. She found them under the sink and took as many as she could carry. When she reentered the kitchen, she saw the men outside the door. She ran over to allow them in.

"Thanks," Colton said as he carried his companion inside. He took action without a moment's delay. In one swift yet gentle motion, he laid Jeremy down on the wooden floor. He took a towel as she handed it to him and set it under Jeremy's battered head. Colton blinked, fighting back against his dizziness.

Emma watched as the man removed the bloody shirt from the unconscious fellow's head. She cringed a little from the sight of all the blood, but held her ground.

"Could you wet one of the smaller towels with warm water?" he asked her without turning his head.

"Of course," she responded without hesitation. Immediately, she did as she was told and handed him what he had requested. She watched intently as he cleaned up the layer of blood covering the top right portion of the man's cranium.

"I think the worst of the bleeding is over. His blood has clotted quickly," she heard him say. "I have to stitch him up, though. Have you called for an ambulance?"

Emma gathered the medical kit from the kitchen counter and set it beside him. "No cell signal. No landline."

"Do you have a car?"

"Umm, yes," Emma blinked. "But it's not here. It's in the shop. I caught a ride here this morning. A friend said she'd bring it back tonight." She watched intently as he cleaned and began to stitch the lacerations on the man's head.

Colton said nothing for a moment, wholly focused on the task at hand. "Well, keep an eye on the phone in case it finds a signal," he mumbled a moment later.

She nodded emphatically, though she knew he wasn't looking at her. She would have thought she'd be more squeamish. Perhaps it had been the calm and confident demeanor with which this mysterious man was somehow orchestrating this whole scenario that kept her at ease. He had a certain aura about him that made it seem as though nothing could shake him, and it was infectious. She now felt cool and collected, even in this drastic crisis she had involuntarily gotten wrapped up in. She noticed that her thinking was in good working order — much better than it had been outside. Her thoughts of panic had ceased as soon as this man had taken control.

:-:

After twenty patient, meticulous minutes, Colton sat back and admired his handiwork. It had been a while since he last stitched someone up, but he was pleased to see that he had not lost any of his skill. He got up to wash his bloody hands in the kitchen sink.

"Sorry about the mess." He smiled when he caught Emma watching. She had impressed him by maintaining her composure throughout the entirety of this ordeal. He would have expected a woman like her to have fainted or at least fled as soon as he began his operations. But she had kept quiet, careful not to distract him, and remained steadfast by his side. Furthermore, she did not appear distressed in the slightest.

"Don't be. What's the prognosis, doctor?" she asked, trying to play off the fact that he had caught her watching.

"I believe he'll live. He's not bleeding excessively anymore — at least externally, but he's lost a fair amount of blood. Not so much that he's in any mortal danger as of this moment, but he'll need a transfusion if he wants a good chance at a full recovery," Colton explained while simultaneously placing a bandage over the gash on his own forehead. "Whether there's excessive internal bleeding, I can't be sure. I'd venture to guess that there is, and that's why we see such nasty bruising. The severity of that is really my primary concern. Everything else seems to be under control, though. His arms and legs are pretty badly scraped up, but fortunately all those cuts ran long and shallow rather than deep. Better yet, his skull doesn't appear to be fractured. Of course I can't say for certain without an X-ray, but when I was prodding around with my fingers, everything felt intact," Colton said. "As bad as he looks, he's incredibly lucky. Except for the few gashes I stitched up on his head, everything else is mostly bruising and minor cuts. I expect his arm is probably broken, but I suppose we'll find out when he comes to or from another X-ray — whichever comes first. How long it will take for him to regain consciousness, I can't exactly say. It could be minutes. It could be hours... Days... Weeks, even. There's no way to know." He paused as a resurging lightheadedness once more besieged him. "A lesser man would not have survived," he added to mask his own troubles.

"What happened?" she finally asked after several moments of silence.

A flood of guilt washed over Colton. His lips quivered and his stare wavered. "It was my fault," he admitted. "He was climbing down from a cliff by Otter Point. He slipped and fell."

"Oh my God," she breathed. "From how high up?"

"I couldn't really tell. My senses weren't operating very well."

"Why? And why do you say it was your fault?"

"Because I had jumped from the cliff's peak into the ocean. After I managed to get ashore, I passed out. He was coming down to help. In his rush, he must have slipped on the wet rock," Colton answered. He shook his head as another wave of guilt and dizziness washed over him. "If I hadn't jumped, we both would have just hiked back down and Jeremy wouldn't be in the critical condition he's currently in."

"Why?" she asked. Confusion and concern swam in her eyes. "Why jump?"

Colton shrugged. "I wanted to."

"You *wanted* to? Whose idea was it?"

"Mine."

"What did *he* have to say about it?" she questioned, pointing to the still unconscious Jeremy.

"He advised me against it."

"And you did it anyway."

Colton nodded in affirmation.

She narrowed her eyes. "Adam said he saw you carrying your friend when you collapsed at the edge of the woods. You carried him all the way here?

"I did."

"How far away is Otter Point from here? How did you know to head in this direction?"

Colton shrugged again. "Like I said, I was a little out of it. I can't judge the distance as well as I normally could, but I would guess I walked for three or four hours. And I didn't know to come here. I wasn't expecting to find anything. I was just walking. If I was in my right mind, I would have navigated deliberately, but it was just random. When I ended up at the wood's edge, I saw the boy — Adam, you called him? Then..." he trailed off, trying to recollect what had happened next. Try as he could, he was unable to remember anything past that moment.

"You weren't breathing when I found you. Your heart had stopped. You're lucky I know CPR."

"My exhaustion must have killed me," he said almost jokingly.

"I've hardly had any sleep the past few days. All the physical stress must have caused my body to simply shut down. At least I hung on long enough to get Jeremy here."

Emma said nothing. She eyed him warily. "Yeah," she finally said. "You look like you could use some rest."

Colton pursed his lips and nodded his head. "Thank you, by the way. I'm in your debt." He turned away to check on Jeremy.

"Mind if I ask your name?" she asked, setting her hands on her hips.

After checking his companion's vitals, Colton stood back up and turned towards the woman. He ran his fingers through his hair and looked away, trying to ignore his pounding headache.

"Look, I understand if—"

"It's Colton," he said at last. "Colton Anders."

Emma nodded. "I'm Emma Payton."

He finally turned his gaze on her. Emma tried to the best of her ability to read him, but ultimately to no avail. Beneath a thin layer of cloudiness most likely gathered from his recent tribulations, his eyes appeared to be remarkably curious, observant, and strikingly perceptive. They were mirrors, rather than lenses, and betrayed nothing of what lied underneath his weathered facade. Feeling suddenly exposed, Emma crossed her arms defensively.

At once, Colton broke eye contact and looked away again. "You wouldn't happen to have any," he began hesitantly. "Spare shirts, would you?"

Emma could not refrain from very obviously glancing over his chiseled chest after he asked. Embarrassed by her lack of restraint, she blushed colorfully. "Oh, yes. Of course," she answered awkwardly. "I'll go chest the closet— No!" She closed her eyes briefly to regain her composure. "Excuse me, I'll go *check* the closet."

"Take your time," he answered gently.

He could not hide from her the ever-so-slight, crooked smile that had just broken across his face. Before, she would have been pleased about finally getting through to him. At this moment, though, she was much more concerned over what an utter fool she had just made of herself. She made her best effort to offer an endearing smile to compensate for her blunder, but felt like even more of a clown in the process. Eager to leave, she stole away at once.

As soon as she was out of sight, Colton lowered himself to the floor to sit on his heels, his back leaning against a low cabinet. He shut his eyes tight and rubbed his temples. When the throbbing subsided, he allowed himself to break into an ear-to-ear grin.

For the first time in a long time, he found himself remarkably amused. Rare was it that someone could make him smile like that — especially a woman. Emma, however, had done it effortlessly and, even more importantly, without intent.

Furthermore, there was no denying she was highly intelligent. The way her discerning eyes had scanned his face for telltale signs of his underlying character was a methodical scrutiny that she had clearly done countless times before. Colton could recognize this, of course, because this neurotic habit was one that he, too, was hopelessly guilty of. The only difference between the two of them was that his tactics were far less aggressive. He was much too tired and distracted to try to match her level of aggression. With an opponent like her, though, all Colton had to do was stand his ground until Emma's own frustration defeated her and told him everything he needed to know.

Knowledge, after all, is power — Colton had grown up under this maxim. The less a man knows, the less power he holds. The more he could discern of another person, the more control he could amass. Colton thrived when in control. Control deterred chaos. Chaos was the manifestation of panic. And if there was one thing he could not tolerate, it was panic.

He crawled over to where Jeremy lay and sat patiently beside the man. Sure, panic had been delayed, but for how long?

:-:

Before Emma opened the closet doors, she stopped and froze. She closed her eyes and breathed deeply. *What just happened?* she paused to ask herself. Her entire day had just turned upside-down, backwards, and inside out with the arrival of this man. Never in her wildest dreams could she have imagined this scenario. Now that she had put a little bit of distance between herself and Colton, her mind once more spun out of control.

And how had he thwarted her attempts to read him? Emma could not remember the last time someone had completely evaded her mental assaults as he had just done. What really disturbed her, however, was that she had allowed herself to become transparent in the process. She had no doubt that he had seen right through her. She had made a fool of herself.

But that look he had given her just before she had walked away... what was that about? It wasn't arrogant. Certainly not malicious. No, it was playful.

All at once, Emma's previous bitter feelings of losing to this stranger faded away, only to be replaced by a content acceptance of the defeat, soon transforming into a lighthearted eagerness towards future challenges. Yes, there would be more of those, she decided. And she would not let him win next time. She would be prepared.

A sudden realization made her smile, for she had, in fact, ended up with one important bit of knowledge. Her embarrassing defeat, it turned out, was not a total failure after all.

His 'Achilles heel' — she smirked to herself at the accidental, although not unfitting comparison of Colton to the legendary Greek demigod — had indeed revealed itself. She could read from that playfully honest, crooked half-smile... that he liked her.

A mysterious aura seemed to envelop this man. Something about him had effectively placated her during that graphic makeshift surgery. Something about him served to almost perfectly shroud his perceivable identity from her... Something about him made her feel more intuitively attracted to him than any other man she had ever met. She shuddered at the thought — not out of agitation, but rather from a spark of aimless, perhaps misguided hope.

Emma browsed through the closet full of hung clothes. After a moment of careful searching, she found a plain white V-neck that she guessed would fit him. She carried it back to the kitchen and offered it to him without meeting his gaze.

He took it and held it up before him. He tried it on, pleased to discover that it fit nearly perfectly. "Thank you," he said. "I can't imagine the consequences if you hadn't given me one of these."

The quip caused Emma to direct her soft hazel eyes right at his. She analyzed the jest with rapid wit and quickly came up with a retort. She calmed herself so that she could deliver it with a couldn't-care-less attitude that she hoped would, if anything, surprise him.

"I can," she began. "I might have walked in on you later on and shot you with a tranquilizer. You look like a bear, wild man."

"What, this?" he responded, clearly amused. He rubbed his chest with one hand and stroked his beard with his other. "Don't judge. It helps me blend in."

"Only with wild animals and perpetually single men."

"Is there a difference?"

"Perhaps that's my point."

"Don't be mean," he joked, smiling. "Perpetual isn't the same as terminal. Perhaps its—"

"A choice?" Emma interrupted. "Yeah, I've heard that before."

"I was going to say lifestyle."

"Well," Emma began in a hushed voice. "Lifestyles change according to the circumstance."

"I suppose they do." He looked away.

She continued to stare at him. He had completely magnetized her with his allure; even if she tried, she could not let go. Until she was once again away from his presence, she realized, she would not be able to think detachedly. Whether with his words or with his gaze, he drew her in with masterful, effortless ease. And as if she didn't already feel helpless enough, it was obvious to her that he wasn't nearly as interested as she might hope.

Emma tore her gaze from Colton when she noticed Adam out of the corner of her eye reentering the kitchen. He stopped just past the doorway and stared at Colton, then at Emma, then back at Colton.

"So, how's he doing?" Adam asked, feeling awkward and uncomfortable.

"He's stable and lucky to be alive," Colton answered.

"Shouldn't we take him to the hospital?" Adam inquired.

"No," a strained voice moaned.

Adam, Emma, and Colton each looked at one another, trying to discern from whom those last words had come. Colton jogged around to the other side of the kitchen counter to where Jeremy was lying on the floor. Much to his surprise, his friend was stirring and slowly opening his eyes.

"Don't take me. Don't take me to the hospital." He brought his hands to his face to dig his fingers into his temples and shut his eyes tightly.

"What? Is he awake?" Emma asked as she ran over. Adam followed. Upon seeing Jeremy, she spoke again. "We don't have a car, but maybe—"

"I'll take my bike and go find some—"

"No!" Jeremy interrupted harshly. "I'm not going anywhere. I don't need any help. I'll be fine... I'll be fine..."

"I really think—" Emma started to say.

"If anyone tries to take me anywhere," Jeremy interrupted again, this time with sharp severity in his tone. "I will fight. I will yell. I will do everything in my power to resist. It's not worth the trouble. Believe me. Please... just obey a wounded man's wishes. I can't go to a hospital."

"Why not?" Adam asked, madly befuddled.

"Because," he began, contemplating what he was about to say. He growled. "I can't go. Just listen to me... Colton," Jeremy appealed, gazing into his companion's eyes. "Let me be."

Colton remained silent for a moment longer, judging the situation carefully. "Okay," he finally conceded. "We'll... let you be."

Adam quietly slipped away without anyone taking notice.

"Thank you." Jeremy sighed. He closed his eyes and, after a moment, opened them once more. "Can you help me off the floor?"

"Of course," Colton said and began to pick him up.

"No." Jeremy waved him off. "Just help me."

Colton did as was requested, gently aiding Jeremy as he tried to get back on his feet. He took several feeble steps with Colton's support.

"I'll show you to the nearest bedroom," Emma said, walking ahead of the two. "If you're to stay here rather than the hospital, it's best if you rest in a proper bed."

The three of them gradually moved towards their destination. To Colton's utter disbelief, Jeremy was limping almost without need of his support by the time they reached the threshold of the doorway.

"There you go," Colton said as he helped his companion into the queen-size bed. "We'll check in on you periodically."

"I'll holler if I need something," Jeremy said.

"Don't hesitate," Emma added.

Jeremy nodded and closed his eyes. Colton and Emma quietly took their leave.

When they got back to the kitchen, Emma looked around to notice that Adam was nowhere in sight. She glanced in both of the adjacent rooms but still found him nowhere. "Adam?" she called, but no answer came. "Adam?" After a few more moments of searching the cabin and outside, she still had seen no trace of him. "Huh," she breathed as she walked back into the kitchen. "Must have gone home. Odd he didn't say goodbye."

"Yes," Colton agreed. He brushed aside the blinds on a nearby window to glance outside. "Very odd."

TEN

A heavy sadness crushed Adam as he rode on between the trees. When he came upon a turnoff, he turned to take it without braking. The wheels of his bike rattled as he drove over a fallen branch. Light from a descending sun flooded in through the tree canopy to illuminate the forest floor in blotted, colorful patterns. An eerie silence pervaded the woodland air. A chill shot down his spine. He detected no movement in his surroundings. As far as his senses could tell, he was utterly alone.

Since arriving in Bar Harbor a week ago, he frequented the forest of Acadia National Park often. The isolated tranquility soothed him when he needed to be soothed. The welcoming emptiness and whispering shadows allowed him to escape and disconnect from the outside world. They were his haven, and no one else's.

He halted as he came to a fork in the path. The left path, he knew, led to the ragged cliffs and boulder-ridden shoreline; the right led back to Bar Harbor. He rarely ventured to the cliffs — they attracted too many tourists. At this hour, though, the sightseers would most likely be bustling through town looking for a place to eat. He doubted he would happen upon anyone if he decided to make the short expedition over there.

Nevertheless, the cliffs were several miles away. Furthermore, darkness would begin its descent before too long. Be that as it may, he felt an ambiguous yearning for the large boulders and deep waters. He bit his lip as the impulsive thought tantalized him.

A briny breeze gently brushed its way through the army of pines. Adam's ears pricked as a seductive taste of the sea settled on the tip of his tongue. He could faintly hear the relentless waves of the distant ocean pounding the immovable stone of the mainland. He breathed in deeply. His eyes glazed over. His troubles were forgotten. Without a conscious thought, he set off for the cliffs of Otter Point.

:-:

He broke through the edge of the forest and halted his bike on a massive, relatively flat boulder. He inspected his surroundings, but saw no one. After propping his bike against a tree, he slowly approached the edge of the boulder. He rested his hands on his hips and breathed in the salty mist. He closed his eyes and stood up straight — straighter than he usually did. Energy coursed through him. For the second time that day, he was happy. Today, after all, was the first day in more than a decade that he had felt a sense of belonging.

Perhaps it was the saline air, but something had heightened his senses. He became hyper-aware of his surroundings, and thus detected a flicker of distant movement in the corner of his eye — something that, under normal circumstances, he never would have noticed. His curiosity caused him to swing his head in the direction of the movement.

At first, he saw nothing. But after surveying the faraway rock more closely, he could faintly make out the silhouette of a man. The figure, dwarfed by the massive crag that loomed behind him, wore dark clothes that blended in with the wet rock. Adam easily understood how he had missed him when initially surveying the area. The only stark contrast between the figure and his stone backdrop was the man's blatantly bald head.

Adam watched curiously as the silhouette appeared to crouch down to inspect something on the ground by the base of the cliff.

Then, in the blink of an eye, the man snapped his head upwards to look straight at Adam. A pang of fear immobilized the boy. Wondering if this was a trick of his capricious imagination, Adam blinked a few times to see if the man would vanish. Alas, the figure remained there, rooted to where he knelt.

ELEVEN

Vincent remained crouching, staring at the boy who stood on the distant boulder. What had he done to attract the child's attention? Nothing. So why was the boy staring at him? Perhaps he knew something about what had happened here... Vincent considered calling out to him. He rose to full height, but the boy turned heels and ran away into the forest just as he did so.

Vincent frowned, unable to make sense of what exactly had just taken place. He could pursue the boy, but it could easily end up being more trouble than it was worth. After a brief moment, he shrugged off the happening and decided to focus on the more important lead he had just discovered.

The chauffeur had spent the day scouring the forest for traces of Colton Anders. He had come across the remains of a campfire earlier, but that had been all until now. He had discovered these cliffs from a distance and immediately identified them as something the loose end would surely have climbed if he was anywhere in the area.

Upon closer inspection of the crag, Vincent had not found Colton, but he had found small pool of blood here at the base. Better yet, drops of blood staining the granite had left a trail leading away from the cliff base. Though he didn't know whose blood it was, he had a strong hunch the loose end had something to do with whatever had happened here. After all, it was the only lead he had right now.

With a final resolve, Vincent followed the blood. When it led him to the woods' edge, he broke through the tree line to study the forest floor. Dead foliage covered the ground in all directions, but his expert eye was able make out slight disturbances in the carpet of pine needles. Slowly, he began to work his way through the forest, following a trail that seemed to be left by a struggling or wounded person.

:-:

Some time later, nightfall was nearly upon him. Stopping to set up camp was not a viable option, though. The trail was relatively fresh and he would not sit by idly to allow it time to fade away. He really had no choice but to work through the night. He pulled an LED flashlight from his backpack and clicked it on.

As daylight continued to fade, a harmonious, natural symphony gradually brought the seemingly empty forest to life. Bugs began whirring. Small animals scuttled along tree branches. Add in the low rumbling of a prowling beast on the hunt, and it was all almost enough to unsettle the lone chauffeur. Still, though, he trudged on. If trouble did bother him, he would handle it. He had dealt with much worse, after all.

TWELVE

Winona Payton had been writing her latest novel on her laptop when her husband walked through the front door. She lifted her eyes slightly to watch him, but he paid her no attention. She could gather by the look on his face that he was deeply absorbed in his thoughts. Even though the market had closed for the day and he was back home at last, work still held his mind captive. Work was always on his mind.

She was grateful that her children were spared from having to see him on a day-to-day basis. He was always his best around them, but they had yet to notice the brooding darkness within him. The shameless narcissism. The cold apathy. The neurotic obsessions. All traits and habits he had acquired from his work over the past decade. He was a different man than the one Winona had fallen in love with so long ago. Scarce now was his endearing charm. Lost was his dazzling wit. Transformed was that crooked smile of his that had so masterfully concealed his youthful mischief. Gone was his infectious happiness. Gone was all true happiness.

In the mornings, before he left for work, Harvey was almost the same man of days long past. Each morning would renew Winona with optimism that that day would be different... That he would come home after work and sweep her off her feet — like he always used to do.

But each evening only brought her the same disappointment.

Day after day. Month after month. Year after increasingly long year... The pattern was the same. Always the same without any exceptions. And yet, she could not liberate herself of it.

No matter how hard she tried, no matter the promises, no matter the courage she would build up, she could never stand up for herself; no morning failed to excite her with the shadow of hope. Her sense of reason begged her to understand that real hope had disappeared with her real husband long ago, but her misguided heart refused to let go. She was a forlorn fool chasing the tormenting shadow of a shadow.

Manipulation, in truth, was his primary trade at this stage of his life. It was a learned characteristic that he had of late embraced to the extreme. A master puppeteer, he had become. And here she was: his faithful puppet, forever bound to the whims of his tempestuous nature, ever-dancing to a monotonous show that would not end — one that after all these years must still somehow provide the master behind the curtains with an inkling of sadistic entertainment.

"How's dinner coming along?" the man himself finally muttered. He had taken a seat on the couch opposite Winona and still had not so much as bothered to look at her. His briefcase remained steadfast by his side. His disinterested gaze held low. His hands were clasped together. One leg sophisticatedly crossed over the other. His 'million-dollar-suit,' lined with light-grey pinstripes, creased across the middle because he had not unbuttoned any of his three buttons. His red silk tie was still pulled tightly up against his white collar.

"Thelma?" Winona called.

"Yes, madam?" the housekeeper answered almost immediately from the kitchen, a room away.

"How's dinner coming along?" Winona asked, reiterating Harvey's question.

"Let me ask Torté," Thelma answered, referring to the Payton's in-house gourmet chef. She hurried away, only to return a brief moment later. "It's almost ready, madam."

"Where's Lance?" Harvey asked. He had not moved a muscle since he had sat down, nor had he shifted his gaze in the slightest.

"In the shower. He only got home twenty minutes ago," Winona responded. She shut her laptop and got up. Her husband's business-like stature was beginning to bother her, and she wanted to somehow gently hint to him that he could lighten up now that he was home. "I'm going to go freshen up before dinner."

In a flash, Harvey jerked his head upward to meet his wife's eyes with his own. He effectively froze her with a bone-chilling gaze. "You've had *all* this time to *'freshen up,'*" he snapped caustically, spitting out the last two words like venom. "Stay *here* and wait for your son with your husband."

Winona sat back down in one hurried motion and promptly averted her eyes from Harvey's corrosive stare. She didn't have the heart to reopen her laptop and resume her work on her novel. She wanted to at least go into the kitchen to get away from him, but she dared not. Instead, she sat there, afraid to move and terrified of looking him in the eye.

Minutes crept by like torturous hours. She could feel his hateful gaze boring holes into her as they sat there in silence. She could hardly breathe. Shock held her completely immobilized. The disgusted look of sheer contempt on his face alone had wounded her deeply. Paired with his vindictive tone and callous words, his scolding had been more than enough to make her want to weep in anguish. She dared not, though. She wanted to quiver and tremble in pained fear, but she dared not. Instead, she put forth her best effort to maintain the illusion of composure. The show must go on.

"Dad!" a voice called minutes later. "It's about time you're home!"

As Harvey spun around to see his son atop of the lavish living room's staircase, a beaming smile lit up his previously scornful face. A handsome young man appropriately dressed in a suit and tie rushed down the steps to greet his father. Harvey stood up as Lance ran to him.

Despite the horror of what had just taken place, a content warmth invaded Winona's heart as she watched father and son meet in a loving embrace. Whereas she was helpless in the wake of her husband's temper, their children truly brought out the best of him. She could unmistakably recognize a look of genuine love on his face as he wrapped his arms around his son.

"It's good to see you, son," Harvey said when the two separated. "Come, now. Dinner is about to be served."

Lance led the way to the dining room. Harvey followed close behind with a gentle hand on his son's back. Winona kept her distance, gliding slowly a few steps behind her husband.

Harvey pulled the chair at the head of the table out and offered his son the seat. Lance kindly accepted and sat down. Harvey took the seat to his son's right. Winona, a moment afterwards, seated herself to Lance's left. Harvey unfolded his napkin and laid it carefully across his lap. Lance mimicked. Winona deliberated a moment before doing the same.

An almost awkward silence hung in the air for a few seemingly eternal seconds. Harvey flashed a slight smile in Lance's direction without a word. Lance nodded his head, returning the slight smile. Winona took a sip of water from her glass and looked away in the opposite direction, absentmindedly tucking a strand of blonde hair behind her ear.

"Ah, here we are," Harvey spoke at last when Thelma walked into the dining room with two platters of food. She set the first plate before Lance and the second before Harvey. As she ran back to the kitchen to retrieve Winona's, Lance gazed with hungry eyes at his dish of six-egg frittata, lobster, and caviar. "My God, son!" Harvey laughed. "I would guess by the way you're looking at your supper that you haven't eaten in days!"

Lance tried to tear his eyes from his meal, but his gaze kept flicking back towards the steaming red lobster. "Well, I must admit I am rather ravenous," he confessed. "I almost forgot what it was like to eat at home."

"Well," Winona began, finally chiming in as Thelma set a bowl of salad and a dish of caviar before her. "I've never heard you complain about Harvard's cuisine before. They don't feed you well there?"

"No," he began, flicking his eyes between his parents. "They definitely do, but nothing compares with Torté's meals."

"Ah, my heart sings with bliss!" a voice boomed as a hefty Samoan man entered the dining room. His long, jet-black hair was tied up in a ponytail and roofed by a white toque. He carried two small, collapsible wooden tables. "I always love hearing that I'm appreciated." Torté smiled. He stopped between Lance and Harvey to set up his little wooden tables. Afterwards, he took two pristinely white cloths from his front pockets and laid one over each of the tables.

"Appreciated and missed dearly, Master Torté," Lance affirmed, turning his head to make eye contact with the tall chef.

"Oh, Master Lance, I've missed you dearly as well," the Samoan reciprocated, still smiling. "But it's my understanding that you'll be dining with us more regularly from here on?"

"If my schedule allows," Lance joked.

"Oh, busy man, eh?" Torté inquired. Thelma entered the dining room to hand the chef two white china plates. He took them and set them side-by-side on one of the cloth-covered tables. "Shall I prepare your lobster, Master Lance?"

"Are your hands clean?" Lance asked, feigning seriousness. The twinkle in his eyes, however, made it obvious that he was just teasing the Samoan. He handed Torté his plate.

"Oh, hush," Torté chided lightheartedly. He took the dish and set it on the second table. He transferred the steaming lobster onto one of the china plates on the other little table. The Paytons watched intently as the Samoan grasped the crustacean with two powerful hands and ripped the tail off in one swift motion. His fingers worked as a well-operating machine, expertly tearing the flesh from the shell. After thoroughly cleaning the muscle out of the tail, he gathered the meat and set it on Lance's dish between the frittata and caviar. Next, he effortlessly plucked the crustacean's arms from its body. A lesser man would have needed a tool to crack the lobster's tough claws, but Torté was able to tear them apart easily with his muscular fingers. After he cleaned the muscle out of the claws and arms, he took the meat and set it on Lance's dish. He mixed it up carefully with the meat from the tail.

Thelma briefly reentered the dining room to hand Torté a small ceramic cup of hot, liquefied butter. She swiftly grabbed the plate that held the undesirable remnants of Lance's lobster and left the room.

Torté poured the butter from the ceramic cup in modest amounts onto the lobster meat. Afterwards, he mixed it up a little more. Satisfied, he offered Lance the dish with a smile. Lance graciously accepted and nodded his thanks. Torté then turned to Harvey. "And yours, Master Payton?"

"Yes, please, Torté," Harvey responded with a light smile while handing the Samoan his plate. "I couldn't do it as well as you could."

Torté smirked playfully and took Harvey's dish. The Paytons

patiently watched as he prepared Harvey's lobster just as he had Lance's. "No butter for you, Master Payton?"

"No, thank you, Torté."

When the chef had finished, he returned the plate to Harvey. Thelma returned once more to take the second china plate full of Harvey's lobster remnants and the cup of hot butter.

"Masters…" Torté smiled, nodding at Lance and then Harvey. "Madam," he nodded at Winona. "Enjoy your meals!" he boomed, clapping his hands together.

The Paytons all smiled graciously and extended their thanks to the Samoan. Torté gathered the cloths and folded them back into his pockets. Then, he collapsed the two wooden tables and tucked one under each arm. He smiled once more to each of them as he exited the dining room.

"I bet you don't get that at Harvard," Harvey scoffed cheerfully as he took the first bite of his frittata.

"We sure don't," Lance agreed, stuffing lobster into his mouth as gracefully as he could.

"I apologize a thousand times over for missing your graduation, son," Harvey said a moment later, between mouthfuls.

"No, no, no, Dad," Lance countered, shaking his head. "It's no big deal. Don't fret."

"Oh, but it is a big deal! I feel like a terrible father for missing your last graduation ever — especially one as prestigious as yours from Harvard's Business School. I would have given anything to have been there with your mother." Harvey paused to try his caviar. He failed to notice his wife roll her eyes. "Alas, I really could not get away from the firm. I was closing a deal — a big merger with Sunfield Oil."

"I know how much that means to you, Dad. Really," Lance

said, pausing to stuff his mouth with the last of his lobster. "It's all right."

"Well, you mean more to me, son," Harvey set his fork down a moment and looked at Lance. He wiped his mouth before continuing. "I know it's not much, but I have a business proposition for you — something of an apology as well as a gift for your graduation."

"Oh, Dad," Lance said, setting down his fork and wiping his mouth with his napkin as well. "I'm so fortunate as it is. You both have done so much for me over the years. I really can't accept anything more."

"I don't want to hear it, son. You've worked extremely hard to get where you are. All we've done is encourage you and present you with the right opportunities. You are the driving force behind your own success." Harvey paused a minute to try a sip of his wine. "I could use a man like you at the firm."

Lance was silent and motionless. He stared anxiously at his father, awaiting what he would say next.

"So I'm going to offer you a position of Junior Partner at the company. You can start whenever you want. You'll only be a single floor beneath me. I've already prepared an office for you. I handpicked the furniture myself. I'm sure you'll approve."

Harvey perceived the evident shock in his son's expression, despite Lance's best attempts to keep his composure. Harvey took pleasure in the genuine reaction. His son was a winner, and winners never presume.

"Dad," Lance breathed. "I don't know what to say." He paused again. "Thank you so much."

"Just promise me you'll keep working hard," Harvey encouraged. "So listen, I've got another big merger coming up in a few days and I'd really like for you to be there..."

Winona tuned out. This was the part of dinner that she knew she would be completely excluded from. She watched as her husband and son carried on a conversation about matters of which she knew nothing about. She took the last bite of her caviar and backed herself away from the dinner table a little. She paused to check Harvey's reaction, but he hadn't noticed. He was still thoroughly absorbed in his conversation with Lance. Nor did he seem to notice as she stood up and walked away.

Winona reentered the living room and began ascending the staircase to the second story. She made her way to her private bedroom and picked up the house phone. She dialed a number that had been ingrained into her memory and sat patiently on the side of the bed while she waited for her daughter to answer her call.

THIRTEEN

"Sorry about that," Emma apologized, walking back out onto the porch where Colton stood at the grill flipping burger patties. "My phone managed to find a signal just long enough for my mom to call and check in."

"Your mother checks in on you?" Colton inquired without turning his head. "Why? Are you trouble?"

"Well, today it would seem that trouble found me, and he's not leaving."

"Who? Jeremy?" Colton joked. "Nah, he's harmless. But I'm sure he's hungry."

"I checked on him while I was in the cabin," Emma said, walking up beside Colton. "He's sound asleep."

"Well I'm making him a few cheeseburgers just in case. We can put them in the fridge if he doesn't want any tonight."

"How many do I get?"

"Oh, I'm cooking for you, too?" Colton asked, feigning shock. "I suppose I can spare you a slice of cheese."

"Now, just you hold on a minute!" Emma exclaimed with a smile. "I think you're forgetting who's providing all the food!"

"Not a fan of cheese?" Colton asked, ignoring her. "How about a leaf of this lettuce?" He turned to her to judge her reaction. Pleased, he continued. "Or would that be too much? Maybe I could scrape the sesame seeds off my buns—"

"I'll have a double cheeseburger," she interrupted. "With onions, tomato, lettuce, mayonnaise, and ketchup," she finished. It was evident to her this time that she had caught him off guard, perhaps for the first time since they met. "Throw some bacon on there, too," she added for good measure.

"No way you can eat all that!" he exclaimed in disbelief.

"And my patties better be well done..." She smirked. "Or else."

"Or else what?" Colton laughed.

"It's in your best interest to not find out."

"That's reassuring. Well, normally I'm a dissident when it comes to authority," he began, placing slices of cheese on a few of the patties. "But I think my inner gentlemen is urging me to give in to your silly requests."

"And they said chivalry was dead."

"Could you grab yourself a plate?"

"Or perhaps it is after all."

"Oh, come on. I don't have to do everything for you, do I? Do you normally get waited on hand and foot back home?"

"How'd you know?"

"I didn't. That's why I asked."

"Well," Emma began, walking over to the wooden table to grab herself a plate and some buns. "I kind of do, actually."

"Oh, am I dining with royalty tonight?"

"Far from it." Emma laughed. "I hate that lifestyle. How else did you think I ended up all the way out here?"

"Well, your majesty, I don't really know what 'all the way out here' refers to. As far as I could tell, you live nearby. So, please..."

He paused, transferring two burger patties from the grill to her plate. "Enlighten me."

"But then I won't be quite so mysterious anymore," she joked.

"I thought I was the mysterious one," he countered, turning the grill off. He grabbed a plate for himself and began building a burger quite similar to Emma's.

"If I tell you," she began, taking her seat at the wooden table. "Then you have to promise to tell me a little bit more about yourself, wild man."

"I think we both already know a lot more about each other than we're letting on."

"Oh, are we being honest now?"

"Sure." He shrugged, sitting down across from her. "I'm in the mood for it."

"Well, then..." She paused to try a bit of her burger. "Oh that's quite good," she managed to say with a mouthful. "Tell me what you already know about me. You seem," she began, pausing again to take a monstrous bite. "Uncannily perceptive."

"As do you, your highness," he began. "Well, for starters, I know you don't eat like that at home, where the rules of social etiquette confine you, nor in your hometown, where you're always being judged." He paused to judge her reaction. He took a bite before continuing. "I do know that you aren't from around here. Your very act of being here, at this cabin sitting on the brink of wilderness, is your idea of an escape. It's your idea of rebellion — just like eating that massive burger, only on a larger scale." He paused again to take another bite of his own burger. He caught a piece of mayonnaise-soaked onion as it tried to drip down his chin.

She interrupted him in the lull before he could continue. "How, pray tell, can you *know* all that?"

"The same way *you* can know things when you perceive other people. This is a game we both like to play. You can't read me like you can everyone else, though." He paused to laugh. "And it bothers you. It's precisely the frustration I see in your face when you fail to read me that allows me to read you. You're so used to being the best, it destroys you to finally meet someone that can best you," he said, opening his bottled water to gulp a sip. "You're very competitive — you were obviously groomed to be the best at whatever you do, and I bet you're very well-versed in a wide range of activities. Your competitiveness causes you to rebel — you succeed and excel and you want people to take notice. But how can people take notice of you when you're at home? How can you succeed when you're being confined? I don't know where you're from, but this isn't home." He paused to eye her. "No, this isn't home at all... this is far from it. There are no boundaries here — all you can do here is succeed at whatever it is you're here to do. You're not here just to escape, though. You have a higher purpose — you're here to figure something out. But what? That, I don't yet know." He took a massive bite of his burger, effectively reapplying a casual aura to their conversation. "Do you?" he asked with half of a mouthful.

"Perhaps..." Emma managed to say. She was making her best efforts to conceal the total shock that had suddenly besieged her. He certainly had read her, and he had missed nothing.

"Not gonna tell me?" Colton inquired after the momentary silence. "That's really all right. I don't mean to pry. I just thought that you wanted us to be honest with each other, so I told you what I knew. I apologize if I made you feel uncomfortable."

"No, it's just that..." Emma began, tearing her gaze from Colton's mesmerizing blue eyes. They seemed to shine in the moonlight of the falling darkness. "Well, you already said it — no one has ever read me like that. I just feel... vulnerable," she admitted. "And I don't like that. But I suppose I asked for it, and you delivered. You hit everything right on the spot."

"Well," Colton began with a shrug. "Not everything."

Emma didn't know how to take that last statement. Was there more that he hadn't said? Or was he implying that he was unable to read some parts of her? She didn't necessarily want to find out, so she didn't press him.

"I suppose it's your turn," Colton said after Emma didn't respond. "Come on, let me have it."

"My turn?" she asked, still slightly confounded.

"What can you tell of me? You've been watching me all afternoon. I know you're savvy enough to infer at least something."

"Oh," she muttered. "Not much. You're kind of an enigma. But I do know a few things. You're paranoid. You try to do it discretely, but you check your surroundings every few minutes. With knowledge of that, coupled with your appearance, I presume you don't hang around in public very much. You're comfortable enough around me, but I would guess that you're not very comfortable in crowds, where there are too many people to keep track of. You, like me, thrive on keeping your identity secure. You feel empowered when you know more about someone else than they do of you. It's only natural to isolate yourself — it's easier and safer that way."

Colton nodded. He felt a little uneasy himself all of the sudden. He hadn't expected much, but she had surprised him yet again. He supposed it wouldn't be too difficult for someone as perceptive as her to deduce that much, though; all she had to do was watch him for a little while and reflect on her own idiosyncrasies — they seemed to be fairly like-minded.

"You didn't like that." Emma laughed. "We're very similar, you know. You're behaving now exactly how you described I was earlier. When you get insecure, you reveal yourself more and more," she said with a smile, but as soon as the words left her mouth, he became inscrutable yet again. He had left his guard down only momentarily, but he put his walls back up the moment his privacy had been breached.

"It's human nature," he offered. "So, then, where are you from?"

"Water Mill."

"The Hamptons?"

Emma nodded.

Colton raised his eyebrows. "Fancy."

"Don't judge."

"You say that like you're ashamed."

"I'm not ashamed," Emma countered with a shrug and sideward glance. "Though it's not something I'm necessarily proud of."

"I understand."

"You do?"

"Yeah," Colton answered lazily. "I mean... after everything I said about you, it would make sense that you would want to achieve things for yourself. You don't want to make it look like you're piggybacking on your parents. After all, that's why you're here, isn't it? To make something of yourself?"

"Yes." Emma smiled. "That's exactly right."

A pensive silence hung in the air as Emma reflected on their conversation. He had not ceased to astound her yet. He really understood her. The discomfort had faded by now. If there was one part of him that she knew for sure, it was that he meant her no harm. He was genuine. She no longer felt vulnerable. All that bothered her now was that she didn't quite understand him.

"So, where are you from?" Emma asked. She watched as Colton tried to stifle a slight smirk. "What? You don't want to tell me?"

Colton caught the sudden edge in her tone. He was quick to rectify the misunderstanding. "It's not that," he answered calmly. "It's just complicated."

"Of course it is," she rebutted sarcastically, although less belligerently.

"I can tell you where I was born."

"So tell me."

"Sacramento."

"What's so complicated about that?"

"And I can tell you where I lived after I turned two."

"All right, let me have it."

"Spain."

"What part?"

"Cerca de Sevilla."

"Is that a place? I took French, not Spanish."

"Près de Séville."

"Close to Sevilla?"

"Yes."

"That's interesting, especially considering you just spoke in three different languages... Are you fluent in each?"

"Yes."

Emma nodded. *Very interesting*, she thought.

"And I can tell you where I lived after I turned four."

"Oh?"

"Trier, Germany."

"Can you speak German too?"

"Ja."

"I assume that means yes"

Colton nodded. "And there are a few more places, too."

Emma raised her eyebrows. "Oh yeah? How many more?"

"Seven," he responded without hesitation. He watched as her eyes opened wide. "Technically, at least. Japan, Italy, Guam..." He paused a moment. "When I turned fourteen, we moved to Afghanistan." He paused again before continuing. "After a two-year stint there, we travelled all throughout India for a few months. After India, I settled down in France to finish high school. Graduated and went on to college. Last three years I've been roaming the globe, never staying in one place too long."

Emma attempted to absorb all that she had just heard. After several long moments, she shook her head, clearly befuddled. "Okay, I have *so* many questions."

"One at a time," he said gently.

"Okay, first of all," she started. "Why?"

"I'm a military brat. My mom and I followed my dad whenever the Air Force transferred him."

"When was he transferred to Afghanistan?"

"After Nine-Eleven."

Emma was silent for a moment before continuing. "You can speak all those languages?"

Colton nodded. "Spent just enough time in each place to learn the native language and all about the culture before moving on."

"It's amazing how easily the brain absorbs knowledge when you're that young and motivated," Emma mentioned.

Colton nodded. "I didn't learn anything in Afghanistan though, and in India I learned a lot of culture but hardly any language. Guam was similar — just bits and pieces of indigenous language, but it was mostly English."

"What's it like to be so cultured?"

"I can go anywhere in the world and feel at home."

"Where is home?"

"Nowhere in particular and everywhere in general."

"Is that a sophisticated way of saying you're homeless?"

"Perhaps."

"Why does it feel like you've told me so much, and yet I still hardly know who you actually are?"

"Like I said, it's complicated."

"Yes, you certainly are," Emma breathed, narrowing her eyes. She couldn't resist letting another smile crawl across her face as she thought of him in light of all that he had just shared with her. Describing him was almost beyond her vocabulary. She had met so many prominent people with remarkably unique stories in her hometown and during her seven years at university, but none came to par with the man who sat before her now. His background was rich beyond comparison, and whereas most people she had met try to flaunt and pretend, here he was, modestly subduing his story. It thrilled her. "What college did you go to?"

"Yale."

Emma's head spun. "My word," she breathed. "What kind of degree do you have and what's it in?"

"I don't have one."

Emma contorted her face into a look of confusion. "You dropped out?"

Colton nodded.

"When? Why? Was it too hard?"

"No, it wasn't too hard." Colton laughed. Seconds afterward, however, his facade faded into an inscrutable passiveness. "I had a few weeks to go in my senior year when I left."

"You just *left*?" Emma burst out, completely befuddled. "You had a few weeks to go in your senior year at Yale and you quit?"

"I couldn't stay."

"Why? What would make you leave?"

"I didn't want to be there anymore."

Emma didn't respond for a moment. He was clearly withholding information from her. "Where did you want to be instead?"

"Somewhere else."

"Oh, you don't say." Emma muttered sarcastically. "Where did you go?"

"Yosemite."

"The National Park?"

"No, the Mexican restaurant." He smirked in hopes of revealing to her is facetiousness. The gesture successfully reapplied a lighter air to the deepening conversation.

"Ha-ha," she pretended to laugh, allowing a slight smile to curve across her gentle features. "To do what?"

A pensive look overcame his face. "To find my purpose," he finally muttered.

"You couldn't find your purpose at Yale?" Emma asked quizzically.

"No."

"What *is* your purpose?"

Immediately, Colton was reminded of his father's question on the peak of the Italian mountain. "I'm still figuring it out."

Emma had felt a bridge of understanding suddenly form between the two of them as he spoke those last few words. Although he was being ambiguous at best, she somehow could relate to what he was failing to explicitly say. She noted to herself the stark differences in the ways he had been conversing with her since they met. He could be charming and infatuating when they were flirting, but the second the conversation turned towards his personal life, his communication skills shut down. No doubt, it was a deliberate defensive mechanism. She did not want to press him, but she was too curious not to.

"So what did you actually do at Yosemite?"

"I climbed El Capitan."

"Which part?"

"The Nose."

"All three-thousand feet?"

"All three-thousand feet."

"That's impressive."

"Thanks."

"How long did it take you?"

"Just under two hours."

Emma's head spun again. He was too good at dropping these bombs on her. She would have to learn to expect anything from him. This certain fact surprised her because she was no stranger to the rock-climbing world, and she knew El Capitan well.

"I know who you are," she breathed as a sudden understanding overcame her. "I know who you are."

Colton raised his eyebrows.

"I interviewed a climber a few semesters ago for a psychology research project. He told me all about you."

"All about me? I doubt that."

"He practically lives there — in Yosemite," she said as the memory came back to her. She could hardly think straight as all the seemingly irrelevant information suddenly flooded her mind. "He's a die-hard climber. He mentioned you a few times. I remember it clear as day now. It adds up."

"Perhaps he was one of my colleagues."

"Seemed like more of a follower," Emma managed to respond. "He said you just showed up out of the blue one day. Next thing he knew, you were half way up the Nose."

"That's not exactly true. It wasn't quite so immediate."

"Seriously, Colton," Emma said sharply. "Stop being so dreadfully modest for just a minute so I can actually wrap my brain around this. Just tell me what happened."

"Okay," he conceded. "I left Yale. Drove to Yosemite. Camped out in the back of my Jeep for a few days. Learned the wall. Made a few ascents with rope to practice. Then, I just did it. No hype. No audience. I just did it. But someone saw. Someone filmed it. Someone even timed me. Next thing I know everyone is going ballistic. Apparently it was the first time anyone had free-solo-climbed the Nose. Setting the overall record was just icing on the cake — for them, I mean. It didn't really matter to me," he said. "That wasn't what it was about."

"What was it about?"

"Finding my purpose."

"That's an interesting way to go about searching for a purpose."

"You don't know what it's like," he breathed, shaking his head. "To be up there. To be up on the rock. There's nothing like it." He paused a minute to stare at Emma. "Almost nothing like it."

"You're right," she admitted. "I absolutely don't. How do you just up and do that? You make it seem like it was no big deal."

"Under the circumstances, it wasn't."

Aha, Emma thought to herself. *Finally getting somewhere.* She knew there had to be more to his story that he wasn't letting on. She had to pursue the opening.

"I see," she began cautiously. "What were the circumstances?"

He didn't seem to hear her. He looked off into the distance. The look on his face was expressionless. The spark of his eyes was lost to a shadow. He and Emma sat in dark silence for several long moments.

"Colton?" she asked, reaching under the table to touch his hand. He recoiled as she made contact. He whipped his head back towards hers. For a moment, a light revealed his eyes. They had taken on a lustrous glow. Emma's thoughts drifted away as a foggy captivation settled over her. As quick as the moment came, however, it passed. Emma kept her gaze locked on Colton, though he had already looked away once more. The dreamlike trance he had seemed to be trapped in no longer appeared to have a hold over him.

"I'm going to clean up," she said a moment later. She grabbed their plates and napkins and slipped through the sliding glass door into the cabin.

She walked to the kitchen and slid the garbage into the trashcan. A slight dizziness suddenly overcame her. She reached out to the counter to steady herself. She opened her eyes wide, stared at the ground, and took a deep breath. She didn't know what to think at the moment because she didn't have any idea what just happened. One moment with Colton she would feel uneasy; the next she would feel completely entranced. On one hand, she wished she had never encountered him, but on the other, she didn't want to let him out of her sight. Once more, her mind swirled. She had never been affected in this manner by another person. A peculiar aura followed the man, and each time Emma thought she had shaken it, it returned.

Emma stood up straight and crossed her arms, only to feel the hairs on her skin standing straight up. A chill shivered through her. She looked at her watch and saw it was a few minutes past ten — much later than she had thought it was.

After another moment of pause, she walked back out onto the porch. "You're planning on sleeping here tonight, right?" she asked Colton, who sat rooted to the same spot. Upon hearing her voice, he perked up and looked at her.

"Well," he began. "I don't want to intrude."

"You kind of already have," she teased.

"Well, I can go sleep on the side of the road," he offered, standing up. "Maybe if I'm lucky I'll find a hole I can crawl into."

"No!" Emma laughed. "Please, stay. You're more than welcome. Besides, someone has to look over your friend. You can't abandon him."

"Okay, okay. I'll stay the night here. Try not being so persuasive next time."

"Next time?"

"Yeah, Jeremy and I were planning on having another accident in a few weeks."

"What makes you think I'll help you again?"

"Well, I hope you would."

"I won't be here a few weeks from now, anyway."

"Why not?"

"I don't live here," she began, stating it as if it was obvious. "My family owns a villa on the outskirts of Bar Harbor. I'm staying there for the summer."

"Then why are you here?"

"I'm running a summer camp."

"For kids?"

"No, for grown men," she retorted sarcastically.

"One could make that argument right about now," Colton said, cracking a sly smile.

"That's very true." She laughed. "Anyway... yes, I run a children's summer camp. Ages vary from three to six. Their parents drop them off at nine every morning and pick them up every afternoon at five."

"Sounds demanding," Colton remarked.

"It really is." Emma nodded in agreement. "And I've only been at it for a day! It was a good day, though, for the most part. I've got some good kids."

"What are you going to do with them tomorrow? Does our being here affect anything?"

Emma bit her lip as she thought up the consequences. It was something that had not come to mind before now. "I'll just have to work around you guys and avoid the cabin as much as possible. We don't really come in here that often, just to wash our hands and use the bathroom — not necessarily in that order, though." She winked. "And I come and get food out of the fridge and pantry for snack and lunch time, but pretty much all of our activities go on outside."

"I just want to make this all as easy as possible on you. You didn't ask for any of this, yet here you are... I don't know what I would have done if you hadn't been here."

"Probably nothing."

"Right." He smirked. "I'd be dead."

"Is that weird to think about?"

"Not so much."

"It would be for most people, I think," Emma said, narrowing her eyes. "It would be for me, at least. I don't know about you, but I haven't come to terms with death yet. I still have lots that I want to accomplish before I'm ready to leave this life. When I think about it I realize I..." she trailed off, apparently lost in thought. "I want to live each day without regrets and leave behind a legacy so I won't be soon forgotten. Scratching the surface of death as you just did... That doesn't put anything into new perspective? You're just going to continue living your life as if nothing happened?"

"Not exactly, no," he began. "I think you misunderstood when I said it wasn't weird to think about. I hang on the brink of death almost every day. So, naturally, the thought of it is constantly trying to weasel its way into the forefront of my consciousness. I try to block it out and avoid focusing on it. I don't want it to prevent me from living the life I have. I think your attitude is the right one — wanting to live each day without regrets and leaving a legacy. Lots of people would agree with that, but most people don't live their days like I do. I come too close to death too often for most people to be comfortable with. The attitude that most people have is to live their life to the fullest *within boundaries*. I don't have boundaries."

"You'll do *anything*?"

"Anything I want to do, yeah."

"What about common sense?"

"Common sense is relative and not at all common."

"You understand what I mean, though," she said, rolling her eyes. "Your judgment skills."

"What about my judgment?"

"Do your judgment skills ever impede your impulses?"

"My judgment and impulses are in sync with each other. What I want to do seems like the right thing to do."

"That seems ineffective and dangerous. Unstable, even," she said, allowing an uncomfortably aggressive edge to creep into her tone.

Colton caught it and assumed the defensive. "That would depend on who you're talking to. For whatever reason, you keep trying to bunch me into your conception of 'most people.' Now, for 'most people,' a judgmental check on their impulses is absolutely necessary. Impulses are impulses because they aren't thought out. Mine are different, though—"

"Wow," she interrupted, shaking her head as a disgusted look crossed her face. "You seemed all modest moments ago, now you're bordering on narcissism."

Colton closed his eyes and dropped his head. She was certainly doing a good job of infuriating him. She knew just what to say. If he were in her shoes, he would be acting similarly. She wasn't in the wrong, just in the dark. He could easily explain if she only gave him the chance.

"My impulses are trained. I spent the first fourteen years of my life in the military, where obedience and protocol reign supreme. I had two constant friends growing up — my mother and my father. I never even went to actual school until I was seventeen. I was never given the opportunity to develop immature, irresponsible habits in my childhood, which are where immature, irresponsible impulses originate. I'm completely stable, and I'm not a narcissist."

Emma could not challenge the authority in his voice. Despite her best efforts to get inside his head and make him lose his temper, she had caused the opposite reaction. His voice had remained perfectly level, and his tone was neither offensive nor defensive. He had complete control over himself and the situation. *Someone like that*, Emma thought. *Is either completely stable or mentally damaged.* She still did not know him well enough to decide which he actually was, so she erred on her gut feeling.

"Okay," she conceded convincingly, although she remained dubious. "I apologize." She noticed no change in his expression. It had remained passive since her aggressive questioning of his character began. Her scrutiny had seemed to have no effect on him, and it bothered her.

"Don't worry about it."

"So," she began. "What do you do for a living that's so dangerous?"

"I climb rocks."

She laughed. "Very sophisticatedly put."

He grinned in return. "It pays the bills."

"By your appearance." Emma smirked, looking him up and down. "I'd say you either have too many bills or none at all. Didn't you say you were homeless?"

"I still have to pay for airline tickets and other travel expenses." He shrugged.

"Airline tickets and travel expenses?" she repeated. "Never thought I'd meet a white-collar hobo."

"Just because I don't technically own a home doesn't mean I'm poor."

"So, you're rich?"

"There's no middle-ground with you, is there?" he critiqued lightheartedly.

"You didn't answer my question," Emma said playfully, drawing an inch nearer.

"Why does it matter, your majesty?" he delayed, taking a small step backwards.

"It matters," she began. "Because you're avoiding the question!" she exclaimed, continuing to inch closer.

"I'm not avoiding the question!" He laughed. "Just the answer."

"Why are you ashamed of your money?"

"Why are you ashamed of yours?"

"You didn't earn it?"

"I've earned a lot," he conceded, looking away. He continued to back away from her ever so slightly as she subtly continued edging towards him. "Just not all of it."

"Then why live the way you do?"

"Why live the way you do?" he asked, once again turning Emma's question back on herself. It was an inherently obnoxious defensive tactic, but in this case Emma didn't find it irksome; she knew it was part of his game, as it was part of hers to play along.

"It's a lifestyle," she answered.

"Well," Colton said, finally standing his ground. "Lifestyles change," he muttered.

As she heard the words, she took one last step towards him, landing less than a foot away from him. The ensuing silence would have made the situation awkward for most, but something else hung in the air. Emma allowed herself to forget her previous doubts about his character to embrace the unspoken essence of the moment.

FOURTEEN

Emma tried to sit down gently on her bed, but she couldn't stop herself as she suddenly collapsed. She landed hard on the mattress and shut her eyes on impact. After a moment, her lightheadedness passed, but she continued to lay there in silence.

What a day, she thought to herself. Her mind jumped from one memory of the past thirteen hours to the next, unable to focus on one for more than a few brief seconds at a time. Every memory that she could recall had one thing, or one person, rather, in common: Colton Anders. He had dropped in on her life like a bomb — although he wasn't necessarily as destructive. The residual effect he had left on her was equal in strength, however.

With her eyes shut and her consciousness wide-awake, she felt the first memory she shared with him flood her mind as if she were reliving it. She once again lost herself to the depths of his azure eyes as if for the first time. They bore so much life for someone who had been dead only moments ago; so much experience and history for a man who, beneath his grizzly beard and weathered face, only appeared to be in his mid-twenties; so much resilience, wonder, passion...

Emma sat up in sudden realization. She had indeed read him. In that initial encounter, in that moment of pure truth, before words or actions could interfere, a connection of understanding had bridged between them. She knew the underlying nature of his character, and it elucidated so much.

She began stringing together all her understandings of his persona as if they were the pieces of a puzzle. There was an evident problem, though... she lacked many of the pieces. In fact, it seemed those that she lacked happened to be the most important ones. Without them, his true identity remained ultimately unrecognizable. She possessed the cornerstones and the highlights, but she lacked that which existed in-between.

Despite all that he had shared with her, hazy gaps sporadically obstructed his timeline. When he had recounted his story to her, he had jumped from one event to the next, leaving her with results and outcomes, but no causes. He had left the in-between stages as murky gray areas. Surely, they would certainly illuminate the reasons explaining why he had done what he had done. Whatever had befallen him was something that she could not divine on her own. The only way she would be able to complete his puzzle was if he allowed her to. In spite of everything, he was still in control. She wondered with near certainty if this was all by his design...

He was a wild card. Entirely unpredictable. If there was one thing she had learned of him for certain, it was that he somehow managed to consistently defy her expectations. Whatever she prepared herself for, he brushed past her defenses to surprise her time and time again. He had control, and he wasn't about to let her in more than he allowed.

The thought made her wonder: was she even playing her own game? Or was she merely a pawn in a much more elaborate ruse of his own? In his presence, she had found herself behaving in a way she didn't normally behave; saying things she didn't normally say; thinking things she didn't normally think. He had an otherworldly effect on her, and she was completely subject to his mysterious influence. *What was that back there?* she wondered to herself, recalling the final scene on the back deck just before she had excused herself for the night. *That wasn't part of my plan. That wasn't forced. What was I doing? What was I expecting?*

The new thoughts made her wonder further... did the game even matter? Could she honestly convince herself that that was what this was about? Colton was certainly different, but he was different in another way as well. Emma could play all the games she wanted. She could even try to make this encounter seem like research — purely for scholarly satisfaction. In the end, though, she couldn't fool herself. Despite all attempted distractions and excuses, there was absolutely no denying that she was inexplicably drawn to the man. She was drawn to him, she suddenly realized, in a way she had never been drawn to anyone else before. It had only taken moments for him to magnetize her. She had given him six hours, and as a result, she now realized she had already completely succumbed to his allure. So much had happened in the past six hours, in fact, it would seem that her life had just changed courses to account for it all. But where would this all lead? That curious question, above all others swirling around in her mind, made her most anxious.

:-:

Colton opened the glass door as he listened to the last of the water slowly trickle out of the showerhead. He grabbed a towel and dried himself off, careful to mind the gash on his forehead. Afterwards, he wiped some of the condensation off the mirror with his towel.

He watched his reflection raise a calloused hand up to his face, brushing the hollowed cheeks that his beard had previously covered up. Afterwards, he ran his wiry fingers through his dark blonde hair, pushing it out of his face. Beads of water accumulated between his fingers. He narrowed his eyes and rested both of his hands on the edge of the sink that jutted out of the wall. He leaned in intently to stare hard at the man in the mirror.

He didn't recognize the face, and it actually took him a moment before he realized it was his own. The tanned skin looked as if it had spent a thousand days weathered by the harshest climates of the wildest places on the planet. The narrow lips looked as though they had gone years without sharing a good conversation. The locks of his wavy, wild hair hadn't been cut in at least a year. The hardened eyes surprised him the most of all, though. They were eyes that seemed to bear lifetimes of experience. They had seen and gone through too much for a man of his youth. They were deep, boundless, and wise far beyond their years. Colton found them almost intimidating.

He could not remember the last time he had seen his own reflection. Was this really what he had become? This was not the man he had known when he had abandoned his former life three years ago. The face that looked back at him now was one he hadn't seen in eleven years. It belonged to a man he thought he would never see again.

He blinked and looked past his reflection, losing himself to thoughts of days long gone. Tears welled up in his eyes as thoughts of his father suddenly engulfed his consciousness.

Colton made a disgusted face, ridden with guilt. He was furious with himself. He could not remember the last time he had given his father a moment's worth of thought. It seemed as though an eternity had passed since he had abruptly dropped out of college, and even longer still since Afghanistan... The slightest recollection of the man tremendously pained Colton. But now, seeing his own reflection — the reflection of his own father — emotions he had not experienced since he was a boy suddenly overwhelmed him.

Resisting losing complete control of himself, Colton forced his gaze back into the mirror. Fighting back tears, he once more examined his own reflection. At first, all he could see was the face of a man long dead.

Gradually, though, he began to take notice of the discrepancies between the face he was actually looking at and the face that had been ingrained in his memory. Though the differences were slight, Colton was indeed a different man than his father. The observation helped him to subdue his emotions.

As Colton stared longer and longer, he noticed more and more subtle distinctions in his own facade. The angular structures of his rugged face cradled an authoritative jawbone that was noticeably narrower than his father's. He had his mother's tapered nose, unlike the much broader and more prominent one that his father had carried so well.

Continuing his examination, he observed a certain softness surrounding his eyes that his father had lacked — not a softness in texture, but rather in expression. It effectively contrasted the intimidating hardness of his infinitely deep eyes. A devoted tenure in the military had eradicated any trace of his father's former soft youth. George Anders had lived according to rule and order, whereas Colton thrived under the liberty of his own decisions. Colton was a free man left at his own devices to explore the vastness of the world. Imagination and wonder coexisted in harmony with his experience and wit.

Why are we here? The thought from nowhere suddenly reverberated through his mind. A dizziness made him cringe for a split second before abruptly evaporating.

The realization that he had died and returned to life suddenly overcame him in full strength. It was not by mere coincidence or accident that he and Emma had met. It couldn't be.

He had walked here half-alive, but why? What had led him here? Fate? Colton didn't believe in such forces, but an uncanny suspicion gnawed away at his curiosity. The day's events could have led to many outcomes, and out of all of the possibilities, it just so happened that he had ended up exactly where he was. It seemed too perfect to be random.

Am I actually in control of my own decisions? he wondered to himself. *Or could I simply be an instrument of some higher power?* Questions continued to besiege him. *Why are we here?*

For whatever reason, Colton couldn't shake the feeling that he and Emma's paths had collided for a designed reason.

He swung open an adjacent medicine cabinet to find a pair of metal scissors. He took them in his fingers and closed the cabinet. He took one more long, hard look at himself in the mirror and began to cut away at his mane of hair.

FIFTEEN

5 JUNE, 2012

Emma creaked the door to Jeremy's bedroom to check on him. He appeared to still be asleep, and after a brief moment she was able to pick up the sound of his deep, heavy breathing. *Definitely asleep*, she decided. She gently shut the door and made her way to the kitchen.

"He still asleep?" Colton asked, standing with his back to Emma while pouring himself a glass of orange juice.

She raised an eyebrow. Somehow he had managed to sense her despite the fact that she had made no noise to alert him. "He sure is," she answered. "How'd you know I was here?"

He shrugged and turned around while taking a sip of the orange juice he had just poured himself. "I don't know. I just did."

Emma lost her train of thought as she took in his new appearance. Much of his face had been hidden to her yesterday, but now, with the absence of his ragged beard, the rugged structures of his streamlined face struck her. With such a handsome face to match such a striking character, he seemed too appealing to be true, Emma thought. She suddenly found herself wishing she had put a little bit more effort into her own appearance this morning...

"Sleep well?" he asked after she didn't respond.

"Yes." She shrugged in response. "I suppose so. How about

you? I know the mattress in your room is a little old and the pillows are a bit worn, but I hope they didn't keep you awake."

"They didn't," he half-lied. In truth, he had only gotten about an hour's worth of sleep, but it wasn't the mattress or pillows that had spoiled his slumber.

"Well, I'm glad to hear that," Emma said with a half-smile. After an awkward hesitation, she made her way to the pantry to grab a box of cereal. "Would you grab me the milk, please?"

Colton did as he was asked and handed her the half-full jug across the counter. "Fruit Loops?" he asked quizzically, watching as she grabbed a bowl from the cabinet and began to prepare her breakfast.

"Don't judge," she defended. "I have a secret weakness for children's sugar cereal. Don't you have a weakness, Superman?"

"Oh, I'm Superman now?" he joked. "I guess I don't look all that wild anymore."

"You didn't answer my question," she managed to say, stuffing a colorful spoonful into her mouth.

"Oh, I don't eat breakfast."

At first, she believed him, but then she reprimanded herself as a fool for not immediately detecting his sarcasm. "Sure you do!" She laughed. "A big muscleman like yourself couldn't make it halfway through the day without starting off with a healthy breakfast!"

If he was at all embarrassed by her remark, he didn't show it. "You know what I really enjoy?"

"I can't say for sure," she pondered. "I mean, you could enjoy any number of things," she retorted, feigning seriousness.

Once again, to her disappointment, she received no reaction. "Raw eggs."

"You're kidding," she muttered in-between bites, once again half-believing him.

"Oh, no," he muttered. "When I'm in the woods, I just pluck them right out of birds' nests. Sometimes I can even hear them squeak one last time in their little eggs before I swallow them whole." He breathed wistfully. "Ah...Delightful."

"Oh, stop!" She laughed and flicked a soggy Fruit Loop at his face. "I know you well enough to know that's a downright lie."

"Maybe so." He smirked.

"Have you already eaten?"

"Nah," he answered before draining the last of his orange juice from the glass. "I'll probably pick something up when I go into town."

"You're going into town? What for?"

"Well I left my Jeep somewhere in Acadia and figured I should go pick it up. After I get it I figured I might as well stop and grab a bite to eat. You need anything?"

"I can drive you up there if you need," she offered, pausing to take another mouthful of Fruit Loops. "My friend dropped my car off here last night."

"I found the keys on the doorstep," Colton said, nodding towards the counter where they now sat. "But no, thank you. I think someone should stay here with Jeremy, just in case. And besides, aren't your children arriving in a little while?"

"Yes, yes, right you are. Maybe you could pick up some fruit for snack-time today? Those ravenous little creatures already ate everything I bought."

"Will do."

"Wait a minute before you leave and I'll give you some money for the food," she said as she began walking away. She made her way down the hall and to her bedroom. She took her purse from the nightstand and retrieved a few dollars from its depths. "Here we are. This should be enough," she called out as she walked back. She handed him a twenty-dollar bill.

"Strawberries? Blueberries? Bananas?"

"All of the above. The kids appreciate a good selection."

"I'll get the best in town."

They made and maintained eye contact, standing face to face, a breath's distance away from each other. Time seemed to momentarily stop as an anxious silence gently subdued the atmosphere of the room. Emma's head was upturned slightly to make up for the half-foot difference in their heights. He bent his head slightly downward at her in return. Then, with utmost subtlety, she just barely bounced her head towards him.

She cringed when he abruptly turned his back on her. In one fluid motion, he made his way to the side door that led outside. She hadn't noticed, but she had been holding her breath. She resumed her steady breathing and impatiently moved a strand of her almond-brown hair behind her ear. She watched as he grasped the door's handle and paused. After what appeared to be a rare moment of hesitation, he half-turned to look at her.

"I'll see you when I get back," he said, nodding. She offered a faint smile in return, but he had already walked through the threshold and shut the door behind him. He was gone, but she remained standing there in a daze.

After a moment, she noticed something stuck in-between the doorframe and the door. She shook her head and snorted in amusement when she realized what it was. She took a few steps toward the door and gently retrieved the twenty-dollar bill. She folded it twice and stuck it in her shorts' pocket. She peeked through the blinds in the window of the door to watch him go, though he was already out of sight. She glanced down at her watch. She had a little less than an hour before the kids would start arriving, and she had much to do to prepare.

:-:

Vincent wrapped his index finger around the cold metal trigger of his M21 Sniper Rifle and peered down the long barrel at his target. "I've got eyes on him," he mumbled just loudly enough for his Bluetooth earpiece to pick up.

"Very good."

"Has there been a change in the objective?"

"No, your orders stand."

"Yes, sir," Vincent acquiesced before ending the call. He disassembled the rifle in a matter of seconds and stowed it away in his backpack. He waited a moment before departing.

When he rose, he remained half-crouching while retreating deeper into the woods, all the while keeping his eyes trained on the loose end entering the forest on the opposite end of the clearing. Vincent broke into a silent sprint between the trees. He wasn't about to allow the boy to slip through his grasp.

:-:

About two hours after he had left the cabin, Colton discovered his beloved Jeep right where he had left it. He felt around underneath his car on the lip of the rear fender and smiled in relief when his fingers found the keys he had hid there. Normally, he would not have done such a careless thing, but he had not planned on being gone very long when he initially left. He had not planned on meeting Jeremy or jumping from the cliffs. He had not planned on watching Jeremy fall to what could have been his death. He had not planned on having a close encounter with death himself. He had not planned on meeting Emma Payton.

No, nothing had gone according to his plan, and yet

everything felt like it had gone exactly according to *a* plan. Someone else's plan. Someone else or something else. Whatever it was, it seemed to have control over every little thing Colton did. The thought, reminiscent of the one from the previous night, shot a shiver through his body. Unable to come to a satisfactory conclusion, he pushed the thought away for the moment and made his way to the driver's door of his Jeep.

As he reached for the handle, the sudden sound of a twig snapping made him freeze. He whipped his head around like an alerted animal to begin scanning his surroundings. After several moments of careful examination, he frowned. As far as he could see and hear, he was alone. As far as he could sense, however, he was not. It was an extremely rare occasion that he felt uncomfortable in the forest, but he felt uncomfortable now. His skin crawled while the little hairs on his arms stood straight up. He scanned the area once more, but to no avail. Eager to leave, he jumped in his Jeep, ignited the engine, and sped off.

:-:

Vincent let out a heavy sigh of relief as he watched Colton drive off in his Jeep. Immediately afterwards, however, he let out a growl of frustration. He slammed his hands against the rough bark of the massive pine tree he had hid behind. Not only had he nearly been discovered, but he was watching the loose end escape before his very eyes.

Quelling his frustration, he set his mind on his next course of action. He thought of two viable options. One was to retrieve his own car and attempt to find Colton in Bar Harbor. Finding his car could take a while, however, and after that it wasn't highly likely he would find the boy. Or was it? Colton's vintage Jeep stuck out like a sore thumb. It didn't exactly blend in with other cars. After a few trips around town, he wouldn't be surprised if he would happen on Colton eventually. *Unless he's already left by the time I get there*, Vincent thought skeptically. *How do I even know he's going into town, anyway? Perhaps he's fleeing the state,* Vincent toyed with the second option he had thought of. *Or perhaps he's driving back to the cabin. And if not now, maybe by later today. That cabin is my best lead right now.* He pondered his plan carefully, deciding his course of action. Afterwards, he began walking in the direction he believed his car to be.

:-:

After Colton had driven away and could no longer see in his rearview mirror the dead end where his Jeep had been parked, he pulled his car to the side of the narrow road and got out. He then quietly and discreetly followed the road back a short distance until the dead end was once again in sight. That was when he noticed a bald man clad in dark clothes emerge from the woods into the small clearing.

Under normal circumstances, a lone man wandering the forests of Acadia would not have stirred Colton's suspicions. This discovery was not under normal circumstances, however. That noise had set him on edge. Now, to see this curious man — who was not at all dressed for hiking — emerge from where Colton had just heard the noise, his level of alertness and paranoia escalated to the next level.

He didn't know quite what to conclude, though. Who the man was and what he wanted was far beyond Colton's fathoming. In that moment of ambiguity, an impulse hit him like a massive wave. His muscles twitched. He rolled his shoulders. He narrowed his eyes. The roles had shifted; now, Colton was the unseen predator.

Before he gave chase, he reevaluated the situation. Perhaps it wasn't the best idea to reveal himself. Not here. Not now. The man was unaware he had been compromised. That meant Colton had the upper hand. To reveal himself now would level the playing field again. That wouldn't do; better to be in control. Always better to be in control. Colton relaxed his muscles and suppressed his rush of adrenaline. He turned to begin retracing his steps back to his Jeep.

With a dissatisfied frown bent across he face, he opened the door to his car. Even though he had the upper hand, he had more questions than he did answers. Nevertheless, he decided that he wouldn't give this any more thought unless he saw the man again. He would pay extra careful attention to details in his surroundings, but there was little else he could do on the matter until he knew more about the circumstances. With a hesitant resolve, he pushed his answerless thoughts to the outskirts of his mind.

Nevertheless, sporadic thoughts of the snapping twig and the bald man plagued his consciousness as he drove down the winding forest road. He needed something else to focus on. Normally, he would ponder where to go for his next great ascent, but the first and only thing that came to mind was Emma. The sudden thought of her surprised him. Nothing ever interfered with his climbing. For three straight years, climbing had remained his sole focus in life. Was she interfering? Or was he subconsciously modifying his focuses?

SIXTEEEN

Jeremy opened his eyes wide. He felt very refreshed. When he tried to move, however, he winced. He struggled at first, but soon discovered that the more he moved, the less he hurt.

"I'm just stiff," he said aloud to himself while slowly sitting up. He rolled his shoulders and tilted his head from one side to the other. Air rushed in and then out of his lungs. He bent his arms to test his elbows. With some gentle encouragement, they eventually eased into proper operation.

He slowly tried standing up, only to let out a stifled shout and collapse against his best efforts. Determined, he tried again. This attempt ended similarly to the first, although not quite as painfully. With a groan, he tried once more and finally succeeded. He slowly straightened himself up.

He walked to the door and cracked it open. He peered through with one eye and listened carefully. Utter silence. Satisfied, he opened the door wide enough to fit through and slowly slipped into the hallway, managing to limp over to the kitchen window and peek through the blinds.

Hundreds of feet away, he saw Emma surrounded by a medley of young children in the oceanside clearing. Confused but not overly curious, he retreated from the blinds and searched the kitchen and adjacent rooms for a telephone. He found a landline, but was disappointed soon after upon realizing that it didn't work. Eventually, he happened upon a purse sitting on the kitchen countertop. He hesitated a moment, then stumbled over to the blinds once more. Sure enough that no one would barge in on him, he made his way back to the purse and searched its contents for a cellphone. Indeed, he found one.

He checked for signal. At first, there was nothing, but as he hobbled around the kitchen he discovered a small area where the signal was good enough to make a call. He carefully dialed a number he knew by heart and put the phone to his ear. The dial tone rang once. Twice. A third time, then a voice finally answered.

"Law Office of—"

"It's me."

"It's about time I heard from you," a weary voice said on the other end of the line, pausing to let out a sigh. "What took you so long?"

"Just some distractions."

"Are we still on track with the plan?"

"We are. I've established contact."

"All right. Let's proceed with Phase Two. Pick up the package from the rendezvous point. You know what to do after that."

"Understood." Jeremy limped over to the window to check outside before continuing. "We almost waited too long, sir. He'll keep pushing his limits until he kills himself."

"Well, I'd imagine Phase Two should preoccupy him enough to forget about tempting death for a while now, wouldn't you agree?"

"There's more."

"Go on."

"There are going to be some... complications with the plan."

"What do you mean?"

"He met Emma Payton yesterday."

The lawyer said nothing. Jeremy could sense his shock, even through the phone. When he remained silent, Jeremy continued.

"I don't know how—"

"Explain," the man interrupted.

"Well..." Jeremy sighed, hesitating. "I met Colton in Acadia, just as planned. We climbed together to establish trust. But then he jumped from the very cliff we—"

"He jumped from a cliff?" the lawyer interrupted again, bewildered.

"Like I said... he'll keep pushing his limits until either it kills him or we step in to intervene. But yes, he jumped from the cliff into the ocean. He collapsed when he got back ashore. So, in the essence of time, I began to climb back down to help." Jeremy paused to catch his breath. His heartbeat raced. "And then I fell."

"My God," the voice breathed on the other end of the line.

"Next thing I know, he and Emma Payton are trying to get me to the hospital. I can't recall anything that happened in between. I guess Colton managed to carry me to safety," Jeremy explained. He turned to examine his surroundings. "I'm in some kind of cabin by the sea, now. I think we're still in Acadia, but I can't say for sure."

"You didn't go, did you? To the hospital?"

"What? No, of course I didn't."

"Good. Well, are you all right?"

"I'm making a quick—" In one fluid motion, Jeremy cut himself off, hung up the phone, and stashed it back into the purse. He nonchalantly stumbled towards the refrigerator as the side door to the kitchen swung open.

"Jeremy! You're up!" a startled Colton exclaimed, closing the door behind him as he entered. "And hungry, it would appear."

Jeremy smirked as he opened the fridge to examine its contents. "That..." he began. "I definitely am. I feel like I haven't eaten in days."

"As far as I know, you haven't. I cooked you a few burger patties last night. If you're feeling carnivorous, then I'm sure we could heat them up in the microwave for you. Still got a few buns left. If you'd rather have something else..." Colton paused to set his grocery bags down on the counter. "That's fine too."

"Actually, some meat sounds wonderful right about now. So I suppose I'll go for that hamburger. It's about lunchtime anyway, right?"

"Yeah, you got it. I'll heat it up for you now," Colton said while searching the fridge for the patty and condiments. "What do you want on it?"

"Don't worry about it. I'll prepare it myself."

"Okay, yeah, sure. And if that's not enough, there are three more with your name on them."

"Thanks, Colton."

Colton nodded and hesitated almost awkwardly. "Look, Jeremy—"

"Don't worry about it," the crippled man interrupted. His words were genuine and his face showed sincerity. "I'm all right. It wasn't your fault."

"But you're not all right!" Colton laughed nervously. "You nearly died!"

"So did you," Jeremy responded grimly.

"But that was my doing. And it was my doing that caused your fall, too."

"Let it go and forgive yourself, because I've already forgiven you."

Colton nodded his head, keeping it and his gaze low. He turned away. "Thank you."

"One thing," Jeremy started to say.

Colton swiftly turned back around and met Jeremy's gaze with eyes widened and brimming with curiosity.

"Don't ever do anything like that again."

Colton cast a sideward glance and slowly nodded his head, albeit with evident hesitation. He pursed his lips slightly and turned away once more. He grabbed two of the grocery bags and headed out through the door.

Jeremy stood still for a moment, staring at where Colton had previously stood. Then, the beeping microwave interrupted the silence. Jeremy ignored it and made his way over to the windows to peek through the blinds one more time. He could see Colton walking towards the middle of the field where Emma was busy entertaining the children.

Afterwards, Jeremy stumbled back over to the purse and recovered the phone from its depths once more. He loaded the call history and promptly deleted the call he had just made, effectively erasing any traces that he had used the phone. He stashed it back in the purse where he had first found it and made sure to arrange everything else as it had previously been.

:-:

"Okay, Cooper's 'it!' Everyone else, run along! Remember, if you're tagged you have to stand still until one of your teammates 'un-freezes' you. Now, go!" Emma exclaimed, and on that note, the children scattered in all directions, shouting playfully.

"Does that mean it's time for your break?" Colton asked as he approached Emma.

"I suppose so," she said in return, flashing her luminous smile.

"Any trouble today?"

"With the kids? No, fortunately. Why?" she inquired. Her bright smile took on a playful edge. "Are you planning on causing some more trouble for me?"

"I wouldn't dream of it," he denied. He stopped several feet away from her and held up the bags of fruit. "I've got some snacks."

"Oh, you're wonderful," she said graciously while taking the produce from him. She turned around and set the bags on a large blanket.

"Jeremy's up."

"Oh, is he?" Emma asked. A look of surprise had lit up her face as she spun back around to face Colton. "How is he?"

"Remarkable," Colton began. "Considering what he's been through. Very remarkable."

"Well I'm very glad to hear that."

"Yes. Interesting character, he is."

"Speaking of interesting characters, have you seen Adam anywhere this morning?"

"No, I haven't," Colton responded. "Why? Are you expecting him?"

"Yes, as a matter of fact, I am. He's supposed to be helping me for community service."

"Oh," Colton said, nodding his head in surprise. "Good for him. Any particular reason?"

"Yes, actually. He's a criminal. If he doesn't help me, he goes back to the Juvenile Detention Center," Emma muttered. "And he's not here helping me."

"That boy's a criminal?"

"A white-collar criminal," Emma specified. "He has an affinity for expensive, shiny things that don't belong to him. He's never hurt anyone, though. That's why he was allowed to come help here... the police don't consider him dangerous."

"Where do you think he is?"

"I'm not sure," she said, looking away. "But I am concerned. He left without a word yesterday and now he's not here."

"You think he might have gotten into trouble last night?"

Emma nodded her head slowly without making eye contact.

"Is there anything we can do? I can go looking for him, if that would help."

"Don't bother," Emma said with a shrug. "The police said if anything like this were to happen, they would detain him for a few days and then decide whether or not to give him another chance. If he *was* caught doing something illegal, I would expect a call from law enforcement before too long."

"Well," Colton began. "Let's hope for the best."

"Yes, let's," she sighed.

"Your life must be pretty stressful right now. I must admit, though, that you're handling it exceptionally well."

Emma let out forced laugh. "My criminal volunteer is missing, I have a heavily wounded stranger making himself comfortable in my cabin, and I'm conversing with a cliff-climbing, world-traveling, Yale-dropout who briefly died yesterday."

"You're handling it exceptionally well," he repeated, setting a reassuring hand on her shoulder.

This time, she believed his words. She subconsciously touched his hand with hers and let it remain there for a moment. His empathetic eyes washed away the stress from her face. She relaxed and suddenly found herself appreciating his company, more than grateful that he had entered her life.

"Who are you?" came a curious voice. Colton and Emma broke contact at once to turn to a little girl. The child stood beside Emma and stared up at Colton with large, curious eyes.

"This is my friend! His name is Colton. Can you say hello, Annabelle?" Emma answered, bending down to put an arm around the girl.

"Pleased to meet you, Mr. Colton. My name is Annabelle," the little girl said very professionally, offering a small hand.

"Well, hello, Annabelle!" Colton laughed, briefly casting a humored glance at Emma. He crouched down and took the girl's hand in his own, gently shaking it in greeting. "I really like that flower you have in your hair. Is that a Meadow Rose?"

"I don't know. I found it growing over there," she answered, pointing to the edge of the woods.

When Emma turned her head to look, she allowed a frown to cross her face. The designated location was exactly where she had discovered Colton and Jeremy yesterday. If the flowers had been there before, she hadn't noticed them. Emma put the thought out of her mind for now. "That sure is pretty, Annabelle."

"I'm going to give it to my mom."

"I think she'll really love that," Colton said.

Annabelle laughed and took Colton's hand again. "You're really nice!" She turned to look at Emma. "Can Mr. Colton come play with us?"

"I think he'd really love that," Emma answered, casting a playful wink in Colton's direction.

Annabelle tugged at Colton's hand with both of her own until he rose to his feet. He allowed her to lead him over to where a bunch of the other children were running around. He turned his head to cast a wide-eyed, worried look at Emma. She merely laughed and waved him off.

:-:

Later, when the last of the kids had been picked up by their parents, Colton and Emma stood side-by-side watching the last car drive away. He abruptly took her by the hand and tugged her in the direction of the grass clearing. She cast him a playfully inquisitive look, but said nothing.

After she began following him, however, he let go of her hand — much to her dismay. Once they had taken little more than a dozen steps, he turned his head slightly to shoot her a mischievous smirk before suddenly breaking into a light jog across the clearing. He stopped after a brief distance to turn around and halfway raise his arms.

"Catch me if you can," he taunted with a crooked smile.

"Oh, now look what's gotten into you!" Emma laughed. When he turned heels and began sprinting ahead, she took off after him. Just when she thought she might catch him, he sprung forward with a burst of speed. She laughed aloud in lighthearted frustration.

When at last they neared the tree line that marked the edge of the forest, they both slowed to a light jog before coming to a steady halt. She smiled and subtly let out her hand, expecting him to catch it as she jogged over to him. When he did not, though, she was careful to conceal her disappointment. She looked at him, but he didn't return her gaze. Instead, his stare was directed downwards. She caught his half-smile and watched as he bent over to pick something from a lush green bush.

"May I?" he asked politely, presenting her with a beautiful flower. She smiled and nodded in consent, slightly tilting her head forward as if to accept a crown. Without another word, he gently stuck the stem through a few strands of her almond-brown hair just above her ear. Once he was satisfied that it would stay — thanks to her ponytail — he retreated.

The full beauty of her face overwhelmed him as it slowly came back into view. Her slender nose perfectly complimented the sleekness of her facial structure. He noticed, for the first time, the soft freckles that dotted her cheeks. Her thin red lips were parted just enough so that he could almost feel her warm breath gently brush across his skin.

Most striking of all, though, were her narrow, hazel eyes that seemed to gaze with enchanting grace right into his very soul. With effortless ease, she had effectively floored the last of his defenses without the utterance of a single word. And yet... he was content in his vulnerability. He decided with sudden finality that she was most beautiful woman he'd ever laid eyes on. He felt humbled to be in her presence, and it took everything he had to maintain his composure.

"How does it look?"

"You look divine," he breathed. The twinkle in her eyes when she smiled in return struck him once more. They shared a moment of happy silence. Neither moved. Both stared into the eyes of the other, straining to read the other's thoughts.

"Would you like to go into town for the evening? You look like you could use some fun," she said with a wink.

"And do what?"

She shrugged and cast a sideward glance, though maintaining a slight smile. "Take a walk on the boardwalk, grab a bite to eat, maybe. I know a place."

He half-smiled and lightly dipped his chin in consent. "I'd like that."

"I knew you would," she grinned, flashing her snow-white

teeth again. "I'll drive!" she shouted as she broke off in a sprint back towards the cabin.

Colton watched her for a moment before lowering and shaking his head. He smiled to himself. He snorted in self-amusement before taking off after her.

SEVENTEEN

Jeremy muted the television to hear the sound of Emma's car fade away down the driveway. When he could hear no more, he turned the television off and slowly rose to his feet. He grabbed the wad of cash that Colton had left him 'just in case' and found the keys to the Jeep on the top of the fridge. He turned off the lights and exited the cabin through the side door.

:-:

Vincent dropped to the ground of the shadowy forest in an instant. He waited in silent trepidation, hoping that the man leaving the cabin had not seen him. After a moment, he turned his head to peek through a bush. He was careful to stay hidden while the lights of the automobile illuminated the falling darkness. After the Jeep had disappeared down the road, Vincent made a second attempt at rising to his feet.

A multitude of questions swarmed the chauffeur's mind. In order to answer them, he emerged from the brush and set out towards the cabin.

The door was not even locked. Too easy. He cautiously entered the unlit premises. He flicked a nearby switch and narrowed his eyes as his pupils adjusted to the sudden light. He began his search immediately.

An unnerving thought gnawed away at his confidence, though.

He failed to believe that mere chance could have been the

impetus in bringing the loose end face to face with — out of *all* people — Harvey Payton's daughter. Colton must be plotting something. He surely knew more than he had been given credit for. He was even more of a threat than Vincent had been led to believe.

This formerly simple job had just become something far more complicated. Furthermore, Harvey didn't know of any of these new complications yet. This only made matters that much worse for the chauffeur; it would be his job to tell his boss that the loose end was indeed plotting something... and that his daughter had been helplessly caught at the crux of it.

Vincent shuddered.

EIGHTEEN

"I'm assuming you're hungry now," Emma said, guiding her white Audi sedan onto a main road that led into town.

"Famished."

"Good." Emma smiled, keeping her gaze on the road. "Because I am, too. Hope you like lobster."

"Lobster in Maine?" he questioned, shaking his head in feigned disappointment. "So cliché."

"Oh, hush. You should be excited."

"I am." He laughed. "I really am. I don't remember the last time I ate lobster." His smile shrank until it disappeared. "I don't remember the last time I ate in a restaurant with another person."

Emma allowed him a few seconds to settle his thoughts. She cast a brief sideward glance in his direction. "Well," she began. "It's not much of a restaurant — if that changes anything. It's about as crude and casual as they come."

"Still..." she heard him mutter. When he didn't continue, she realized that she had completely lost him to his introspection. She remained silent.

"Have I been missing out?" he asked out of the blue after several minutes.

His tone alarmed her. His guard was down. His confidence

gone. Regret, anxiety, and uncertainty had taken hold of his voice. He was afraid. Somehow, it made her afraid, too.

"Not at all," she finally said. "Everyone takes different paths. The one you decided to take is nothing to regret."

He nodded.

Her answer obviously hadn't satisfied him. She sighed. "We can continue this conversation once we're seated," she said. "We're here."

"Looks like a charming little eatery."

"It's one of my favorites," she said with a half-smile. "I've only been here in Bar Harbor a few weeks, but I've already lost count of how many times I've eaten at this place."

"Your mother would be proud, I'm sure."

She let out restrained laugh as she parked on the side of the road. "If you served her the lobster they serve here rather than the lobster that gets made for her at home, she'd never know the difference."

"It's that good?"

"It's that good," she affirmed, turning the vehicle off. She adjusted the flower in her hair and opened the car door. She turned to look at him before exiting. "You ready?"

"Absolutely." After stepping out of the car, he took a moment to acquaint himself with his surroundings. "Stunning view," he breathed, taking notice that the restaurant, crude as it was, was situated right beside the ocean. Its deck, in fact, was suspended over the water. Rows of rope lights hung above the seaside patio, effectively illuminating just enough of the falling darkness. A live band was playing on a makeshift stage at one end of the deck. Colton was a little surprised by the size of the crowd, considering it was only a Tuesday evening. In the summer days of Maine, though, every evening called for celebration.

Emma led him up a short wooden staircase to the front door, which he held open for her as they walked inside. The waitress seated them outside at a two-person table situated beside the railing that overlooked the open sea.

"Can I start you two off with something to drink?" the waitress asked. Her northern accent was heavy.

"I'll have a water, please," Emma answered, briefly looking up from her menu.

"Water for me, too, please," Colton added.

The waitress muttered something under her breath and rolled her eyes before leaving.

"Wonder what that was about..." Emma said once the woman was out of earshot.

"She said that we're boring."

"You could hear that?"

"I read her lips."

Emma blinked and shook her head. "Of course you did. I think your choice of water with your dinner tonight might be the only boring thing about you." She bowed her head to take a look at the menu. Colton mimicked.

"Who knew you could do so many different things with a lobster?" Colton asked, almost overwhelmed by the selection. "Lobster Bisque. Lobster Stew. Stuffed Lobster. Steamed Lobster. Fried Lobster. Lobster Primavera. Lobster Risotto. Lobster Rolls. Lobster Shish-Kabobs."

"Shish-Kabobs? That's new."

"No." He smirked. "I was kidding about those. But seriously, how am I supposed to know what to get? Too many options."

"Are you asking for my recommendation?" she asked, peering up at him from her menu.

He met her gaze briefly and offered a shamed smile before continuing his search. "Maybe."

"Okay," she consented with a wink. "Well, they're *all* really good. If you're feeling classy, I recommend the Steamed Lobster. If you're just plain hungry, then I recommend the Lobster Primavera."

He contemplated in silence, reading the descriptions of his options on his menu. "Believe it or not, this is one of the hardest choices I've had to make recently."

"Yeah, you don't seem like the kind of guy who has an overwhelming amount of difficult decisions constantly plaguing his mind."

He shot her a harmless 'stop talking' look. She smirked slightly and focused her attention back at her own menu.

"I'll just get the Lobster Primavera," he finally muttered after several long moments.

"Not feeling classy?"

"Nope."

"Well, all right then!" she exclaimed, disappointed that he had not supplied a witty retort. She decided on what she would get, closed her menu, and set it down on the table. Leaning back in her seat, she took a brief look at the ocean before settling her gaze on Colton. He was absentmindedly staring at the rolling waves. It was apparent that he was lost deep in thought. "Penny for your thoughts?"

"What?"

"Here are your waters," the waitress, who had just returned, began. "Are you two ready to order yet?"

"I think so," Emma answered with a smile, handing over her menu. "Steamed Lobster for me, please."

"And I'd like the Lobster Primavera."

"Of course." The waitress took Colton's menu and walked away.

"No attitude this time," Emma noted. "So?" she asked after a moment of shared silence.

"So what?"

"What are you so intently thinking about?"

"You tell me."

"I can't read your mind."

"Sure you can."

Emma paused and stared him down. He stared back at her, daring her to try to read him. "You're trying to convince yourself that you should be feeling guilty about not wanting to be here."

Colton said nothing at first, but narrowed his eyes. "Spot on," he finally said, looking away.

"Part of you wants to be here," she continued. "But the other part is completely terrified."

"Not terrified," he countered. "Just..." He paused to take a sip of his water. His eyes wandered as he did so. "Uncomfortable."

"Because you're paranoid."

He shrugged. "I'm watchful."

"And *why*, I beg to ask, is that?" Emma inquired. "What happened to you three years ago? What are you hiding from me?"

Colton turned the full power of his unnerving gaze on her. She had expected it, but she could not have prepared herself for it. She gave her best effort to keep her ground. If she showed weakness, she knew he would not tell her — perhaps ever. She had made her move; now she had to stand by it.

His penetrating stare was unrelenting. She didn't know how much longer she could last before breaking. The anxiety viciously ate away at her determination. At last, just as she was about to yield, he lazily closed his eyes and released a deep sigh. She held her gaze a moment longer, then allowed herself to take a sigh of relief.

"You don't really want to know about my past," he muttered, looking away.

"Yes, I do."

"Why? Because you saved my life? I didn't ask for that. Yeah, I get it — you think I'm indebted to you and therefore you deserve to know everything about me. Well, maybe you do have the right, but you don't deserve it. You deserve better. I'm bad news, Emma. I'm no good for you. Not now, not ever. Keep your hands clean of me and any trace of me."

"If you're so eager to steer me away, then why are you here? Why bother leading me on? You've stuck around for some reason, and I'm bright enough to know it's not for your pal Jeremy."

He didn't respond.

"You don't even know," she prodded confidently. "You've done a better job of lying to yourself than you have to me."

He pursed his lips and shook his head. "You don't know what you're getting into. You think you want to know, but you don't. You won't like what you hear."

"It's not about liking what I hear. It's not about hearing what I want. It's about the truth. I'm tired of these games."

"Well, you tire quickly. The games had only just begun."

Emma rolled her eyes and shook her head, letting out a sigh. Several minutes passed before either of them spoke another word. It was Colton who finally broke the silence.

"It all began long before three years ago," he started to explain.

As Emma turned to look at him, she was reminded of the lustrous glow his eyes had taken on in the moonlight the night before — the last time she had last asked him about his past. He had effectively shut down then. This time, Emma hoped, would end differently.

"The life I had been born into... It was always only a matter of time." He took a long pause. His empty gaze had shifted in the direction of the ocean, as if he were searching its depths for his memory.

After several minutes had passed of him staring neurotically into the waves, Emma wasn't sure if he would continue. She was patient, though, and at last, he did.

"The military was my father's life. For the first sixteen years of my life, never once did he take leave from service. His conviction was too strong. A man like that... You wouldn't think he could be equally dedicated to his family, would you?" A grim half-smile weakly meandered across Colton's face as he shook his head in disbelief. His gaze never wavered from the rolling surf. "But he was. He absolutely was. He was the ultimate man. I couldn't have asked for a better father. And yet..." Colton trailed off. He clenched his jaw and pursed his lips. "When he died, I was angry. I was furious with him." He shifted his gaze back to Emma.

"*I* was *angry*," he breathed as a crazed spark gleamed in his eyes. A caustic bitterness had crept into his tone, and although Emma cringed from it, she knew it was not directed at her, nor even at his father. It was directed instead at himself. He held his gaze on her for a moment longer before abruptly turning to watch the ocean once more. "I woke up that morning and he was gone." He flicked his eyebrows upwards as he stared with vacant eyes past the swarming shadows. His mouth remained parted ever so slightly — the forthcoming words expertly balancing on the tip of his tongue. "As if he had never even existed." He lightly shook his head. "You'd like to think that... that when someone leaves this life the world actually notices... that the air is a little emptier and the light is a little dimmer." Silence caught his breath and a sight not of this world captured his gaze. "But that's just a fantasy." His unreadable eyes swirled with nameless emotions. "My dad died and the world just continued on. It didn't stop spinning. It didn't pause... not even momentarily to steal a quick breath. It just spun on... On and on," he drawled hypnotically, his words becoming whispers. "So I spun on, too."

Absolute silence settled like a thick fog between the two of them for several moments. Colton abrasively penetrated it in an instant, though.

"Never found his body. Declared missing in action and, after a while, assumed deceased. My mom... she kept believing. Everyone else had given up hope but her. She ended up losing her sanity before accepting the truth." A dark, humorless shadow of a smile crept across his lips. "Or so she would have led us to believe... I think she knew all along. She had everyone fooled — including herself. It was her own duality that drove her mad."

Another pause interrupted his dialogue. Emma stared hard at him. His vacant eyes and detached words reeking of rampant apathy drew her in — as if she were feeling the emotion that he was somehow completely devoid of.

"I gave up, too. Hell, I was the first to give up. When tragedy strikes, you have to recognize it for what it is. Go ahead and be afraid, but don't let it paralyze you. You've got to let go and move on before hope moves in. Let a little in, and you're already compromised." He frowned and shook his head. "Hope," he snorted in contempt. "It's just misfortune's way of toying with you. It's just trying to prolong the pain merely for the sake of sadistic entertainment. I told myself I wouldn't let it make a fool out of me, though. 'Take it all in stride,' I said. 'Spin on.'" A grim half-smile again curled across his thin lips. "Funniest part of all? It's not really misfortune, it's just life. Sometimes, life will beat you down; sometimes it'll raise you up. Other times, it'll throw you aside, forget about you for a while, then come back to beat you down again once it sees that you're back up on your feet. Then, just for good measure, it'll start kicking you. Sooner or later, you have to realize you're utterly helpless against the whims of our capricious universe. Most people realize too late... I decided I wasn't going to be most people. The truth is ugly. It doesn't mold itself in accordance with our opinions and desires. It answers to no one. People like to think they have a certain amount of control, but life's a gamble. It's a fool's game. No one makes it through in one piece. Only way to minimize damage is to roll with the punches and keep your head low. And to do that, you have to recognize reality for what it is."

"I don't think a little faith is such a bad thing to have, though, Colton. You may think in retrospect that it was better to detach yourself from your father's death because he never was found. But if... if he *was* found... if he *had* come back to you... don't you then think that it would have been worth it to keep some hope? It would have made that initial misfortune a little more bearable. It would have kept despair at bay."

Colton narrowed his eyes and shook his head. "That which actually happened is all that concerns me. Even with the tragic cards life dealt me, I played my hand right. I would have lost everything if I had bet on hope because, as it turns out, my dad never did return. There's no use in imagining what *could* have been. He's dead, and I accept that. But if I had bet on hope, perhaps I'd *still* be waiting to see how it all plays out. Even though I'd probably already know deep in my heart that I was betting on a ruse, I would have kept at it even still... because it would have given me a shadow of comfort." He paused a moment as sorrow subtly appeared to replace his anger. He lowered his gaze. His next words were thoughtful whispers. "That's exactly the trap that my mother fell into, after all." He paused once more before raising his gaze and his voice once again. "No, you can keep your passive hope and blind faith, and I'll take the despair. Because at least the despair is real. I'd rather live in a grim reality than a comfortable delusion."

For a long moment, he held his tongue. He ignored Emma's stare. After a while, she finally spoke. "Tell me more about your despair."

Colton's eyes glazed over as he leaned away from the table to shift his gaze back at the restless sea. "Not too long after my dad's 'accident,' a 'suspicious' photographer was detained at our base in Afghanistan. For whatever reason, my mom was constantly visiting him in his cell. I don't know why they spent so much time together, but whatever he was telling her, it was changing her." Colton paused momentarily. "Then the man somehow escaped."

"You think your mother helped?"

Colton nodded faintly. "I have reason to believe so. Naturally, we fled after that. The three of us. I didn't even know the guy — Lenny was his name." He snorted and tossed his head from side to side. "I didn't know my mother anymore, either. We were all strangers to each other, and yet... the only people we could trust was one another," he said. "We hitchhiked our way to India. Traversed the entire country in a year. Then Lenny convinced my mom India wasn't safe anymore. So we flew to France. Lenny found a private boarding school for me, and then they left. Abandoned me for good."

"I'm sure they had their reasons. Whatever was going on, it sounds like it was too dangerous for you. Your mother was only trying to protect you, I'm sure."

Anger danced across Colton's façade. "My mom tried to replace my father with some random guy... and then she deserted me." His expression hardened in a flash. Once again, he became unreadable. "That's a unique way of protecting me. I haven't felt safe once since the moment I learned my dad died. I didn't lose one parent that day, I lost both." For a long while, he stared silently into the descending darkness, listening carefully to the waves as if they were whispering stories of long-forgotten memories. "After she abandoned me, I never heard from her again," he muttered, breaking his trance with quick raise of his eyebrows and a subtle side-toss of his chin. He lowered his gaze to stare blankly at the wooden table. His eyes were still voids.

Emma couldn't summon any words to speak. Pity held her helplessly mute.

"Three years ago, a lawyer contacts me while I'm hiking in Colorado during Spring Break of my senior year. Tells me my mother and stepfather were killed in Uganda."

Though his voice was steady, his body trembled. Emma judged it as a restraint of fury rather than a shiver of grief.

"My mom *married* that man?" Colton asked wildly, looking Emma in the eyes as if she were responsible for answering the rhetorical question. His resurging anger was now prominently evident. "How could she keep that from me? How could she carry a secret like that to her death? How could she—" Colton cut himself off with a vicious jerk of his head, thus putting an end to his noticeably escalating rage. As the hatred receded from his expression, a cold, apathetic impassiveness moved in to take its place. "A funeral was held once what remained of their bodies arrived back in the States. The lawyer got in touch with me so we could handle the legal matters. I figured if I'd ever hear from my mom again, at the very least, it would be in her last will," Colton said. He shook his head. "I guess even that was too much to expect. Only thing she left for me to remember her by was Lenny's loads of money."

Emma said nothing. Sometimes, she figured, there's just

nothing worth saying.

"So," he began again. "After the funeral, I went back to Yale. Tried getting back into the swing of things," he trailed off, shaking his head again. "But I couldn't keep going on with that life. I didn't want anything to do with who I used to be," he explained. "So, the same day I had returned to New Haven, I turned around and left for Yosemite once and for all. Never told any of my friends where I went. I dropped off the map of civilized world. Only reason anyone might know who I am nowadays is because of my rock-climbing accomplishments. After the extreme sports culture found out about my free-solo climb up the Nose of El Capitan, I got sponsored. That was the beginning of my new life." He paused one last time. "I spent the last three years climbing to the highest peaks of some of the least accessible places on the planet, and I never once set foot in a restaurant with another human being." He snorted and shook his head, then took a sip of his water.

She reached across the table to touch his hand. "You're not alone anymore, Colton. I'm here for you."

"And here we are! Steamed Lobster for the lady and Lobster Primavera for the gentleman!" A tall, lanky, scruffy man — possibly the restaurant manager, based on his etiquette — exclaimed as he brought their dishes. "Sorry about the wait, but I can assure you both it was well worth it. So how does everything look? Can I get either of you anything else?"

"Looks delicious," Emma said, slightly perturbed that he had interrupted them — better now, though, than a few minutes ago, she reasoned. "Could I get some hot butter, please?"

"Of course. Anything for you, sir?"

"I'm fine, thanks."

The man nodded and walked away. Their waitress, however, was the one to return minutes later to give Emma her butter.

"How's your Primavera?" Emma asked Colton once they were alone again.

He chewed a mouthful and swallowed before answering. "Very tasty."

"Glad to hear it," she responded as she began cracking apart her lobster.

Colton stopped himself from offering to help just before the words were about to leave his tongue — she appeared to be more than capable herself.

"Good enough to regret missing for the last three years?"

"Almost."

"I wouldn't regret them, if I were you."

"No?"

"No. Definitely not. You're one of the most courageous people I've ever met, Colton. You've refused to allow tragedy to consume you. You let it in and made it your motivation. You embraced it and made yourself stronger by it. Most would have yielded and given up, but you made something of yourself. No one else could have done what you've done." She paused to judge his reaction. He was inscrutable, of course. Nevertheless, she pressed on. "The so-called 'civilized' world — the world you've been lucky enough to avoid — is more corrupt than ever. I shudder when I look beyond my protective little bubble and take on a global perspective. People are so blinded by the subtlety of the downward spiral that our species is headed in. Do you know why?"

"Do you?" he lackadaisically challenged, unsure where she was going with this.

"Weakness. The human race is weak," she said, answering her own question. "Tragedy is an everyday product of living, and, despite its sometimes discreet nature, it can't be avoided. It's inevitable. But people, because they're so *dreadfully* weak, lose every trace of control when it strikes. They let tragedy destroy their lives and they become the hollow remnants of what they remember as a nightmare. All at once, nothing matters anymore. They simply stop caring. They don't believe they can positively influence the world anymore, so they grow apathetic," she stated bluntly. "When you have seven billion people on a planet, and the large majority allow apathy to rule their lives, do you know how destructive that can be for the future of our kind?"

"I do. And I agree," Colton conceded skeptically. He narrowed his eyes. "How is this relevant?"

"You don't fit the mold, Colton. You're not a product of our corrupt society. You don't fit in with the apathetic machine that our civilization has become. You're strong, you're brave, and you're special." She paused a moment to let her words sink in. "You would betray me, humanity, and yourself if you actually regret these past few years." She paused again. "Ask me why."

"Why?"

"Because," she started to answer before the word had even left his tongue. "The only thing that can counteract all this gloomy apathy, selfishness, and fear... is inspiration, hope, and the desire to achieve. *You*, Colton, are a living manifestation of everything that this world needs. I commend you. I respect you. I wish these seven billion people could strive to be even half as admirable as you."

"Those sound to me like the words of someone who's never lost anything before," he retorted, stunning her with his bluntness. Indeed, she said nothing for several moments while he stared her down. "Listen, Emma, I appreciate your admiration, but I don't think it's deserved. I'm not what you think I am. I *did* give up. Tragedy *did* consume me, and I've done nothing worthwhile since. And, honestly, I'm not even trying to. I'm entirely despicable. Climbing rocks... what good does that do?

Absolutely none. I enjoy it, sure, but dedicating all this time to something like that is completely selfish. And yet it's self-defeating at the same time, because doing everything purely for myself is completely unfulfilling."

She shook her head with widened eyes. "It's not your fault these terrible things have happened to you. Taking a few years to get away from it all and find yourself is perfectly understandable. These things happen to countless others as well, but if you're so disgusted with yourself for acting as anyone would have, then be different. Combat the despair you've willingly embraced and make something from yourself in the fight. Do some good in a world that desperately needs it"

He said nothing. In fact, he seemed to have withdrawn to wholeheartedly focus on his Primavera. His uninterrupted bites were ravenous.

She sighed, completely at a loss at how to reach him. She signaled a passing waiter for the check.

NINETEEN

Vincent made his way back to his post on the edge of the woods. Unfortunately, his search in the cabin had not yielded any new information. In fact, it hadn't yielded much information at all. There were hardly any signs that people were even living there, save for a little bit of food in the fridge and pantry and a half-full garbage can. As if that frustration alone was not enough, now he had to call Harvey and be the bearer of bad news.

Vincent was not an easily intimidated man; he had traveled to the harshest and darkest corners of the planet, encountering some of the most wickedly terrifying human beings along the way; he had seen and done things usually only ever experienced in nightmares; he had schemed, plotted, led, and crushed rebellions; he had killed men, women, and children alike.

Nevertheless, Harvey Payton frightened him.

With a heavy heart, Vincent retrieved his satellite phone from his messenger bag and began dialing his boss's number.

"What is it?" the man spat on the other line after the fourth ring. "You've already called once tonight. You're interrupting my time with my family. You'd better have something important to tell me."

Vincent closed his eyes and remained silent for a moment. He had to gain at least some authority in this conversation before telling Harvey about Colton and Emma. Allowing Harvey to disrespect and trample all over him could only lead to one, very painful end... His dignified silence should put a check on the man's attitude.

Sure enough, it did. After a few moments of total silence on the line, Harvey tempered himself before continuing. "I'm sorry, Vincent. Go on ahead with what you were going to inform me of."

Vincent knew Harvey well enough to know that it pained him to apologize like that and, as a result, it wasn't completely heartfelt. Vincent wasn't overly concerned about the sincerity of the apology, though. It was, in fact, just sincere enough to give him the respect he needed to continue. "Very well," he began, allowing as much authority to creep into his tone as he could possibly allow, fully aware of the bombshell he was about to drop on his boss. "I urge you to prepare yourself, sir. This news is disturbing and unexpected."

A dreadful silence regained hold over the line before Harvey responded. When he finally did, a nervous chill shot along Vincent's spine. "Tell me."

"Do you know where your daughter is, sir?"

Again, Harvey didn't respond for a moment. "Bar Harbor, Maine," he finally muttered under forced breaths. Vincent knew that he had already caught on.

"Well, I've found the loose end," Vincent stated. "And he happens to be with your daughter as we speak."

Another malevolent silence hung on the line. Neither spoke, but Vincent was well aware of the indescribable fury that had possessed Harvey on the other end. Vincent knew better than to say further. The silence seemed eternal.

Finally, after what must have been five minutes, Harvey finally spoke. "Did *you* know about *this*?" His suppressed rage gave a maniacal edge to his wicked tone.

"I can assure you, sir, I only just learned of this moments ago."

"You *knew* where to find Colton! You *knew* Emma was there, *too*! And *you* didn't tell *me!*"

"I did *not* know Emma was staying in Bar Harbor, sir. I assumed she'd be going back home, like she does every summer." It took Vincent everything he had to give off the even the slightest air of confidence. He knew if he allowed any weakness in his defense, Harvey would exploit it and tear him down. His life — or perhaps even more — was on the line at this moment. It was necessary, though, that Harvey find out about this now. If he ever learned that Vincent kept this information from him for more than a day, his not-so-trusted chauffeur would never escape the consequences.

"Very well," Harvey muttered with a final resolve that was hardly soothing. "Continue on with your current orders until I contact you again. I need to reconsider our plans. We have no choice now but to take action. We can no longer assume our safety. There is no room for error, Vincent. Stay vigilant. I'll call you tomorrow with your new instructions."

"Yes, sir," was all Vincent could say before Harvey hung up. He closed his eyes and suddenly noticed how quickly his heart was beating. His lungs fought to fill themselves with a substantial amount of air.

It was done, though. He had narrowly dodged the wrath of Harvey Payton, and almost felt sorry for whoever wouldn't be so fortunate.

Seemingly on queue, headlights lit up the falling darkness in the distance. After a moment, Vincent recognized the distinct shape of Colton's antique Jeep. He huddled against the forest brush to stay out of sight as the vehicle neared the cabin. He waited patiently as the car came to a gradual halt at the end of the gravel driveway beside the cabin's porch. He held his breath as the lights flicked off and narrowed his eyes as the engine ceased its rumbling. He watched as the same unknown man as before exited the vehicle. Vincent assumed it was the same man, at least — he could not see his face clearly enough, but this figure had the same crippled hobble that the man who entered the Jeep an hour or so ago did.

:-:

Jeremy stumbled through the doorway and limped over to the couch as fast as his aching legs could carry him. He flung his knapsack down on the cushion beside him as he collapsed. He breathed heavily and winced in pain as he resisted the urge to clutch his quadricep. Though he hadn't done much, the little bit of walking he had done and even pressing the gas and brake pedals on the Jeep had taken a serious toll on his entire right leg. After he had left, it hadn't taken long before he realized he couldn't use his right arm to drive. From his shoulder down, his arm was in tortuous agony that very nearly rivaled the pain in his leg. Worst of all, though, was his pounding headache. His vision had blurred on the drive back, and searing spikes of pain in his head had distracted him during the rendezvous.

Nevertheless, he had obtained what he had set out to obtain. That was all that mattered. He had accomplished his mission — brief as it was — and now he could relax and recover. He wanted to find the medical kit that he knew was stored somewhere in the kitchen, but he couldn't bring himself to get back up. He winced again and brought his hands to his head. He closed his eyes and focused on ignoring the pain. He had, after all, dealt with much worse before. Pain was pain, though, and no amount of ignorance could ever completely eradicate all traces of it.

All the same, though, he recalled the mental exercises he had learned in his training and started to put one into effect. The first few seconds were the most difficult, mostly because his agony was distracting him from concentrating. Gradually, though, a hazy mental fog began to settle over the sensation of pain. Almost immediately, he began to feel the effects. With that, he pushed onwards. The next part, without quite as much pain distracting him, was less difficult. He was able to focus more clearly and block out even more of the pain.

Minutes later, the previously excruciating hurt had become nothing more than a distant afterthought. His energy was spent, and he wanted nothing more than to fall asleep. So that's exactly what he did.

TWENTY

After Colton paid the bill — something he had insisted on doing, he and Emma made their way down to the pier. The mood between them wasn't awkward, though it wasn't necessarily comfortable either. Dinner hadn't gone as well as Emma had hoped. She freely admitted it was her fault, though. She had forced Colton's hand. He shared the secrets of his past with her — something he was obviously very uncomfortable doing.

"What made you decide to tell me?" she asked.

"I trust you."

"Oh, you do?" she said skeptically. "Why?"

He shrugged lazily. "Because I can recognize a trustworthy person when I see one."

"Well, that may be true, but that's not the real reason. And it's not because you owed me, either. It was a decision you made completely on your own."

"You're absolutely right," he affirmed after a moment.

Though it was exactly what she wanted to hear, Emma was shocked that he actually admitted it. "So, tell me why. Tell me the real reason."

He remained quiet as they reached the end of the pier. They stood together in the dark, listening to the waves crashing against the rocky shore. "Life's thrown a couple of curve balls at me. Last night was another game-changer."

"What changed all the sudden?"

"I saw my reflection in a mirror last night for the first time in years," he began. "But I didn't see myself... I saw my father. I saw him, clear as day, just as I remembered him. He was right there in front of me." He shook his head. "The guilt came like a terrible flood. All the numbness I had built up over the years was all just washed away. I realized I despised myself for trying to forget him."

Emma could hear a painful edge creeping into his tone. Emotional scars so deep could never be completely concealed, she decided, no matter how great the effort.

"I realized I simply couldn't do it anymore. I'd been living a lie, acting as though I never cared that he had died. After all these years, I realized it was time I accepted his death once and for all, no matter what the cost."

"And telling me over dinner was the most effective way to do so."

He nodded after a moment of evident hesitation. "It took your prodding to get me to see the opportunity, but yes. It's a gradual process, as I'm sure you're well aware of, but spending time with you is making me realize just how much I've been wrong about. Humans need one another to balance out the thoughts in their heads. When you're alone, there's no one there to tell you that you're losing it. Thank you, Emma, for being here for me. I may not have wanted it at first, but it's exactly what I needed. If there's one thing I regret these past three years, it's that I'm just meeting you now."

Once again at a loss for sufficient words, "I'm glad we met," was all she could muster up as a response.

At last, he let loose a long-overdue, contagious smile. Emma couldn't resist letting a silly grin crawl across her face in return.

"I'm glad we met, too," he said, reaching for her hand. "So," he said, snorting in fake amusement. "Are you having fun yet?"

"I'm," she began with a smile, judging her response carefully. "Enjoying our time together."

"I know I've been in a pensive mood since we left, but I think I've finally got everything out of my system. Would you like to go have some real fun before we head back?"

"Depends on your idea of fun," she began warily. "Does it involve climbing rocks or jumping off cliffs?"

"Would you respond unfavorably if it did?"

"Perhaps."

"Well it doesn't," he admitted. "Not this time, at least."

"That's a relief. What, then?"

"Swimming."

"You're joking. Here?"

Colton nodded. "Yeah, why not?"

"Because it says no swimming around the pier. Because it's getting dark. And because the water has got to be sub-sixty."

Colton simply slid his shirt over his head and tossed it to the side. He yanked his shoes and socks off and sat them beside his shirt. He rolled his jeans up just past his ankles, took one look at Emma, and jumped in.

Emma hollered in laughter as frigid water droplets splashed up at her as Colton hit the water. "You're insane!" she exclaimed after she saw him surface.

"Come on in and join me!" he shouted back.

She bit her lip, surprisingly tempted by his offer. She didn't know what had come over her, but she was suddenly much less concerned with the consequences.

"Come on!" he repeated, splashing water at her. "Just let go and stop thinking so much! You'll never have any fun if you always let your common sense dictate what you do and don't do."

That was all she needed to hear. She wasn't about to let him think she was boring, after all. She could make all the excuses she wanted to, but in the end, she knew she wanted to jump.

She slipped her sandals off and tossed them beside Colton's belongings. She undid her ponytail and gently set the Meadow Rose on one of her sandals.

She didn't think before she leapt. She laughed aloud just before making contact with the ice-cold water, almost forgetting to hold her breath. Once submerged, a cold shock traversed her body as she felt her lungs shrink. When she surfaced, she rubbed the saltwater from her eyes and pushed her hair behind her head. She inhaled deeply, fighting to balance the oxygen level in her body.

She swam over to Colton, grinning proudly. "You didn't think I'd do it!" she exclaimed between gasps.

"No, I knew you would," he said calmly in response, edging nearer to her. She noticed that the bone-chilling water didn't seem to have much of a noticeable effect on him.

"Oh, did you?" she challenged.

"Of course."

"Do you know what I'm about to do next?"

He didn't respond right away. "I might," he finally muttered.

Not another moment passed before her lips met his. At once, a warmth resonated throughout her. The sensation was unmatched by anything she had ever felt before. She stopped treading water when he wrapped an arm around her. She ran her fingers through his hair as they kissed again. And again.

PART II

ANTEBELLUM

TWENTY-ONE

9 JUNE, 2012

Colton and Emma had spent the rest of the week together, watching over the kids during the day and exploring Bar Harbor and the surrounding area in the evenings.

Jeremy was recovering rapidly, though he still was not one hundred percent — and understandably so. He kept to himself mostly, seemingly more interested in television than whatever Colton and Emma were doing.

Emma had still not heard from either Adam or the police. Though her concern grew ever so slightly with each passing day, she was far too occupied with Colton to worry about the juvenile delinquent.

Because it was Saturday and Emma didn't have to work, she and Colton made plans to spend the entire day together alone. They had left the cabin just before five in the morning to grab some breakfast at a small cafe in town before heading out to Acadia.

When they finally arrived at their destination, an eerie chill crawled across Colton's skin as the memory from five days ago raced through his mind. He and Emma had come to the cliffs of Otter Point to go kayaking. The two paddled out a decent distance from shore before coming to a steady halt. They were just in time for what they had come for.

The rising sun bathed the world in an orange hue as it broke the Eastern horizon. Emma watched as the color seeped into the surrounding water. She turned to gaze at the cliffs behind her. They, too, had taken on a lustrous scarlet tint — the water droplets on the rock reflecting the rays of the sun. Overcome by the surreal beauty, Emma swung her head to look at Colton. He was leaning back in the seat of his kayak, motionless and gazing deeply into the ascending sun. He appeared to be lost to his thoughts.

Emma paddled over to him, silently drawing up beside his kayak. She looked him over, then turned to face the sun. Together, they watched as some invisible force seemed to lift the gleaming sphere higher and higher in the sky. Colton and Emma rocked back and forth, gently cradled by the incessant motion of the ocean.

Emma suddenly felt an intimate connection bridge between her and her natural surroundings, allowing her to, for the first time, really understand how Colton was ever able to completely disconnect from modern civilization. She wondered how many times he had done something like this.

"Do you know why we're here?" he asked out of the blue, though still maintaining his unwavering gaze on the radiant sun.

He had caught her off-guard. At first, she wanted to blurt out, "To watch the sunrise, of course!" Upon second thought, though, she knew that there must be more to his question than she might have initially presumed. She pondered in silence for a moment.

"Does anyone?" she finally asked in response.

"That's no excuse for not wondering."

She narrowed her eyes as she weighed his words. "I think everyone wonders. I think everyone has their own idea."

"I disagree."

Emma raised her eyebrows and turned to look at him. When he didn't meet her gaze, she looked away. "You don't have much faith in humankind, do you?"

He shrugged. "I think we've lost our way."

Emma snorted. "When did we ever have it?"

"Which begs the question, why are we here?"

Emma opened her mouth to retort, but realized she didn't have an answer. "I don't know," she finally said, shaking her head. "Why do you think?"

Colton shrugged. "I don't know, either. Everything we do is so infinitesimal in the grand scheme of things. Even the things that matter most to us don't *really* matter at all. In the blink of an eye, we could all disappear and the universe would simply carry on as if we never even existed — and perhaps even for the better." He paused. "I'd like to think we have a purpose, I just don't know what it is."

Emma nodded her head, casting a sideward glance. "What makes you ask?"

He shrugged again. "No reason, I guess."

Emma pursed her lips. Something was troubling him, she could quite easily see. "I think," she began. "That even though we can't answer *that* question, we can answer another, more impactful one."

Colton finally turned his head to look at her. His eyebrows were raised most subtly in faint curiosity.

"Why are *you* here?" she asked, meeting his gaze.

He narrowed his eyes, but said nothing. He turned back to face the sun. "I'm still searching for my purpose," he muttered.

"I think we all are," she agreed, turning back towards the sun.

"Most of us, at least." She paused. "That's why I'm here in Bar Harbor, after all."

He turned to look at her, though she maintained her gaze on the sun. He said nothing.

"I only have one year left of school. I have to figure out what I'm going to do with my life."

Colton turned away. "I understand."

A half-smile curved ever-so-slightly across her face. "I know you do," she said. "You're the only one I've told."

"Don't spend too much time thinking about it," he said in response to her earlier statement. "Just keep yourself open. The ideas that make us who we are often come rather unexpectedly. The less time you spend toiling and fretting and the more time you spend simply doing what you love doing, the sooner it will come to you."

Emma narrowed her eyes as she weighed his words. "Is that why you became a world-traveling rock climber?"

"Ultimately, yes."

"You were chasing an idea?"

He nodded.

"But you haven't found it yet?"

He turned to look at her. She turned to him.

"My journey has led me here, and by no accident," he said. "I'm closer than ever."

Emma nodded. One thought concerned her. "You said you don't stay in any one place for very long, right?"

"I like to keep moving."

"How long are you going to be here?" she asked nervously.

The question startled Colton. He hadn't given it much thought. Under normal circumstances, he would probably be preparing to leave in a few days. "I wouldn't want to overstay my welcome," he answered, turning away.

"You're welcome to stay as long as you want, Colton. You know I wouldn't force you away."

"I appreciate that."

By now, the sun had ascended far above the horizon and the world had mostly reverted back to its usual colors.

TWENTY-TWO

Jeremy had woken when Colton and Emma had bustled around in the kitchen that morning, but he had not spoken with them before their departure. He didn't know what their plans were for the day, but he knew where they were, at least — thanks to the GPS bug he had planted in Colton's Jeep a few days ago.

He opened his laptop to check up on Colton's current whereabouts. According to the GPS, he appeared to be by the coast of Acadia National Park. Satisfied, Jeremy shut the laptop and set it down beside him on the couch.

He was far from being wholly satisfied, though. Out of anxious habit, he retrieved his M9 handgun from his knapsack and routinely began disassembling and thoroughly cleaning it. He had to be sure that it worked, after all. He couldn't allow the possibility of it failing him when he needed it.

He had obtained the laptop, GPS tracker, M9, and photos five days ago from his contact at the rendezvous point in Bar Harbor. The laptop and tracker were to keep tabs on Colton. The photos were for Phase Two. The M9 was for threats like Vincent Gaffeur.

Several days ago, Jeremy had spotted the mercenary hiding out on the edge of the forest across from the cabin. Surely, Vincent had no idea that he was being watched while he kept watch on Colton. If he had any suspicions concerning Jeremy, Jeremy would most likely not still be breathing right now.

Furthermore, perhaps Vincent had been asleep and had missed Colton and Emma's departure, but, for whatever reason, he had not followed them when they left this morning.

As long as Vincent was here, Jeremy would remain on-edge. The fact that the mercenary was so close and still hadn't made a move led Jeremy to believe that he and Harvey were plotting something. Jeremy had no idea of their plans, and he had no idea how to learn of them. He did know, however, that as long as Colton was in Emma's presence, Harvey wouldn't allow Vincent to take violent action.

All of Jeremy's impulses were pushing him to walk out of the cabin right now and remove Vincent from the situation, but three things made him refrain. First, his boss would not approve unless there was no alternative. Second, he wanted to see if he could catch wind of Harvey's schemes before any actions were taken. Third, there was no way Jeremy could handle Vincent right now even if he wanted to — not in the condition he was currently in. Even under normal circumstances, Jeremy doubted he could match Vincent's experience and prowess.

No, Jeremy would take the defensive if need be, but until Vincent made an active offensive, all he could do was wait and prepare. He finished cleaning his M9 and reassembled it, making sure it was loaded. He stowed it back away and retrieved the photos from his bag. He flipped through them, pondering how and when he would initiate Phase Two.

Yes, he had much to do to prepare. The storm was imminent.

TWENTY-THREE

"Did you bring any sunscreen?" Colton asked Emma. They had been paddling along the coast of Acadia all morning, and the sun was finally beginning to reach its zenith.

"Of course I did," she responded. "Why?"

"I think it's about time I put some on."

"*You* use sunscreen?"

"Yeah," he answered. "Why wouldn't I?"

She shrugged. "You look like you've spent every day under the sun for the past three years. I didn't think a wanderer such as yourself would concern himself with sunscreen."

"I *always* wear my sunscreen," he argued. "I've heard skin cancer can be quite unpleasant."

Emma laughed. "I can't believe I'm hearing this from you!"

Colton looked at her wildly, not understanding what was so hard to believe.

When she saw the confusion on his face, she elaborated. "Oh, please. If there's one thing I know about you, it's that you don't fear any consequences. You do whatever you want and don't think twice about it. You conquer death day after day simply for the thrill of it. And yet... you're afraid of getting a sunburn?"

He waved her off lightheartedly.

She laughed again as she stopped paddling to retrieve the sunscreen from her bag. She began applying it on herself first.

"Don't forget your face," he said without looking at her as she smeared the cream over her skin. She smiled at the reminder.

When she was finished, she tossed the bottle to him while he wasn't looking. She knew it was a little mean, but she wanted to test his reflexes.

He didn't disappoint — he caught it one-handedly without even turning his head. She opened her eyes and mouth wide as she laughed in astonishment.

"How'd you do that?" she asked wildly.

"When you're sending a rock—" he began, opening up the bottle.

"Sending a rock?" she interrupted.

"Climbing."

"Oh."

"You spend a great deal of time developing your peripheral vision," he explained, beginning to slather his arms with the sunscreen. "Being on the rock heightens your senses. You have to stop thinking so much and allow your skills of perception to take control."

"So," she began, narrowing her eyes. "Your senses are so maxed out that you can see a bottle of sunscreen flying towards you without actually seeing it?"

"Something like that," he answered lackadaisically.

"I want to hear more about your climbing," she informed. "Raconte-moi une histoire."

He raised his eyebrows in subtle surprise, but continued rubbing sunscreen on himself rather than turning to look at her. "What lovely French. You ever spend any time overseas?"

"Don't try changing the subject. I asked for a story."

"All right, all right," he acquiesced, searching his memory. "About a year ago, I was traveling in southern Chilean Patagonia. My destination was the Torres of the Eastern Andes, a series of rock spires jutting out of the earth. They're so steep, the only way to reach the peak is by climbing. The only way down is to jump."

"Sounds like your kind of rock."

"Oh, you can't even imagine," he said with a nostalgic smile. "Anyways, I was traveling alone, as usual, but a few days into the trip I began to get suspicions that I was being followed."

"And the suspense grows!" Emma chimed in, eyes widened.

"It took several days to make my way through the National Park, so I had to camp out in this massive field every night. Well, my second night there, I noticed the smoke of a campfire not too far behind me in the distance. At that point, I didn't think much of it. The next night, though, I noticed it again. That seemed curious to me, because even though I had made a lot of headway that day, the smoke of this campfire seemed to be the exact same distance behind me as the one the night before. My nerves were really beginning to get to me when the pattern repeated again the following night."

"Uh-oh, this is getting intense," Emma interjected once more.

"My last morning there, I woke up earlier than normal to get a head-start. I thought I was just being overly cautious and perhaps maybe even a little paranoid, but, as it turned out, that decision saved my life. When I started to close in on the mountain, I heard a series of gunshots. Not machine guns, but single-shot rifles."

"You were being hunted?" Emma asked wildly.

"I got the feeling that I was, yeah. Bullet after bullet pounded the rock around me as I started to climb one of the spires. They never hit within a radius of fifty feet or so, but the shots were still too dangerously close for comfort. After a while, the shots stopped, but when I got about halfway up, I heard voices from the base of the spire. I looked beneath me — something I never do — and saw what appeared to be a group of armed men. I couldn't see them well enough to be certain, though, and I couldn't hear them well enough to discern what language they were speaking in. At the time, that was all beside the point, though. I kicked into high gear and realized I had to climb as fast as I could. They tried shooting a few more times, but they never really got close. Anyways, they didn't try to come after me. They just hung out at the base while I sent the spire. I guess they figured they would just wait it out, assuming I had to come down eventually. I did, after all, leave all my camping gear down there."

"So what did you do?" Emma asked wildly.

"I finished my ascent," he answered. "And jumped."

"Oh, did you?"

"Ever heard of wingsuit flying?"

"Oh, yeah, I do it all the time. They call me Batman."

He ignored her sarcasm and continued. "After I got to the peak, I found a relatively flat platform and dug my wingsuit out of my compact climbing backpack. Then I jumped off the opposite side of the spire."

"And you flew?"

"Technically, I glided... Like a giant flying squirrel."

"Oh, how majestic..."

"I soared for a few miles before I finally opened up my parachute and crash-landed in a lake."

"Oh, how majestic," she repeated.

"I feel like you're not taking me very seriously," he said with a wry smile.

"I just enjoy bothering you," she teased.

"Well, you do a good job of it," he said, splashing her.

"Oh, do I? I was beginning to think I couldn't get under your skin!" she exclaimed, splashing him back.

"I just do an excellent job of hiding it."

"You're excellent at a great number of things, it would seem."

He smiled, twirling his finger around in the seawater, but didn't say anything.

"Who were those men?"

"I never found out," he muttered pensively, still focused on the mini whirlpool he was stirring up with his finger.

"You didn't run into them again after you crash-landed?"

He shook his head. "Nope. I wasn't able to circle back and get my hiking gear, either, so I had to live off river water for a day and a half as I made my way back to my Jeep. It wasn't so bad. I've been through worse."

"It's hard to imagine worse than that."

"No, not really." He laughed grimly. "That story only ranks ninth on my list of near-death experiences.

"Where does saving Jeremy five days ago fit in?"

"Eleventh."

"Really?" Emma questioned, astounded. "The fact that you *actually* died and came back doesn't help its case at all?"

"No, it does. If I hadn't briefly died, it would be somewhere in the mid-twenties."

"How long is your list?" Emma asked wildly.

"Long," he said. "Very long."

"I want to hear," she began, paddling over closer to him. "Every single story on that frightening list of yours."

"Too bad," he said, looking up at her as she neared him. "That's all you're getting for now."

"Oh, *why* must you torture me so?"

"I have to let the anticipation build back up," he answered. "And I do enjoy bothering you."

She leaned over and gave him a kiss. "Well, you don't do a good enough job at it to keep me from doing that," she said afterwards.

"Shame," he said, kissing her again. "I'll have to try harder."

"Oh, please don't," she said, giving him one last peck before pulling away. "I'm hungry."

"You're always hungry."

"Want to pull over and have our picnic now?"

"I have a feeling no matter what I say, you've already made up your mind."

"You know me so well."

The two of them made their way over to a wide outcropping on a nearby crag. They pulled their kayaks up on the rough rock and stepped into a small cave-like formation.

"This is cozy," she said.

"I've slept in one of these before."

"Of course you have. What about high tide?"

"That was the interesting part."

She laughed. "Your life seems to be comprised of those."

"Does that make me an interesting person, then?" he asked

with a spark in his eye. "Aren't we all simply the product of our experiences?"

"It would seem that way. Humans aren't quite so simple though. Experiences are important, but it's our reactions to those experiences that really show our character."

"Where do we learn to react the way we do?"

"Our environment. Culture. Society. Civilization."

"That sounds like a recipe for disaster."

"Again with the cynicism."

"You don't like the cynic in me?"

"I don't," she said, allowing a slight edge to creep into her tone as she handed him the food she had packed.

"But you do understand where it's coming from."

"I suppose I do," she said. "But I don't think it's entirely deserved. I think there's a lot out there you that would impress you."

"Nature impresses me, Emma; mankind doesn't."

Emma pursed her lips. "Well it's saddening to hear that you've given up on your own kind."

"And you haven't?" Colton asked, allowing a defensive edge to become evident in his tone. "Maybe you've forgotten, but I seem to recall you yourself telling me about the big downward spiral our race is headed in; about how apathetic we've all become; about how *dreadfully* weak humankind is."

Emma nodded, fighting back a look of disgust. "Yeah, well, I suppose I did. But maybe, even though so many others have already given up, I don't want to see you do the same. I know we're capable of something better. We just need some heroes to step up and lead us."

"Yeah, well," Colton muttered, looking away apathetically. "My heroes are dead in all but books and memories."

Emma blinked, hurt deeply. "Well, enough of that. Let's eat."

TWENTY-FOUR

Adam threw the ball against the peeling wall and caught it single-handedly as it bounced back at him. *Four hundred thirty-seven*, he counted. He was lying on the sheet-less cot of the tiny seven-by-seven room he was renting. He was actually beginning to like it here. It helped him think. *Four hundred thirty-eight.* He supposed some fresh air couldn't hurt, though. *I have to see her.* He would have to wait until Monday, though. *Four hundred thirty-nine.* He knew that showing up out of the blue on the weekend after being out of contact for so long would unsettle her. He didn't want to unsettle her.

The emotional trauma from last week's happenings had mostly subsided by now. He had forgiven Emma. *I have to see her.* That was the reason he was here, wasn't it? *Four hundred and forty.* To see her? To spend time with her? *Four hundred forty-one.* To get close to her? *Four hundred and forty-two.* What had he been doing here for the past week? *Four hundred and forty-three.* He was wasting time. *Four hundred and—damn.*

He let his arm fall like dead weight down to the cot as gravity dribbled the bouncing ball across the old wooden floorboards. He stared at a wet spot on the ceiling where water from the upper floor must have leaked through. He and that spot were in this together. They had become quite close over the past few days. Together, they had shared in this lovely loneliness... Adam made a perplexed face. *Sharing loneliness?*

He sat up and rubbed his eyes. He crinkled his nose. A foul odor seemed to emanate from the walls. Or maybe it was just his feet... *I suppose a shower might be in order before I see her again.* He stood up and marveled at his prison. The smothering walls. The dusty, cracked window that stubbornly refused to open. The upside-down, tetanus-infested nails jutting up from the floorboards, patiently awaiting some warm flesh to bite into. That curious bubble behind the wallpaper on the far side of the room that seemed to grow with each passing day. The 'kitchen' faucet flaunting its rust as proudly as if it were a suit of armor. That black widow that had claimed that corner of the ceiling as its humble abode. Adam breathed in deeply, allowing the stale air to pour into his welcoming lungs. He simultaneously slid on a pair of old socks while stumbling about the room to look for his shoes. Less than fifty square feet of space, and he still managed to lose his only pair of shoes... *Aha!* There they were. He swore he didn't remember setting them in the sink.

He jammed the crevice between his toes on a nail as he turned towards the door and tripped on that stupid ball afterwards, but he eventually made it through the threshold without any mortal injuries. He slammed the door shut behind him and proceeded to nearly fall head-first down the staircase. *Damn shoelaces.* He would need to cut them off later. This was beginning to become a persistent problem.

TWENTY-FIVE

Colton and Emma had eaten their lunches mostly in silence, neither wishing to discuss the previous topic of conversation further, though neither willing to move on.

Growing increasingly bored, Colton took the last of his sandwich and stood up.

Emma watched him as he looked around and stepped behind a wall that she had not noticed until now.

"Woah," he said with half a mouthful. "Check this out."

Emma couldn't see him, but she could hear his muffled voice. "What is it?" she asked, beginning to stand up.

"It's a tunnel. Come look."

"What? Really?" Emma said, peering around the wall. He had indeed found a tunnel that appeared to lead underneath the crag.

"Let's check it out," Colton urged, disappearing into the earth.

"Colton!" Emma exclaimed upon watching him vanish.

"What?" he asked, reemerging a moment later.

"Do you think that's such a good idea? What about high tide?"

"High tide isn't until much, much later. And of course it's a good idea," he stated matter-of-factly.

"Is that your impulse or your reason speaking?"

A wild look sparked in his eye. "Both," he said before disappearing again.

Emma growled in frustration as she took off after him. She had an easier time watching all twenty of her day camp children than she did keeping up with Colton. She wondered if he had given the same no-nonsense, headstrong argument to Jeremy when the poor guy had tried talking him down from jumping off the cliff. This was who he was, though, she realized, and there was no changing that. When he sees something that intrigues him, he goes after it. Simple. Always so simple.

"Pretty cool, right?" he asked after she caught up to him.

Though the gesture was minimal, it meant something to her that he had actually waited for her. "Yes, I suppose it is," she said, putting her hair up in a ponytail. They both had to crouch, though, and there was hardly any light. Emma still felt unsure about the whole thing, but the spirit of adventure had kindled deep inside of her.

"Looks like there's an opening up ahead," he said, beginning to walk forward.

"If you say so... I can't see hardly anything. You lead the way."

They walked carefully on the wet, rough rock for several minutes, crouching the whole while. Emma had taken hold of Colton's hand so that she wouldn't slip and fall in the darkness. She really didn't understand how he could see anything. As soon as the thought crossed her mind, though, she could make out a faint light up ahead. As they progressed, it grew larger and larger, but never brighter. Eventually, they entered a large, cavernous opening.

As Emma adjusted to her surroundings, she took note of what they had just discovered. The chamber was an imperfect ellipse about twenty feet in length and perhaps fifteen feet at its widest, as Emma judged it. The ground receded towards the center, where a pool of ocean water resided, extending the whole length of the cavern. Emma turned her head upwards, looking for the source of light. Perhaps fifty or sixty feet up, she could make out a narrow string of daylight that had found its way through a very narrow gap between two ridges, one on either side of the ellipse.

"What is this place?" Emma asked in wonder.

"It's a grotto."

"How did it get here?"

Colton laughed. "Water, sweetheart."

"How?"

"Water is a restless artist; a patient sculptor doomed to carve away at land for the rest of eternity. Give it enough time, and it can create some pretty remarkable structures... Like this one. Breathtaking, isn't it?

"It is," Emma breathed in wonder, looking around as the faint light reflected off the wet rock.

Colton walked over to one of the walls and felt the rock as if he were learning everything he needed to know about it merely by touch. He looked upwards and opened his mouth to speak, but Emma interjected before the words could leave his mouth.

"No," she said firmly. "You're not going to climb that. Not now. Not here with me."

He began to object, but stopped when she gave him a look that checked him. "Fine," he conceded.

She lifted her chin slightly with an air of victorious authority, but said nothing.

"Next time, I suppose," he said as he walked away, longingly staring back at the wall as he did so.

"Are you ready to go?" Emma asked, beginning to lead the way out.

"We only just got here!"

"What else do you plan on doing in here?"

"I don't know. Explore!"

"No, I think we're done exploring. Let's go back and make sure our kayaks are still where we left them."

"Okay, you lead the way, your majesty."

What a character, she thought as she ducked her head back into the dark tunnel. One moment he's so disillusioned he won't even talk to her, the next he's completely enthralled in the natural wonders of his surroundings. *Nature really is his remedy for emotional discomfort.*

"Don't worry, I won't let you walk into any walls or fall on your face," he said in a not-so-reassuring manner.

Now that she was in the lead, she found that the tunnel turned and twisted much more than she had thought it had during their descent. Nevertheless, she did eventually emerge, and when she did, she was thrilled.

"That was fun!" she exclaimed.

Colton gave her a puzzled look as he exited the tunnel behind her. "You didn't seem like you were having much fun while we were in there."

"Well, to get out and look back on what I just did, it makes me feel accomplished!"

"You should try climbing with me sometime," he offered.

"Maybe someday. But I'll need lots of rope."

"Bah," he grunted, waving her off lightheartedly. "You're no fun."

"I could sit and watch you, if that would make you feel better."

"It wouldn't."

"I simply can't wrap my head around how you can climb a vertical mountain face without any rope. I don't see how that's physically possible, and I don't see how anyone could ever convince themselves that it'd be worth it."

"There is no wrapping your head around free-soloing; you either do it or you don't. There's nothing more to it. It's just one of those things that if you don't do it, you can't understand it."

"Well said."

"I'm sorry." He chuckled. "There's really no explaining it. I will say one thing."

"All right."

"The physical endurance is only half the battle. The other half is the mentality. You can't climb with the perfect body if you don't have the right mindset. No one but the most experienced climbers fully understands that. Sometimes, the mental focus is even more important than the physical aspect. It really just depends on what you're climbing. That's really what it all boils down to."

"So if you have both of those then you're safe?"

Colton chuckled again, taking a seat on the rough rock. A wave battered against the crag and sent a salty spray of seawater up at him. "No," he said. "You're never safe on a cliff face. It only takes a split second for the faintest trace of uncertainty to weasel its way into your consciousness. You ask any free-soloer what he or she is most afraid of, and they'll tell you it's losing their confidence when they're sending a rock. Nothing is more dangerous. You can build up all the mental barriers you want, but you're never completely safe."

Emma nodded, narrowing her eyes as she took a seat beside him. Together, they gazed out at the open ocean. "I see," she began, flicking a pebble at a wave. "That explains a lot."

"A lot about me? Yes, I suppose it does."

"And I suspect you developed that mentality naturally as a result of all of your hardship."

"There's a bit more to it than that, though."

"Explain."

"I was in a bad place after my mom's funeral. I had already abandoned my former life, but I hadn't yet adopted my current one. I didn't know where I belonged and, frankly, I didn't know if I even belonged anywhere. Death had taken so much from me, so I dared it to take everything else. I challenged death and climbed the Nose of El Capitan. There wasn't the slightest part of me that cared whether I survived it or not."

"So you're apathetic towards living?"

He nodded. "In a sense. That's what sets me apart from the other climbers. That's why no one else can do what I do. Everyone else has something to fear, whether they admit it or not."

Emma narrowed her eyes again, judging his words. "I think you're wrong."

He shot a look at her — curious, rather than belligerent, though.

"I think you *do* have something to fear, and I think that faintest trace of fear is the only thing that actually motivates you."

He said nothing, too intrigued to interject.

"You still don't know where you fit in, Colton. You might have found your new life after you conquered El Capitan, but to this day you still haven't found your purpose. I know you well enough to know that, although you're willing to take risks no one else will, you're going to make sure you don't fail because you still have unfinished business in this world. Now, I don't know what it is you have to accomplish, and perhaps you don't either, but you *do* know there's more, and you're afraid of dying before you can accomplish it."

He looked away. A long silence ensued. Emma wasn't sure what he was thinking, but she was terribly anxious to hear what he had to say. At last, he turned his chin ever so slightly to look off in a different direction. Emma thought he was ready to respond, but she was wrong. She waited even longer still.

"You're right," he finally muttered in consent.

"But you already knew that," she said, looking at him. "You just haven't willingly admitted it to yourself until now. I understand that you don't want to be afraid, Colton. You think that fear comes from weakness, but you have to understand that no weakness bred this fear." She paused a moment as her mouth curved into a proud grin. "You *do* care, and that's something admirable."

"Yeah, well..." He met her gaze before leaning in to give her a kiss. "Just don't tell anyone," he joked, standing up.

"My lips are sealed," she said, gathering the picnic materials and packing them away in her bag.

"Oh, don't tempt me," he said, launching his kayak back into the water. "Here," he said, motioning towards her bag. "I'll hold that while you board."

"Thanks," she said, handing it over and then launching her own kayak. She boarded and took back her bag from him. "What do you say we head back?"

"And go where?"

"My villa?"

"Sure."

"I'll even cook for you. I picked up some food from the grocery store last night and dropped it off for tonight."

"Oh, so this is planned?" an impressed Colton asked as they paddled back in the direction of the mainland.

"Maybe," Emma said, raising her eyebrows and casting a sideward glance.

"Is this part of your elaborate scheme to tie me down?"

"At the end of the night, let me know how it worked."

TWENTY-SIX

18 JULY, 2002

It was dry. It was hot. And it wasn't even breakfast time yet. This was summer in Afghanistan.

Colton scanned the surrounding landscape. He was completely lost. Fortunately, though, he was not alone. "Dad?"

"Yeah?"

"How do you always know where we are?" Colton stuffed his hands into his pockets and kicked at a pebble. It bounced across Earth's stony shell before coming to a gradual halt twenty feet away.

"Who says I do?"

"You're lost?" Colton looked at him, the growing terror in his eyes evident.

"No." George Anders came to a standstill and turned around. He pointed a weathered finger to the heavens. "See that star?"

Colton turned around as well, mouth agape as he fixed his eyes on the lone star his father was directing his attention to. "Yeah," he affirmed.

"I can't say exactly where we are right now, but I do know that Base is directly beneath that star right there."

"So if we keep walking in that direction, we'll eventually get back to Base?"

"That's right."

"What if it disappears before we make it back?"

"Then we'll be abandoned out here forever. No one will come looking for us. We'll have nothing to do but wander aimlessly in circles. It's hard to say what we'll die of first... dehydration, sun poisoning, a stampede of wild goats... I'll probably have to end up eating you to last a little longer. Hope you understand."

Colton smiled and playfully shoved his father. "You're not worried about the enemy?"

"The enemy?" George raised an eyebrow, beginning to walk in the direction opposite of the star. "What do you know about the enemy, Colton?"

"That they want to kill us," the teenager stated as if it was blatantly obvious.

"Have you ever encountered 'the enemy?'"

Colton opened his mouth to speak, but checked himself. After a moment of hesitation, "No," he admitted.

"Then how do you know they want to kill you?"

"I don't know." Colton shrugged. "That's what everyone says."

George raised his eyebrows, pursed his lips, and cocked his head as he looked ahead into the empty distance. "I see. That's quite the convincing argument."

"Are you saying they're not the enemy?"

"If everyone says something, it must be hard fact, no?"

"Well..."

"Listen, Colton," George began in a gentler, but more serious tone. "Don't ever let anyone tell you what to believe in. Remember this: every other person you'll ever meet on this planet has one thing in common; they're human. Just like you. Just like me. And none among us is any greater than his brother. No matter how many of us there are, just because we all believe something doesn't mean we're right. Cultivate your own beliefs and be your own person. One of the worst things you can be is unoriginal. Do you understand?"

Colton nodded, deeply contemplating his father's words.

"So, until you have a firsthand experience with the locals of this country, it's not your right to determine whether they are your enemy or not. Don't misinterpret my message, though; I'm not encouraging you to be careless and naïve in this land. There are bad people here. And some of them want to hurt you. But most aren't bad at all. And most wouldn't even think of hurting you. But sometimes, good people do bad things. And in many of those cases, those good people are doing bad things for good reasons."

Colton remained silent, content with merely listening and thinking.

"In truth, there are no good people. There are only the decisions we make and the circumstances we live in. You could have just as likely been born here, Colton. And if you had been, you might have been born into poverty — like many of the boys in this land. Perhaps your father would have been a goat herder. Perhaps, one day, when you were as old as you are now, you would be out in the countryside tending to the herd when a bomb suddenly dropped from nowhere. You manage to escape with your life, but all that remains of the herd is smoldering ash. And with the goats, so goes your parents' livelihood. Without the herd, your parents have no milk to sell. They have no income. And if they can't earn any money, how are they supposed to provide for you and your three brothers and sisters? You're the eldest son, though. You feel it's your responsibility to help, especially because you were there when the bomb fell. But how?

What can you do? Where on Earth are you going to find the money to buy even one new goat? You have no savings. Your parents have barely been making enough to get by as it is. You could steal a goat, but would you really risk penalty of getting your hand cut off... or worse? Then, one day, you hear that there is a way... A way to get your parents not just one goat, but six. Then they can breed them and continue to sell their milk and make enough money to raise your younger siblings. This is the only way, and you only have to do one task: strap a bomb to your chest, wander through the Hindu Kush until you find some American soldiers, and blow yourself up as soon as they get close enough."

Again, Colton only answered with silence. He gulped a heavy breath of air.

"Hatred has no place in your heart, son. Empathy does."

The morning sun was just beginning to break over the distant mountain range, and with it came an array of multicolored light to flood the desert valley. Colton raised an arm to shield his eyes before looking away in a different direction.

"What if that was you, though?" the boy asked, his voice trembling at the thought. "I don't think I could keep myself from hating whoever was responsible for blowing you up."

George sighed. "Someday, Colton, I'll be gone. And that day could be today. It could be tomorrow. It could be thirty years from now. There's no way to know. Everybody's time comes eventually. And if I happen to die here, then I'd be the person responsible for my death, because I'm here by my own choice. War isn't a personal battle. One side puts up their soldiers, and the other side puts up their own. And in war, that's all we are... soldiers, not people. Soldiers are supposed to die. That's just how war goes. You can't hate the other side for it. After all, we're doing to them what they are to us."

"So you're not afraid? Of dying?"

"There's no use fearing what I know will come one way or another."

"What are you afraid of, then?"

"Wasting any minute that I'm still alive on anger or regret. There's too much to appreciate and look forward to for me to get stuck on the things that only ever want the worst for me. There's too much to do for me to do to waste the precious minutes I still have on the things that only ever want to hold me back."

"What do you have to do?"

"Raise my son into a man that I can be proud of." George turned to smile at his son. "And I'd say I'm doing a pretty good job of that so far."

Colton smiled faintly, but did not respond or look at his father.

"What about you? What do *you* have to do?"

Colton raised his eyebrows and exhaled. "I don't know. What should I do?"

"That's not for me to decide. Only you can answer that. That's something worth keeping on your mind, though. You've been given many gifts, and it's up to you to figure out how to use them for the greater good. You're fortunate enough to not have to tend to a herd of goats all day long. You don't have to worry about starving or freezing to death while you sleep tonight. You have clothes on your back and shoes on your feet. You have your own personal tutors to give you a solid education. And you have two parents who love you very, very much. There's no excuse. Do you understand me?"

"I'll make you proud," Colton said confidently, though reflectively.

"You already do." George slowed to a halt and turned around, staring up at the heavens in search of the star. "Looks like the star disappeared after all."

"How are we supposed to get back?" Colton asked, trying to suppress his concern.

"You tell me."

Colton opened his mouth, prepared to blurt out that he hadn't the slightest clue, but stopped himself. His father was testing him, and he didn't want to disappoint. He could feel his father's eyes watching him think. "That way," he decided, pointing in the direction completely opposite the sun.

"Oh, yeah?" George asked skeptically.

"Yeah," Colton said definitively. The boy could sense in his gut that his father had just implicitly validated his suggestion. Colton's ability to read the man was growing each day — and his father was not an easy man to read. "West."

"West it is, then." George affirmed, setting off in that direction. "I guess we'll find out. I better not miss my morning recon mission because you led me astray."

"You won't."

With the sun at their backs and the distant mountain range running alongside them, father and son trekked westward through the Afghan desert with naught but nature to guide them home.

TWENTY-SEVEN

"Welcome to my humble abode," Emma said as they pulled in the driveway of her villa.

Colton opened his eyes wide as he took it in. If there was one word that simply couldn't be used to accurately describe the villa, that word would be 'humble.' It was a magazine-cover-worthy seaside mansion, complete with the appropriate porthole windows, sun-dried tan brick, and navy blue trim. It even had a three-story-tall turret that gave off the appearance of a lighthouse. Its house-wide veranda had nautical rope looped through short wooden posts in place of standard railing. The walkway leading up to the front entrance was made of the wooden boards that one might find at a pier.

"We built it a few years back as a vacation home, but…" Emma trailed off as Colton pulled the Jeep to a gradual halt at the end of the driveway. "We don't come out here much as a family. My dad doesn't really take many vacations."

"It's lovely," Colton managed to say as he unbuckled and turned the engine off. He opened the door and hopped out. "I really like the whole marine theme you guys were going for."

"I think we pulled it off pretty well. A friend of my brother's came up with the architectural plans and my dad found the contractor. My mom and I came up with most of the ocean-inspired idiosyncrasies."

"You haven't talked much about your family," Colton pointed out as they walked up the boarded walkway together.

She brushed her hair as if she were moving it out of her face, even though it was in a ponytail — a motion that Colton perceived as a sign that she was uncomfortable breeching the topic.

"And if you don't want to talk about it, that's okay with me," he added before she could respond. "I respect your privacy."

"Oh, please," she said, shaking her head. "I owe you some explanations in turn for everything you've shared with me."

"Don't look it as a mutual exchange. That's not what this is. That's not what we are," Colton countered. "I shared my past with you because I wanted to, not because I expected anything out of it. I'm interested in your family because I'm interested in you. What you feel comfortable sharing is completely your choice. No pressure at all. Honestly. Understood?"

"Understood," Emma said with a sigh, raising her eyebrows. "I just don't normally like discussing my family, sort of like how I don't like discussing my wealth. I'm not necessarily proud of either. My dad's a slave to work. My mom's a slave to money. My brother's a slave to society and appearance. They're all so incredibly myopic. They each always have one and only one thing on their mind. One motive to spur all their patterned and predictable choices and actions."

"What do you have to cling to?"

"Adventure," she said with a smile as they finally reached the front door. She took out her keys and turned the lock. They entered together.

Colton held his breath as he took in the lavishness of his surroundings. They were simultaneously overwhelming and inviting.

"Not in the sense of adventure that you're associated with, of course, but rather an adventure into the unknown regions of the human psyche."

"I can imagine that there's plenty of uncharted territory there," Colton said as he followed Emma into the living room.

"You can't even imagine how much, though," Emma said as she plopped herself down on a plush white leather couch. Colton took a seat on a complementary armchair beside her. "And that's what fascinates me. I went to Cornell and majored in Psychology, now I'm headed into my final year at Georgetown in hopes of earning my PhD."

"And you don't know what comes next?"

Emma shook her head as she stared off blankly at a wall. "Nope. You know as well as I do. That's what I'm here to find out."

"Like I said before, it'll come to you naturally... eventually."

When she didn't respond for a few moments, he continued. "So your family members are blinded prisoners to worldly obsessions and you're the avant-garde explorer marching to her own beat. You're sure you weren't adopted?"

Emma laughed at the thought. "You know," she said, smiling. "It would explain a lot." She paused, lost in thought. "But I suppose I'm too like my dad in too many ways. Both my brother and I are, but in very different ways. We both inherited — or learned, rather — our father's unwavering fixation to win, but where I'll work hard or come up with a different method to achieve, he'll simply cheat." Emma tried to subdue a disgusted look, but ultimately failed.

Colton didn't have the heart to press further. He could see the topic of her brother was a tender one. Unless she took it upon herself to elaborate, he wouldn't question her.

"And your mother? Where does she fit in?"

Emma shrugged. "She doesn't, really."

"Well, she must care for you. It must mean something if she calls to check in on you."

"She never called to check in while I was at college," Emma said, raising her eyebrows again as she stared off into the distance. "She's only calling now because she wants me back home. Things are out of order, and she doesn't know how to deal with it. She thinks if she calls and can convince me to come home, everything will go back to normal.

"Well," Colton began, searching his mind for a suitable argument. "If she wants you back home that must mean she misses you."

"Oh, yeah," Emma said, loosing a spiteful smile as she shook her head in disgust. "She misses me, all right. Not in the normal way a mother would miss her daughter, though. She only misses me because her little 'system' has been disrupted. During the majority of the year, when I'm off at college, I'm *supposed* to be off at college. That's just part of her big 'plan.' But during the summer, I'm *supposed* to be at home in the Hamptons. Instead, I'm way out here and she can't show me off at home like she normally does during the summers. She can't brag to all her uppity neighbor 'friends' about my studies and accomplishments at graduate school. Now she can't take me on bizarre outings introducing me to random strangers to give off the impression that she's actually a legitimate mother, as if she's done anything to help get me where I am."

"Emma," Colton interjected gently. "I wouldn't really know, but are you sure you're not being a little too harsh? She must be proud of you if she wants to brag about you and show you off. She *is* your mother."

Emma shook her head, rolling her eyes. "I wish I had a

mother, growing up. I wish I had a mom to talk to when I didn't have anyone else. Instead, I had a parent who mostly ignored me. My dad was around a fraction of the time, but I at least got the sense from him that he actually enjoyed being around me. I at least felt loved, appreciated, and wanted by him."

Colton looked away without saying anything. He refrained from speaking his mind. He didn't want to make this about him. "Well," he began. "You are where you are and doing what you're doing because of the way you reacted to your past experiences. All that hardship shaped you into the woman you've become. And where you are, what you're doing, who you've become," he said, looking at her. "Is nothing to be ashamed of."

"You're sweet," she said faintly, looking over at him and gently grabbing his hand. Fatigue had washed over her face.

"In fact," he continued. "I'm rather fond of the woman you've become."

"Oh, stop." She giggled and squeezed his hand affectionately.

"And, unless I'm mistaken, I'd dare to say I'm more fond of you than any other woman I've ever met."

"You're making my job awfully easy, you know. You're falling right into *my* elaborate plan. I'll have you tied down in no time at this rate. You'd better be careful."

"Is that a piano?" Colton asked, looking the other way.

Emma snorted in feigned contempt. "Are you *trying* to ruin the moment? Or do you simply have A-D-D?"

"A little of both, perhaps," he said, still fixated on the grand piano that occupied a corner of the grandiose living room. "I have to allow the tension to build up, after all."

After a brief moment of longing, he got up and approached the instrument. He ran his finger along the polished side as he found the seat. He gently laid his fingers on the keys as he sat down and played an eight-fingered octave chord.

"Can you play?" Emma asked, intrigued. She craned her neck to watch him.

"Play me a tune."

Emma arose from her comfortable seat and sauntered over to a shelf that bore an iPod connected to the home stereo system. "What are you in the mood for?"

"Anything but classical," he said, replaying the same chord, but this time brokenly.

"Still not feeling classy?" she hummed, browsing the selection. "Ooh, John Mayer," she muttered to herself, choosing one of his songs at random. Emma watched as Colton stared intently at the keys of the piano, listening carefully.

"Okay, pause it," he requested.

She did as he was she was told and he began playing the basic notes with his right hand. When something didn't sound right, he would try different notes until he could carry the tune.

"Okay, start it over," he said without looking up.

Emma narrowed her eyes in curiosity as she once again did as she was directed. As the song played a second time, he played along with basic cords. Not long afterwards, he was adding in a basic melody. He played through the song, learning as he went. When the song ended, he asked Emma to play it again. So she did, and he played along one more time, embellishing upon the notes and chords this time around.

"Again?" Emma asked when it had finished the third time.

Colton shook his head and started playing the song. With his left hand, he played the chords and background tune. With his right, he played the exact melody, note for note.

As he played, Emma fell into a dreamlike trance. Surely, this couldn't be real. She had no reason to believe he could play like that. She never doubted his intelligence, but she had never witnessed such a feat of genius before. All cynicism aside, though, his music was beautiful. She listened, captivated in wonder as he serenaded her.

Still half in disbelief, she walked over to the couch beside the piano. She collapsed on it gracefully and hung her head over the side to watch his fingers. They were flying across the keys, hitting each note precisely on target. She flicked her gaze upwards to his eyes. It was evident that, to him, there was only one thing in his world right now, and that was the piano.

Emma leaned back and closed her eyes, allowing the melody of his music to reverberate through her soul.

Several minutes later, the notes came to a gradual and graceful finish. Now that it had stopped, Emma jolted upwards and gave Colton a wild look. "*What* was *that*?" she asked with widened eyes.

"That was a crude rendition of whatever tune you just played for me."

"That was hardly 'crude,' Colton," Emma said, still in disbelief. "Tell me that wasn't the first time you've done that. Tell me you've played the piano before."

"That wasn't the first time I've done that. I've played the piano before," he said with a wry, crooked smile.

"You never cease to amaze me," she said, shaking her head.

"My mother used to tell me that." Colton stood up from the piano and made his way back to his armchair. "And she didn't always mean it in a good way."

"Oh, I can't imagine *you* ever causing your mother any trouble," Emma remarked sarcastically.

He shrugged. "I was curious and adventurous and sometimes

I would get bored. The way I saw it, the world was out there waiting to be discovered and it was mine to claim. You can imagine what I would get myself into. Most of the time, my dad was working and my mom was left with the responsibility of keeping a watchful eye over me. I would always finish my school lessons early and then sneak off while she wasn't paying attention."

"Ooh," Emma breathed, interested. "I want stories."

"Maybe later."

Emma rolled her eyes before repositioning herself. "What do you mean you 'got bored?'"

"My school lessons bored me, so I would finish my work early and then run around and explore to blow off steam."

"Were they *actually* boring? Or did you just grasp the concepts before your tutors could finish explaining?" Emma asked with a raised eyebrow.

He shrugged and looked away. "I don't know. I always preferred reading to listening to my tutors drone on and on, anyway. That way I could go at least go at my own pace."

"You seem like a pretty fast-paced kind of guy."

"You think so?"

"And a pretty smart guy."

"That's what they say."

"You don't think so?"

"I don't really like to think of myself that way. I look down on people who think they're smarter than everyone else."

Emma weighed his words. "So you had a lot of free time, from the sounds of it?"

He nodded.

"And you taught yourself how to do various things like... play the piano?"

He nodded again. "Yeah, but I always had an inspiration. My inspiration for the piano was my dad's flying partner. He and my dad would always get transferred together, so we were always at the same base. At most of the bases there happened to be a piano of some sort, and he would play whenever he had the chance." Colton raised his eyebrows and shook his head slightly. "And he could play like no other. He would play by ear, I would watch, and then I would try it myself. It took practice, but I took to it fairly naturally. I never got as good as him, though. He was an entertainer, I tell you. He could always lighten up the mood, no matter what the situation was."

"Sounds like a wonderful inspiration to have. What else have you taught yourself to do?"

"I can sing."

Emma opened her eyes wide and shot him a look of sheer shock. "You're lying!" she said, half-believing him.

He laughed. "Of course I'm lying."

Emma curled her lip in disappointment. "Oh, something you can't do?"

"There's plenty I can't do."

"What else?"

"I can't paint."

"Yeah, painting doesn't seem like it would be your forte. Too much sitting and patience."

"Spot on."

"I, on the other hand," Emma began, slowly standing up from the couch. "Love to paint."

"Who knew you had any artistic talent?"

"Want to come see?" she asked, ignoring his playful jab.

"Of course," he answered without hesitation, standing up as well. He followed her up the stairs as she led the way to her studio.

When they reached the room, Colton was once again impressed. The whole back wall of the spacious room was composed of ten-foot-tall glass windows, allowing for a breathtaking view of the ocean.

"The view from here faces East," Emma said, extending her hand towards the windows. "So at dawn, the sun bathes the whole room with its orange light, not unlike what we experienced this morning."

"Must be magical," Colton breathed in wonder as he gazed out at the rolling ocean. At last, he captured his wits and began evaluating the contents of the room.

The space was equally a gallery and a studio — the walls were garnished with dozens of paintings, but much of the floor space was dedicated to Emma's artwork in-progress. For an active art studio, Colton was surprised how neat and tidy everything was. He turned his attention to the completed canvases on the three walls that weren't glass.

"Did you paint all these?" he asked in awe.

"Yeah," Emma affirmed, flicking her eyes from one painting to the next. "As you can see, nature is a big inspiration for me. I think you would understand."

"I definitely do," he said, still gaping at her artwork. She was very talented. "These are incredible, Emma. When did you get the time?"

Emma began to walk around the perimeter of the room to look at each canvas individually. Colton followed. "Even though we don't come up here much as a family, that doesn't keep me from coming up here by myself. I get some pretty decent time off from my studies, and rather than going home to New York, I come up here. Painting helps me think clearly when I'm puzzling over a psychological conundrum." She paused, stopping to gaze at a watercolor illustration of a sunrise. "Everyone needs an outlet — a physical way to channel pent-up stress. Stress comes in many forms, and it's entirely unavoidable unless you're living under a rock. It can be very damaging if we try to hold it all in. So it's up to the individual to choose how she relieves her anxieties. Some choose to be productive; I think a lot of beautiful artwork — whether it's a painting, music, or even a novel — is the result of releasing stress. Others, unfortunately, choose to channel their stress in negative ways. Others, even still, climb rocks," she said, turning to give Colton a wink.

He didn't respond how she had expected him to. In fact, he didn't really respond at all. He simply stared blankly at the watercolor sunrise. "Can I ask you a question?" he finally asked. He tried to keep his tone flat, but Emma caught the slight emotional anxiety.

"Of course," she answered. "Anything."

He remained silent a moment longer, carefully judging his ensuing words. "I've got a pretty good handle on you by now — mostly because we're quite similar in a number of ways. That being said, when I discover something that interests me — a cliff, for example — I learn everything I need to know about it and then conquer it. You're equally interested in psychology as I am in rock-climbing, I gather." He paused before continuing.

Emma gulped. She knew where he was going.

"So I have to ask, are you keeping me around to learn from me? To study me? Or are you keeping me around for the same reason I'm choosing to stay here?"

"I want you here because I want to be with you," she

answered as genuinely and straightforwardly as she could. "I'd be lying if I said I wasn't learning from you, but that's unavoidable. You intrigue me greatly, but because I like you, not because I'm studying you merely for scientific gain."

He nodded, his facial expression lightening by the moment. "That's reassuring. I hope you're not bothered that I asked. That's what I thought, but I had to be sure."

"No, not at all," she said, resuming their walk around the studio's perimeter. "I understand completely. I'm glad you asked, in fact. I have nothing to hide."

Colton nodded. He believed her. There was no doubt in his mind that she had spoken the truth. He could detect lies as well as he could read people.

Nevertheless, something still bothered him. Over the years, he had developed an uncanny knack for sensing misfortune. The night he had met Emma, he had gotten the feeling that he was being directed by a much greater power. He experienced a similar feeling now, ambiguously sensing that something dark was lurking in his near future. Even more troubling, he couldn't shake the feeling that it seemed to be directly linked to his relationship with Emma.

TWENTY-EIGHT

Vincent sighed in boredom. He had spent the entire day doing absolutely nothing. It wasn't too terrible, he figured; he had been forced to do nothing under much worse conditions before. He was so incredibly anxious, though. Very rarely did he ever become anxious, but this occasion rightfully called for it. It did, after all, happen to be more than a decade overdue.

His orders were to wait, though. He had to standby helplessly just a little while longer. He had seen Colton and Emma leave before dawn this morning, but had already been instructed not to follow them today as he had every day prior. Instead, he was instructed to lie low and keep watch on the buffoon in the cabin. Vincent still had no idea who he was, and neither had Harvey when Vincent had mentioned the man's presence.

Curiously, the buffoon had not left the cabin once in the last five days. He could be either of two things, as Vincent reasoned: a very high level threat, or a harmless nuisance who was inconveniently obstructing the plan. Vincent was convinced he was a harmless nuisance, hence the title 'buffoon.' Harvey, however, was more cautious, which was ultimately why Vincent was rotting away at his post here rather than following the loose end; Harvey wanted tabs kept on the buffoon, and he also didn't want to take any chances on the loose end getting spooked. No, not today. Action was about to be taken, and Harvey didn't want anything to go awry.

After all these years, action was *finally* about to be taken. Vincent smirked at the thought. Although he and Harvey were equally ruthless, the manners in which they executed their ruthlessness were polar opposites. Vincent preferred a quicker, more direct approach to taking care of his problems. Harvey, on the other hand, was much more deliberate, contemplative, and indirect. He was excruciatingly careful, but understandably so; any man with so much to lose has no choice but to be careful.

All the same, Vincent would always harbor a deep contempt towards Harvey for allowing this threat to hang over their heads for over ten years. If it had been up to him, all loose ends would have been removed before even becoming active threats. It wasn't up to him, though. Harvey was his boss, so he had to abide by Harvey's slow, methodical approach.

In the end, though, the result would be the same, and this *was* about to end. Of that, Vincent was sure. And when it finally did, he would walk away a *very* rich man. And walk away he would. This would be his last job with Harvey. He had decided that long ago. When this was all over, he would disappear into retirement. Perhaps he would spend the rest of his life sipping mojitos on the empty, white-sanded beach of a random Caribbean island. He liked the thought.

TWENTY-NINE

Jeremy, ravenously hungry, stumbled into the kitchen. In his nervous anxiety, he had forgotten to eat at all today. At last, he would forfeit his comfortable position on the couch to search the contents of the refrigerator.

While he was up, he peeked out the window to see if Vincent was still at his post. Jeremy searched for the telltale sign of the mercenary's bald head hardly visible through the underbrush. After a moment, he saw it. It was faint, but it was all Jeremy needed to be consoled.

He grabbed some leftover pasta and set it in the microwave to warm it up. He turned the dial to three-minutes and stared off blankly in the distance while he waited.

In truth, he wasn't consoled by Vincent's presence. In part, he was, but in a much larger part, he wasn't. The fact that he was still here ultimately meant one thing: he had a plan.

Earlier this morning, when Jeremy had been much more confident, he had assumed that Vincent and Harvey had merely set some vague plan in motion guided towards some ambiguous goal. Earlier, he could presume that Vincent hadn't followed Colton and Emma because he hadn't known that they had left.

Now, though, he found himself much less confident. Vincent was after Colton, but Colton, clearly, was not here. Surely, Vincent was well aware of that by now. Why, then, was he still *here* if his target was *not?*

Because he had a plan. Because he had a direct objective. Because Harvey himself was giving him specific orders.

As the microwave sounded its alarm, Jeremy realized that he had already completely lost control of the situation.

He shook his head, expelling his thoughts of doubt. No, not all was lost. Not yet, at least. Vincent was here, so that meant Colton wasn't yet in any imminent danger. Of that, Jeremy was convinced. Harvey might be a depraved, corrupt, self-obsessed man, but Jeremy knew he would never send any of his other thugs after Colton as long as the boy was around Emma. Vincent was the only other person Harvey trusted, and Vincent, after all, was *here.*

THIRTY

After spending an hour or so talking in the art studio, Colton and Emma had made their way to the kitchen so Emma could start preparing their dinner.

"I'll do what I can to help, but you'll have to give me very specific instructions," Colton said as Emma got all the food and utensils out and ready. "In the wild, I can do all the makeshift cooking you can imagine. Put me in a kitchen, though, and I'm witless."

"That's okay," Emma said with a smile. "You probably haven't had to do much kitchen cooking at any point in your life. You can start by chopping this onion, though. Slice it into half first, then chop one of the halves into quarters. After that, take the four quarter slices and chop them into little bits."

"Whoa," Colton said, raising his eyebrows, looking around wildly for a knife.

Emma pointed out the cutlery set for him while she simultaneously carried out four other tasks.

"Okay, thanks," he said as he grabbed the largest knife he could find, setting it down on the marble counter. "And the other half?"

"Just bag it and put it on the bottom shelf of the fridge," she answered without looking up.

"Where are the—"

"In the last drawer behind you on the far right," Emma interrupted, predicting what he was going to ask.

Colton spun around and found the drawer Emma had directed him to. He opened it and grabbed a Ziploc bag from its box. He shut the drawer and walked back to his post at the counter, only to find that Emma had already set out the cutting board with the onion sitting atop it. She had also switched out the massive knife he had selected with a better-suited, smaller blade. He nodded his head and pursed his lips, feeling dreadfully stupid. Nevertheless, he got to work.

When he finished that job, Emma applauded him and gave him something else to do.

With renewed confidence, he accomplished task after task while Emma subtly directing him as she carried out her own business. Whenever he was about to do something wrong, she would catch it out of the corner of her eye and gently show him the proper way to do it. Time after time, he would accept her help graciously and then set out tenaciously to do an even better job.

"Wait, what are we making?" he asked in the midst of carrying out his fourth job.

"You still don't know yet?" Emma asked, raising her eyebrows in slight surprise.

"No, not really," Colton said, looking around at all the ingredients. "No."

"Well, it'll be a surprise I guess. I hope you don't have any allergies."

"I'm allergic to surprises," he said, resuming his steadfast work.

"Oh, hush. Let me have my fun."

"Fine. But only this once."

"Deal."

They worked for about a half an hour. Colton was largely unaware of whatever Emma was doing; he was very focused on the task he had at hand. When he finished, he watched as she took his work and her work together and tossed it on a pan. She set the pan on the range and flicked the burner on.

"Now can you tell what it is?"

Colton squinted his eyes and cocked his head, completely clueless as to what dish they were preparing. "No. I don't have the slightest idea."

"Me neither!" Emma exclaimed. "I suppose if I had to classify it as something I'd call it stir-fry, but I really just made it up as I went along."

"I hope you know what you're doing," Colton said warily.

"Oh, I do. Trust me. It'll be one of the best meals you've ever had. I promise. You know how you said your dad's flying partner was your inspiration for piano?"

"I do," Colton affirmed, wondering what she was getting at.

"Well, we have an in-house gourmet chef back home... He sort of took me under his wing as his apprentice when I was younger. He taught me a lot, and I caught on quickly."

"So I can play songs on the piano by ear, and you can create gourmet recipes on a whim?"

"Talented bunch we are, eh?"

"And did I mention I can sing?"

"Oh, hush," she said giving him a playful shove.

He came back and interlocked his lips with hers. He pushed her up against the countertop, leaning on her. They quickly fell into a rhythmic beat, exchanging kiss after kiss. He supported her back with one arm, holding her side with his other. She gripped his back muscles, pulling him closer.

After a few heated minutes, Emma tried to gradually pull away, against her wishes. "I have… to stir… the pan," she said in-between kisses. It took another minute for them to completely stop, but at last they did when Emma practically threw him off of her. "Sorry," she apologized. "I knew it was only a matter of time before I wouldn't be able to stop. I have to tend to our dinner before it gets burnt. We'll continue later."

"Don't apologize," Colton said calmly, wiping his lips with the back of his hand. "I'm looking forward to it."

A desirous shiver shot down her spine when he walked up beside her. She stirred and tossed the contents of the pan, but her scattered mind was elsewhere.

:-:

"Okay, grab a plate," Emma said twenty minutes later.

Colton walked over to the dining table that he had set and grabbed both his and Emma's plates.

"Oh, thank you," she said when she saw that he had brought them both. "I'm giving you a heaping portion, and I expect you to eat it all," she said, piling a sizable mound onto his plate.

"I won't disappoint," he said, staring ravenously at his delectable dish. "Can I get you anything to drink before we sit down to dine?"

"Sure," Emma said, piling food onto her own plate. "The wine cellar is downstairs. You can't miss it."

"Any preference?"

"Something old and Spanish."

"Por supuesto, Señorita," he said, disappearing down the staircase.

She smirked and shook her head as she cleaned up the

counters and washed her hands. Afterwards, she found two wine glasses in the cupboard and set them on the dinner table beside her and Colton's plates, respectively. She dimmed the lights and lit several scented candles.

Minutes later, Colton emerged from the basement, vintage wine bottle in hand. "Sorry I kept you waiting. The selection was overwhelming."

"Ooh, good choice," Emma said, inspecting the bottle. "Yeah, my dad's a bit of a wine aficionado. Another way he's rubbed off on me, I suppose." She pulled the cork and poured them each a splash. Afterwards, they gently touched their glasses together, acknowledging the official start of their dinner.

"This is excellent, Emma," Colton said with half a mouthful. "Really excellent. Thank you."

"Give yourself some credit," Emma said, taking another bite.

He shook his head. "No, this is all your genius. I owe you."

"Then you can start repaying the favor by telling me more stories from your past."

Colton grumbled, but didn't complain. "All right," he conceded in-between bites. A few long seconds later, he continued. "I used to get in fights as a kid."

Emma almost spat out her food in surprise. Fortunately, she managed to hold it in. "What?" she asked wildly after she had swallowed her bite. "You? Really?"

"Yes, believe it or not. Not until after my dad died. I guess that, for a while, it was a way for me to release with all my pent-up stress."

"Did you ever get beat up?"

"Yes," Colton said with a reminiscent grin. "I had my share of beatings. But, like I do with everything else, I learned. I adapted."

"But your fighting days are over, right?"

"They pretty much ended when my mom died."

Emma raised an inquisitive eyebrow. "They didn't end before you enrolled at Yale?"

Colton gave her a look and chose to take a massive bite rather than respond.

"You didn't start an underground fight club of any sort, did you?"

He gave her another look, but simply chewed his food. After he swallowed, he was silent for a moment longer. "Do you want to hear about that or the time I got into it with the gangs in India?"

"Both."

"Choose one."

"Why must we play this game?"

"Part of my elaborate scheme to keep you interested."

"It's working."

"Is it?" Colton asked, taking a sip of his wine.

Emma nodded, biting her lower lip. "Tell me about India."

"Okay," Colton said, setting his wine glass down. "I was a very unhappy kid in India. When trouble wouldn't find me, I went looking for it. It was never too difficult to find. No matter where we stayed the night, the slums were always just around the corner. So anyway... one night, I get particularly angry. I refuse to stay in the hotel with my mom and Lenny and I run off. They don't personally come looking for me; they send the local police instead. The cops chase me through the streets and alleys. Through houses and on the rooftops. They never catch me, but eventually I find some real trouble." He paused to take the next bite of his dinner. "I end up accidentally running in on a gang in the middle of some shady drug business. I can't tell exactly what's going down, but I know by the looks on their tattooed faces that they're less than pleased to see me. And they've got guns. So I turn tail and run. I run like I've never run before in my life. So now I've got the cops *and* a crew of career criminals after me, right? Well, I know I can't go on forever in a city I don't know, so I come up with a plan. Well, it's not really much of a plan, but it's solution."

"Introduce your pursuers to each other?"

Colton nodded. "Bingo."

"Did it work?"

"For the most part, yeah."

"For the most part?"

"Well, they did eventually run into each other. They get into a little firefight, and I run away. I guess two of the gang members come after me again, though, only I don't know it this time. So I get a little distance away and finally stop running to hide. I'm not expecting them to find me."

"Uh-oh," Emma said grimly.

"I try putting up a fight, but they beat me to a pulp. After they've had their revenge or fun or whatever they think it is, they run away and leave me for dead."

"How did you get out of that?"

"I don't. The next morning, a local finds me crumpled in a bloody heap and calls the police. When the cops find me, they take me to the hospital. I have two broken ribs, a broken nose, need stitches in five different places on my face, and have internal bleeding in my chest."

"Oh, my God," Emma said, deeply concerned.

"But I recover, obviously."

"Obviously," Emma repeated, completely relieved all of the sudden.

"Without any permanent damage, fortunately."

"So where does that experience rank on your list?"

"Seventh."

Emma raised her eyebrows and took a sip of her wine.

"Anyway, I never wanted to get beat up like that again. So, ironically, I went looking for more fights. Fights that I knew I wouldn't end up in the hospital if I lost."

"I see," Emma said, taking another sip of her wine. On the one hand, she didn't like imagining the violent side of him. She had come to know him as such a gentle, calm, in-control person, and she really admired him for that. On the other hand, though, the thought of him fighting stirred a deep primordial longing within her. In the end, she decided she liked him that much more for it; it added a whole other dimension to his ever-deepening identity.

"Does that bother you?" he asked, sensing her thoughts.

"No."

"What's on your mind, then?"

"A week ago, who could have predicted that tonight I'd be dining with..." she trailed off. So many words came to mind. In the end, though, only one seemed truly fitting. "With *you*?"

"I know the feeling."

"Do you?"

"Of course I do," he said, penetrating her with his eyes. "How on Earth did I end up here? It seems... unreal."

"Does that mean you're planning on sticking around?" Emma asked hopefully.

He shrugged and looked away. A moment later he turned his

nonchalant yet captivating gaze back on her. "Do I look like a guy with a plan?"

"You look like a guy who doesn't know what he wants," Emma said, subtly raising her eyebrows. "Even when it's right in front of him."

He snorted and looked away again. "What are you suggesting?" he asked after a minute.

"That you stay here," she said bluntly. "With me."

"Why are you so eager to tie me down?" he asked, turning to once again stare at her.

"Because I've decided that I like having you around. And the thought of letting you go leaves me feeling..." Her eyes darted around while she searched for the right words. "Like a glass without its wine."

A long silence hung in the air while he gazed into her eyes from across the table. "All right," he said at last.

Emma raised her eyebrows and opened her mouth, wanting him to say more. She didn't know what 'all right' meant in this context.

"I'll stay."

She took a deep breath, relieved beyond understanding as her heart leapt with untold joy. Afterwards, she let loose a beaming smile. "I'm so very thrilled to hear that."

"At least for a little while longer," he said, standing up to take his empty plate to the sink.

"Yes, of course," Emma said, still smiling. She knew she had already turned him. She got up to follow his lead.

"I can handle this part," he said, taking her fork and plate from her.

"What a gentlemen," she complimented, gliding back over to

the dinner table. "Would you care for some more wine?"

"The night's young. Why not?"

"Yes, why not?" she repeated to herself, filling both of their glasses a tad less than halfway. She took both in one hand, each slid in-between her fingers, and sauntered back over to Colton, who was just finishing up at the sink. As he grabbed a dishtowel to dry his hands off, she walked up behind him to wrap her free arm around his waist. She put her lips to his ear and whispered, "Now how about we continue with what we started earlier?"

THIRTY-ONE

Jeremy spun his cellphone nervously between his fingers as he stared off blankly at a wall. His opened laptop showed Colton's current location: the Payton's waterfront residence in Bar Harbor. By now, Jeremy assumed that Colton and Emma would not be returning to the cabin tonight.

When he had last checked, Vincent was still in the exact place he had been all day long. But would he try to sneak away under the cover of darkness? The ambiguity of the situation was driving Jeremy mad. Never in his career had he been so indecisive.

He stopped spinning his cellphone and stared at it with burning anxiety. He hadn't planned on calling his boss again until the photos had been planted, but the situation wasn't exactly going according to plan. Jeremy needed help. He needed guidance.

He dialed the number and put the phone to his ear. He didn't have to wait long for the man to pick up.

"I was wondering when I was going to hear from you."

"Yes, here I am," Jeremy muttered grimly in response.

"Is something wrong?"

"I haven't planted the photos yet."

"What? Why not?"

"I've been waiting for the right time."

"You've had five days! How long were—"

"Vincent Gaffeur is here," Jeremy interrupted flatly.

A silence caught the lawyer's voice. "What do you mean?" he asked, half-terrified a moment later.

"He's been watching the cabin we've been staying in since Tuesday. I didn't want to put Colton in further danger by giving him the photos. I don't know what or how much Vincent knows."

The voice let out a heavy sigh. "You did the right thing. I trust Vincent and you haven't established contact of any sort?"

"We haven't. He knows I'm here, but I don't think he knows who I am; otherwise, he would have made a move against me for the photos. He hasn't done anything, though, which makes me that much more unsettled. This tension is messing with my head."

"Focus, Jeremy. I need you. Colton needs you."

"I know," Jeremy said firmly, shutting his eyes. "What I need to know is what to do about tonight."

"What's the situation?"

"I'm at the cabin, but Colton and Emma are at the Payton's villa in Bar Harbor. I have reason to believe that they won't be coming back tonight. Vincent has been here all day long, but I'm concerned that he plans on taking action against Colton once night falls."

"You don't have to worry about Vincent tonight."

Jeremy opened his eyes, narrowing them in response to the subtle tint of fear he detected in his boss's voice. "And why is that?"

"Because Harvey Payton just went mobile," the lawyer answered. "His jet is on track for the Hancock County-Bar Harbor

Airport. He'll be arriving in an hour."

Jeremy opened his eyes wide in alarm. "So what do you want me to do?" he asked wildly.

"Nothing."

"Nothing?"

"Harvey is coming to assess the situation and draw out any leads he can. Nothing will happen as long as Emma is involved. As long as Harvey is here, you can't do anything that would give him reason to be alarmed. Lie low and protect the evidence until he's gone. Understood?"

"Yes, sir. And then what?"

"And then..." the weary voice trailed off, pondering. "The storm breaks. No more waiting. Take action before Vincent does."

THIRTY-TWO

10 JUNE, 2012

Colton and Emma spent the majority of their Sunday lounging around the house. They talked and laughed and shared stories and enjoyed each other's company. Emma couldn't resist hoping that they might spend countless days just like this one together in the future. She wondered if Colton was having any similar thoughts.

Now, they were sitting on the balcony of their bedroom sipping wine and looking out at the ocean. Colton had just finished telling her about the time he narrowly dodged an encounter with armed terrorists while hiking in a prohibited area to reach the 'Nameless Tower' of Northern Pakistan.

"I have an idea," Emma announced.

"Let me hear it," he said, taking the last sip from his glass.

"It's a beautiful day. Why don't we go sailing?"

Colton looked through the balcony railing. A grassy slope ran from the rear of the villa to the water's edge, at which point a grand seaside dock harbored a luxurious sailboat. "Do you know how to?" he asked.

"Do you?"

"Yes."

"Then let's be off!"

:-:

After traveling far out to the open ocean, Colton stopped maneuvering the boat. They slowed to a steady glide, allowing the light breeze to carry them wherever it pleased. The distant shoreline had become a narrow strip, barely detectable to Emma's eye.

"So where did you learn to sail?" she asked him.

"My dad first taught me in Japan. We sailed a few times in Italy and Guam, too. In France, I bought a sailboat with Lenny's money to live on so I didn't have to stay in the boarding house with all the other boys."

"Why didn't you stay with the other boys?"

"We didn't really get along."

Emma didn't delve deeper into the topic.

"Want me to teach you how?" he offered when she didn't respond.

"Maybe another time," she said with a smile. "It's my lazy day, remember?"

"Of course, your majesty," he said, lowering the sail. The wind had subsided for the moment.

"Oh, enough of that," she chided playfully.

"Enough of what? Enough of me?" he asked, feigning seriousness as he neared the starboard edge of the boat.

"No," she drawled. "I could never have enough of you!"

He unbuttoned his long sleeve white shirt and tossed it onto the deck beside him.

"What are you doing?" she asked him.

He turned around and jumped off the boat, falling into a dive before he hit the water.

Emma cursed under her breath and ran to the edge of the boat when she watched him vanish over the side. Seeing him surface a moment later, she let out a heavy sigh of relief. A moment later, she threw her hands up in the air. "Why?" she asked wildly.

"Why not?" he shouted in return.

She shook her head, failing to understand. "You really couldn't help yourself, could you?"

He grinned and shook his head proudly in response.

"There are white sharks in these waters, you know."

"I don't taste very good. Care to join me?"

"Not this time."

"Where's your sense of adventure?"

"Cowering behind my sense of better judgment. Get out of there before you give me a heart attack."

"Toss a rope over the side."

She looked around and found a thick rope. She tied one end around a cleat and threw the rest over the edge. She watched helplessly as he swam back to the boat and reached up to grab the rope. Without seeming to exert any effort at all, he nimbly scaled his way back up the side.

"See? That wasn't so bad," he said as he climbed up over the edge and onto the deck. He stood dripping before Emma.

"It never is with you, is it?"

"What do you mean?"

She shrugged, turned around, and sat down. "Nothing's ever a big deal with you. I mean… if you told me to jump off the boat, I would have given you a dozen reasons why I vehemently refuse to. To you, though, there are simply no consequences. I know what you just did doesn't even begin to compare with climbing a cliff, but to hear you talk about your daring feats and to actually witness one are completely different things. You're so confident. You're so headstrong and impulsive and daring... I wonder if you're too confident; too headstrong, impulsive, and daring. From all the stories you've already shared with me and all the stories I might not even want to hear, I honestly can't believe you're not dead yet."

He sat down and looked away.

"I have to ask, do you know your limits? Do you even *have* limits? How far are you going to push yourself before you convince yourself you've gone far enough?"

He gazed out at the open ocean and remained silent. A westward breeze swept against the wisps of his hair.

"Do you think that in the midst of one of your daring endeavors you'll suddenly divine your purpose? Do you think a rush of adrenaline will bring you the epiphany you're searching for?" she asked intensely. "Come on, Colton. Work with me. I'm just trying to make sense of this."

"All I know is," he finally began to mutter in response. "The more I push myself, the more distant my past becomes. Then, I can move forward. I can actually progress. My purpose lies in my future, right? I figure eventually I'll catch up with it."

"You can't if you're dead," she countered bluntly.

"Yeah, well, I seem to have an uncanny knack for thwarting certain death. Seeing as how it hasn't taken me yet, I have my doubts that it plans to anytime soon." As Colton spoke the words, a shadowy chill fell over him. He shuddered as the westward breeze intensified.

"Don't assume you're invincible, Colton," Emma warned warily. "Death doesn't pick favorites."

He snorted in amusement. "I beg to differ," he mumbled.

"I'm sorry?" Emma asked sharply, checking to see if she had heard him right.

"Do you know exactly how many different vertical-cliff-face-routes I've sent in my career?" he asked, matching the severity in her tone.

"No."

"Four-hundred and sixty-eight."

Emma tried to keep her jaw from dropping, but ultimately failed.

"Do you know how many I've sent without rope?"

"Colton, I—"

"Four-hundred and sixty-eight. I've gone base-jumping, wingsuit flying, and parachuting — dozens of times each. Eleven different people in the last three years alone have tried too kill me. I've been shot. I've been stabbed. I've had malaria. I've been in *two* plane crashes." He turned his cold gaze on her.

She didn't want to believe him, but she had seen and felt the scars of his stories last night. His scars weren't just stories, though, they were truly horrifying memories that had been engraved into his very flesh.

"Now, look at me and honestly tell me that death doesn't pick favorites. Look at me and tell me that death doesn't fear me."

She couldn't bear to look his way.

"Come on, tell me. I want to hear it."

At last, she looked at him. A wild look had glazed over his eyes. At first glance, his composure appeared to be calm, but upon closer inspection Emma noticed he was trembling.

"Do you believe in God?" she asked with as much control in

her tone as she could instill.

He closed his eyes and turned away to face the East. A tiredness had washed over his face. "Why do you ask?" he inquired faintly.

"I want to know what you attribute your alleged invincibility to. You said several days ago you don't put stock in faith, but... the way you describe your relationship with death... doesn't sound natural."

He said nothing for a few moments, allowing the westward breeze to brush against his hollowed cheeks. "Human beings have an incredibly narrow perception of our universe — that is, we are simply a relatively young species that lives in just another era on just another comparatively small rock that orbits one, average-sized, fairly remote star out of the billions that are in this galaxy that is itself one in a cluster of maybe a billion other galaxies that are all ultimately contained within an ever-expanding universe that may very likely not actually be the only universe out there." Colton paused. "As insignificant as we are, we can't afford to narrow our perspectives even further with specific beliefs, because they have a habit of closing our minds. Keeping our minds open — with dissatisfaction towards unanswered questions and rational skepticism towards the answers we have — is the most progressive way to live. Belief, however, is content. It's stagnant. It's what so many of us settle for when we give up. But the will to understand and explain... That, on the other hand, is an extremely powerful method of motivation."

"I agree that this will to understand can give us a purpose that simple belief often cannot," Emma interrupted. "But I think one could still abide by that attitude while also having a relationship with God. I don't think belief necessarily negates the seeking of universal truths."

"It does if you tie yourself down to any one dogma or set of dogma without freeing your mind to explore other possibilities. I see belief as an anchor; if you adopt a belief, then you're chained to that anchor. Yeah, you can explore a little, but you're really more or less a prisoner of that belief. It limits the extent of what you can experience and understand. Some people are able to stray quite a bit from their anchor without having any trouble finding their way back. Others are too afraid to venture out hardly at all. You can only do so much seeking if you keep yourself anchored. I prefer to have no anchor, because having firm beliefs would restrict my mind's ability to explore."

"Total liberty may sound appealing to you, but because it is inherently amoral I could see how the lack of a so-called-anchor could drive you towards hedonistic tendencies. If you have no foundation, how do you know you won't get lost? Without a moral code, how can you know right from wrong?"

"You don't have to have a moral code to be an agent of progress."

Emma narrowed her eyes. "And what do you define as progress?"

"Actively pursuing the ideal world, even if it's ultimately unattainable."

"Well, what is the ideal world?"

"The exact opposite of the hedonism you touched on — a world where every man fully empathizes with his fellow man. I think that if something as simple as that were true, the ripple effects would be truly world-changing."

"So then you do have a moral code. You do have a belief. You believe empathy can lead to utopia, and so you've adopted empathy as your moral code."

"But that's a different kind of belief than the one that we were talking about, which is the belief in a god — whether that god be a deity, or entity, or force, or whatever — and the effects and implications are therefore very different. I don't worship or pay homage to some great, unfathomable creator because of my belief. I don't assume that there's a greater authority that has direct power over my life because of my belief. I don't relegate my self-importance and the decisions I make by imagining that I'm merely a pawn in some mysterious, grand plan. If this empathy-utopia relation is my belief, then it's still distinctly different than a religious belief. I tend to think of that as more of my personal philosophy than a belief, but you may see it differently."

"No, I see what you're saying, but it's mostly a moot point to the topic at hand. What's your problem with believing in a higher authority, especially if it is indeed worthy or respect and maybe even worship?"

"You can't fully understand and explain that which you call God. And if you could, then you can no longer call it God — or any god for that matter. Right?"

"I think any believer would admit that."

"Well, where others may accept that as a thing of beauty, I reject it as a total cop-out. Theists, no matter how rational, will always reach a point in their line of thought where they conclude: 'God is unfathomable, and therefore we cannot know.' And if they don't reach that conclusion, then 'God' is not the conclusion they've reached. As you just confirmed, after all, any believer would admit that 'God' is unfathomable. I completely reject the notion that anything humankind has ever experienced is inherently unfathomable. Once again, that seems like such an absolute cop-out to me, especially because belief in any sense of the word 'God' pretends to answer questions while actually just opening the doors to countless others."

"Such as?"

"Who created God?"

"Maybe nothing at all."

"So, our existence requires causation, whereas God's does not?"

"Perhaps," Emma muttered, casting a sideward glance.

"If you believe divine, attentive creation is necessary for existence, then God can only exist if he himself had a creator." Colton paused and raised his eyebrows, staring intently at Emma. "And his creator must have had a creator as well... And so forth. It's endless, and it ultimately answers absolutely nothing. I think it's far simpler and far more realistic to say that *we*, human beings, were created instead over the course of billions and billions of years by no more than chance and probability under ever-improving conditions and nature's trial and error."

Emma had nothing to say. As a woman who valued logic, she could not outright refute his argument. But his reasoning unsettled her greatly, for it disrupted the very foundation upon which she had built her life. Her emotions urged her to simply ignore his words and shut him out, but her sense of reason had already been sparked, and the curiosity it bred was working hard to open her mind.

"Like you, many are satisfied with not knowing where their God or gods came from," Colton continued. "And yet they continue to perpetuate the belief all the same. They hear it from their parents, they grow up, and they tell their wide-eyed children. And not a single person in this endless cycle, mind you, *actually* understands what they're saying. Because anyone who has rationally arrived at the conclusion of God wouldn't be so insecure as to presumptuously inoculate the very same belief into their unsuspecting children."

"You make this *inoculation* sound so mechanical and, frankly, evil. I think it's most often actually done out of love."

"I think we convince ourselves that we do this out of love when it is actually done from a deep-seeded desire for self-validation; by convincing others to believe what you believe, you feel that you were right all along. Any uncertainty that one may have had before now evaporates so that feelings of superiority can take its place. You, as a psychologist, should certainly know this or at the very least be able to understand it."

"Well," Emma sighed, looking away. "You have once again succeeded in making those, such as myself, who are helplessly guilty of this seem unjustly cruel and horrifyingly egotistical, but I have to agree. Your idea is dangerously reasonable."

"After all, a rational believer in God would want their children to arrive at whatever conclusion seems most rational to them, no? And yet, belief isn't spread that way — through reason. Instead, it's spread through emotion; it's an exploitation of the emotional weaknesses that so many of us are born with — an emotional weakness that I myself am a victim of: the fear that my brief existence here on this Earth has no meaning. These stories we tell one another are so readily adopted because they give us meaning, and before too long these stories become beliefs, and those beliefs ultimately become a grand delusion. Which method of spreading belief seems more unsure of itself to you — the one that preys on our emotional weaknesses in order to acquire our nervous acceptance or the one that encourages us to think for ourselves and cultivate self-awareness and confidence?"

"I think most, myself included, would concur with the latter."

"Do you think an almighty creator would be satisfied with believers who were emotionally compromised into believing in him or would this creator prefer believers who examine all known evidence and then use impartial reason to then arrive at the conclusion of his necessary existence? If your answer is the former, then that creator is anything but almighty; he is power-hungry and insecure and he is not fit for worship. If your answer is the latter, then I ask you: why does such an overwhelming portion of the world's believers portray attributes that support the former?"

"So you're saying that..." Emma narrowed her eyes, pausing to digest his dense words. "If God existed, then believers would find his existence to be true by using reason and logic rather than emotion-based faith, right? But that since so many believers actually subscribe to religion through faith instead of reason, then God most likely does not exist?"

"What I'm saying is simply that it just doesn't line up. You would think that something as important as God would use something as important as logic to support its existence. But time and time again, I see cases of believers admitting that God is beyond logic. That seems so dreadfully self-defeating in my opinion. If God existed and he *actually* wanted people to believe in him, then he would utilize logic — not faith — as his primary method of acquiring believers. Alas, I think I've clearly stated multiple accounts in which logic refutes God, in which case belief can then only be perpetuated by faith. But faith is inherently weaker than reason, and I argue that it is because it is arrived at through the lack of cognitive effort. Faith, simply put, is what we're left with when we decide we can't understand something. But if I were God and I gave the average human being the average human brain — a remarkable, intricately complex organ currently unparalleled by anything else in the animal kingdom — then I would value the cognitive efforts that a man makes infinitely more than the blind faith that he preaches. Logic is our greatest gift, and yet it refutes the very thing we believe gave it to us. The discrepancy alone is enough to lead one to be skeptical of the existence of God, because that seems like the one mistake that a god would have been careful not to make."

"And yet," she began. "I get the peculiar feeling that there is some unfathomable force currently acting in your life that you're at a complete loss of rationally explaining."

Colton stared at her, his bronzed skin dulling the brightest rays of sunshine.

"You know what I'm referring to. It's that feeling you get when you wonder how you've trumped death so many times despite your wildest endeavors. It's that feeling you get when you ponder your ever-evasive purpose. It's that feeling you get when you stare at me, because ending up here after everything you've gone through seems far too perfect to be random."

Colton had looked away. His jaw was set. His gaze was tense. Emma knew that he was likely more in tune with her words than even she herself was. But in the end, she didn't know where she herself stood. She wanted to compromise, but the only middle ground was the lack of an opinion. Ambiguity had begun to settle in, and she knew Colton could feel it, too.

Emma looked at him. He watched intently as the rim of the falling sun carefully touched the distant blue horizon of the western ocean. Something about the sight struck her core. In unsettled silence, they drifted along, gently swaying back and forth in the steady rhythm of the ocean's melody.

:-:

Before the last of the daylight had disappeared, Colton had steered the sailboat back to the mainland. They returned just as dusk silently claimed the eastern seaboard.

"Someone's here," Emma voiced as Colton tied the vessel to the dock. Even in the twilight, she could make out the presence of a black Mercedes in the villa's driveway.

Together, the two walked back up to the villa, growing evermore curious as they neared the veranda. When they finally reached the entranceway, Emma slowly opened the front door; even though she had locked it when they had left, it was unlocked now.

They had taken only a few careful steps into the living room before Emma recognized the intruder. She gasped in surprise.

Harvey Payton looked up from his comfortable seat on the white leather armchair. He swept his empty gaze past his daughter to stare directly at the man he recognized as Colton Anders.

THIRTY-THREE

"Hello, Emma," Harvey said as he stood up. "I hope you don't mind I let myself in."

"Dad!" Emma exclaimed in return, still bewildered. "What are you doing here?"

"I was in the area for business," he answered as he approached them. "Thought I might stop by to say hello to my favorite daughter. I apologize... I didn't know you had company."

"Oh, it's a pleasant surprise! I'm sorry, Colton," she said, turning to him. "This is my father."

On queue, Harvey extended his hand towards Colton. Colton shook it, not overly surprise by the man's firm handshake.

"Glad to meet you, Mr. Payton. The name's Colton Anders," he said, returning Harvey's unwavering gaze.

"Harvey Payton. The pleasure is all mine, son. I wish I could say I've heard all about you, but unfortunately I am unable to. Emma's become quite the independent young woman of late. She doesn't keep her worried parents as informed as they'd like. I wasn't aware that she was seeing anyone."

Something about the way he spoke made Colton uneasy. For one thing, the man was clearly lying. Almost everything he had said so far had been a lie, in fact. Colton was careful to conceal his suspicions.

"Oh, please, daddy," Emma chided. "I don't have to tell you and mother everything, do I? I only met Colton a week ago."

"Well the simple fact that you've spent even that much time around him speaks volumes," Harvey said, keeping his gaze focused on Colton. "Any man on par with your standards is a man worth getting to know. I'm rather intrigued. How about the three of us go into town to dine together tonight? My treat. I presume you two haven't already eaten."

"I think that sounds lovely." Emma looked at Colton. "What do you say?"

"I'd love the opportunity to get to know your father," Colton answered, finally averting his gaze from Harvey's eyes to look at Emma. "Dinner together with him tonight would be wonderful."

"Then it's settled!" Harvey exclaimed with a triumphant smile, clapping his hands together. "I know an exquisite place in town. They serve the best steaks in Maine. Not much competition, surely," he said with a refined chuckle. "Come, now. I'll drive."

:-:

After the three of them had arrived and had been seated, Harvey decided to take the initiative and order a New York Sirloin Steak for each of them. "I do hope you're not a vegetarian, Colton," he said with an over-confident smile.

"No," Colton said, looking to Emma. He was put off by the fact that Harvey had ordered for him without first consulting him. He didn't complain, though. "I couldn't live without—"

"So, how did you two meet?" Harvey interrupted. He took the first sip of his champagne and made a satisfied face.

"Meat," Colton said, finishing his previous sentence. He was careful to repress his ever-growing irritation.

A look of annoyance crossed Harvey's face as he set down his glass. "Yes, where and how did you two meet?" he asked again, misunderstanding.

"Last Monday, he—"

"We ran into each other at the grocery store," Colton answered, cutting Emma off before she could betray the truth. "It was really quite a mundane encounter. Nothing to tell stories about." He ignored the perplexed look Emma shot his way. Harvey, wholly focused on Colton, didn't notice Emma's confusion.

"So you must live around here?" Harvey asked as he set his hands on the table, pressing his fingers together.

"I'm new in town, actually."

"Oh? Where do you hail from?"

Emma narrowed her eyes and looked curiously at Colton. He hadn't yet told her where he had been before coming to Maine.

"I've been traveling through Europe for the past few months," Colton answered, maintaining eye contact with Harvey.

"Well, you certainly look the part. I've imagined abandoning my life to take a personal pilgrimage around the globe before, too. Of course, I could never get away with such a thing. I have far too many ties. Loved ones. Bills to pay. A career," Harvey said, trailing off. "What part of Europe?"

Colton's feelings of distaste intensified. On top of the pathological lying, the man was now blatantly trying to drive a wedge between Colton and Emma. "All over the continent."

"Ah, of course. Must have been quite the experience. Traveling is awfully expensive. Where did you get the money?"

Now, why would you ask that? Colton wondered to himself. "The same way any man my age might get his money—"

"Rich parents?" Harvey interrupted, raising a gray, presuming eyebrow.

"Hard work," Colton countered firmly. "Besides, when you don't have to pay for fancy suits, Rolexes, mansions, and five-hundred dollar haircuts, you'd be surprised how much money you have left over. Sure, my watch doesn't scream insecurity the same way yours does, but it still manages to tell time. Don't get me wrong, though, your hair looks... really fantastic. Does your barber do Donald Trump's hair, too?"

Emma fidgeted uncomfortably in her seat.

A look of rage lit up Harvey's face for a fraction of a second. Almost immediately afterwards, though, he opened his mouth into a wide, malevolent smile while casting a quick glance at Emma. "Hah! Your boyfriend is quite the character, Emma. Colton, you're a sharp one. Where did you attend university?"

Colton shrugged and quickly fabricated an answer. "I spent a couple semesters at a community college back home. My grades were too low, though, so they kicked me out. No big deal. I learned everything I need to know in Kindergarten."

"I see," Harvey mumbled. "Where *is* home?"

"Colorado."

A tension-filled silence ensued.

"Colton's something of a genius," Emma chimed. "He's too modest to even hint at it. Don't let him fool you."

"Oh, I'm not being fooled," Harvey hinted, narrowing his eyes as he stared piercingly at Colton.

A moment later, a waiter brought them their steaks. Before any of them could take a bite, Harvey raised his glass of champagne. "Allow me to propose a toast," he began. "To... new acquaintances. To new friends. To new relationships. I wish you and Emma the best of luck together, Colton."

Colton's ears pricked in foreboding as they sensed the outright lie behind the toast. He matched Harvey's knowing gaze as he lifted his glass to his thin lips.

The remainder of their dinner carried on in a similar pattern. Colton and Harvey continued to lie to each other, neither betraying his suspicions of the other. As their war of attrition wore on, each man further complicated his web of falsities. Harvey would continuously backtrack to make sure Colton stuck to his original story, but Colton was ever-careful not to fall into any traps.

Dinner had grown increasingly more unbearable for Emma. She had wholeheartedly decided that she regretted accepting her father's offer to take them out tonight. As Colton and Harvey exchanged deceitful banter, Emma had been all but excluded. She chimed in when the opportunity was right, doing her best to hold the middle ground. Overall, though, she was at a complete loss as of what to think. These were the two most important men in her life, but they clearly didn't trust each other.

Furthermore, Emma was deeply disturbed by how brilliantly Colton was weaving tales of pure fiction as his life's story. Had he been putting on the exact same show for her this entire past week? She had believed that she had come to understand him, but seeing him in this light put everything she thought she knew into jeopardy.

Of course, though, her father was acting rather strange — stranger than she had ever remembered seeing him. He was rude; he was deceitful; he was presuming; he was clearly looking for the worst in Colton. Why? What had Colton done to him? Perhaps her father's behavior was putting Colton on the defensive, and understandably so. Everyone at the table knew something that the other didn't, but no one was willing to share exactly what he or she knew.

More than anything, Emma wanted to get up and leave. She wanted to berate the both of them for twisting such lies. Nevertheless, she knew she couldn't. She knew she didn't completely understand what was going on here. Until she did, she couldn't put the blame on anyone. She couldn't be angry with her father because she didn't know his motives. She couldn't be angry with Colton because she understood that he was merely protecting himself. Furthermore, everyone else here was maintaining face. Couldn't she? She was the psychologist, after all.

All at once, the conversation had come to an abrupt end. Colton and Harvey had both averted their gazes from one another and Emma was left to look back and forth at each of them cluelessly.

"Well, I'll let you two have the rest of the night to yourselves," Harvey spoke up at last, hailing the waiter as he spoke. "Check, please," he requested. "I'll drive you both back and then I'll be on my way. I have business to tend to early tomorrow morning."

"You can stay in the villa if you like," Emma offered. "I should stay in the cabin tonight anyway. I haven't prepared at all for next week of camp and I don't have any more time to put it off."

"I would," Harvey said, signing the bill with his elegant signature. "But my dealings are further upstate. I'll drive up tonight and try to catch a few hours of sleep in a hotel."

"Well, I'm sorry to have kept you out this late," Emma offered in consolation. She stood up, following her father's example.

"No, no. Don't apologize. It was my idea, remember? Getting to know Colton, here, was more than worth it. In fact, I think it made my whole trip worthwhile. I was skeptical about coming up here in the first place, but now I can rest assured it was time well-spent."

"I'm glad we had the opportunity to meet," Colton said, offering Harvey his hand. They made penetrating eye contact one last time before departing.

THIRTY-FOUR

The sheets smelled of vomit — not his own, but someone else's that had long ago been ingrained into the very threads he now buried half of his face in. Crust flaked from his eyelid when he blinked an eye open. A stinkbug had fluttered down from the heavens to settle on his limp arm, effectively waking him from his sleepless slumber. He stared at it lazily.

The strength of the tiny creature was admirable. Even with hollow pins as legs, it could somehow carry that impressive shield on its back. Adam pitied the creature, though he did not know why; it appeared to have adapted accordingly to its unwieldy load.

A sudden realization startled Adam out of his wits — he could see a face on the stinkbug's shield-back. Two stern eyes. A low-hanging nose held up only by the likeness of a mustache. No mouth, though... perhaps the thick mustache concealed it? Without meaning to, Adam laughed aloud to himself. The sound of his own laughter unsettled him, though; he was quick to reassume his previously long-held muteness.

He carefully snatched up the insect up with his thumb and a thin, ghostly pale index finger and crushed it without a second's thought. He apathetically flicked its remains into the distance.

He let out a groan and rolled off the mattress, landing hard on the wooden floor. He picked himself up a moment later and meandered over to the TV remote huddling quietly in a forgotten corner of his cell. He fetched it and scraped a film of some unknown substance off the power button. He then hurled the device across the tiny room at the wall above his bed. It hit the nauseating wallpaper with a resounding thud and promptly fell victim to gravity, first bouncing off the springy mattress and then shattering to pieces upon landing on the wood floor.

Adam cursed to himself and quickly rushed over to assess the damage done. He recovered the plastic and was pleased to discover that nothing had actually broken. The battery cover had popped off and the batteries themselves had disappeared. Nevertheless, panic quickly set in. Those batteries could be anywhere by now. How on earth would he ever be able to find them? The panic consumed him, whipping him into a mad frenzy.

He ripped the vomit-stinking sheets from his bed first. Then he tore his pillows from their cases until they sat as naked in the musty air as a newborn abandoned to the streets of a cold, lonely city. He dug his fingers into his tangled black hair and stared with widened eyes at his spinning walls. The floor called to him, so he fell to meet it face to face once again.

Then he saw it: a single AA battery sidled up cozily beside a dust bunny under his bed. He reached out to it, but it rolled away playfully at the touch of his fingers. As his hand flung about, he came into contact with a great number of forgotten things, among them a sheet of paper that he chose to take in his hand and inspect with a closer look.

The document was proof of a pledge he had signed only last week at the grocery store — a pledge to be more energy-efficient to save the environment. Turn out the lights when he left a room. Take shorter showers. Reduce. Reuse. Recycle. Of course, he never turned the lights on in his room to begin with; there was no bulb. He couldn't take shorter showers because he didn't take showers at all. Sure, though, he reused. He reused practically everything, in fact. He was not one who could afford to be so liberal with his few belongings. And... just yesterday, was it? Yes, yesterday he recycled an empty Pepsi bottle he had seen lying on the sidewalk. He smiled triumphantly. What a responsible member of society he was becoming. He cared. It was good to care.

Another sudden realization made him freeze. The paper slid through his grasp and gently fluttered to the floor, retreating back to its dark sanctuary beneath the bed.

He cared, but how could he be a responsible member of society if he was ignoring the only real responsibility he was required to tend to? One, single responsibility that no one else could possibly fulfill.

The one responsibility that had led him here in the first place. The one responsibility that would change his life the moment it was finally carried out.

No more delaying. No more procrastination. No more lonely thinking. Tomorrow, he would fulfill his duty.

THIRTY-FIVE

"So, what was *that* all about?" Emma asked after she got in the passenger side of Colton's Jeep. Harvey had dropped them off as promised and they had all said their farewells. She and Colton were about to head back to the cabin for the night.

"Dinner?" Colton clarified, igniting the engine of his Jeep.

"Yes. You have some explaining to do."

"I understand you probably didn't like seeing me lie like that. Have some faith in me, though, and believe me when I tell you I haven't lied to you about anything I've told you. You have my word. You can trust me. I can trust you." He paused momentarily. "I can't trust your father, though."

"He was rather off tonight," Emma conceded, staring out the window into the darkness. "He's not normally like that. I wonder what got into him."

"Makes no difference. First impressions are difficult to erase. I doubt our next encounter will be any more friendly."

"Don't think like that. He *is* my father, after all."

"I know."

Emma sighed. "But I understand. Just try not to let him come between us."

"He won't."

"Promise?"

"I promise."

They drove on through the night, mostly in silence. Both were too preoccupied to voice their thoughts. A nervous sensation had been rising gradually in the pit of Colton's stomach the past week, first kindled on the evening he had met Emma. It had escalated when he discovered that bald man following him in the woods the day afterward. Now, it had reached a fever pitch, gnawing away at him with vicious intensity. There was no denying it or putting it off any longer; something was *very* wrong.

THIRTY-SIX

Harvey Payton, comfortably seated in luxurious, custom-designed, personal Gulfstream jet, dialed a number on his cellphone.

"Do you have orders for me?" a voice from the other end of the line answered.

"I do," Harvey answered. He paused a moment to look out a porthole window at the starry night sky. The new moon hung invisibly in the heavens, far above even Harvey's impressive altitude. "I want you to terminate the loose end."

"Of course, sir," Vincent complied, pleased to finally hear a decision be made. "Should I not first find out if there are any copies of the photos, though? Or if he has shared their existence with anyone else? I can get him to talk. You know my methods are... effective."

Harvey snorted in amusement. "That won't be necessary, Vincent. He hasn't seen the photographs. He didn't recognize me when we met."

Vincent was too stunned to respond right away. Colton Anders was *the* loose end. They had tracked down and dealt with everyone else who may have been a potential threat. No one remained. If Colton didn't have the photos, then Vincent and Harvey were in the clear. It was indeed time to remove the last trace of this mess. Nevertheless, as incomparably ruthless as

Harvey was, Vincent was surprised to hear his boss give such a blunt and explicit order; the loose end had quite obviously become an important part his daughter's life. "Yes, sir. Right away," Vincent finally said, masking his curiosity for the moment.

"I do have one single request of how it be done, though. I'll leave the rest to you and your imagination."

"Anything, sir."

"Catch him alone. I don't want Emma to see something that might scar her for the rest of her life."

"Of course, sir," Vincent said, still pondering about this conclusion to their decade-long hunt. Next time he and his boss would speak, this would all be over. Although it didn't really matter, if there was ever an occasion to ask his boss's motives and satisfy his curiosity once and for all, that moment was now. "I have no qualms with you orders, sir. I, personally, believe that the task must be done. Nevertheless, I feel compelled to ask—"

"Why?" Harvey interrupted. "Why *kill* the innocent boy? Because, Vincent, I'm tired." He sighed. Indeed, he sounded weary. "The enemy is no more. The threat, dissipated. And yet, the game goes on. Whether Colton Anders knows it or not, he is a player in this game, and as long as he still breathes, the game cannot end." He paused to sigh again. This sigh was markedly different than the last, though. Accompanied with it was a dark air of arrogant satisfaction that Vincent could detect even over the line. "It's time the game ends. It's time we win once and for all."

THIRTY-SEVEN

11 JUNE, 2012

It was very early morning — Jeremy guessed somewhere around three A.M. He was too preoccupied to actually glance at a clock, though; his mind was focused on one and only one thing.

The coast was clear inside the cabin; Colton and Emma had gone to bed long ago. The coast outside appeared to be clear, too. The new moon would provide the cover of darkness he would need to sneak out to Colton's Jeep without alerting Vincent. It was still a risky move, but it was a risk that must be taken. Action was crucial. He couldn't afford to wait another day.

He grabbed the keys to the Jeep that Colton had tossed onto the countertop upon his return hours ago. He was careful not to turn on any lights as he made his way through the kitchen; he didn't want to betray any sign of activity in case Vincent happened to be awake and watching.

He moved to the side door of the kitchen stealthily and silently. Colton's Jeep was parked right outside at the end of the gravel road. Once outside, Jeremy wouldn't have too far to go in the near-pitch-black darkness.

He reached the kitchen side door and opened it as slowly and carefully as possible; the slightest creak of the hinges would completely betray his presence to Vincent. He held his breath in anxiety as he gradually swung the door open wide enough for his lean body to slip between. He made his way through with utmost quietness.

The trek to the Jeep felt farther than it actually was. The shadows rendered Jeremy completely and hopelessly blind. Fortunately, he had made note to himself earlier when Colton had arrived where he had parked his car in relation to the cabin. Jeremy could estimate where he was now only by the count of footsteps he had taken. He took his steps slowly and lightly.

Eventually, his outstretched arms touched cold metal. He breathed a sigh of relief. He gradually made his way around the car to the driver's door. He felt around the door until he found the slight raised bump that he assumed must be the key slot. He inserted the key he had swiped from the counter and turned it until he heard the distinct *click* that meant the latch had been successfully unlocked.

He pulled the handle and gently swung the door open. He swung his knapsack over his shoulder and retrieved a manila envelope from within. He pursed his lips and tapped it nervously against his chest.

Proceeding with Phase Two, he thought to himself. He gently set the envelope on the cloth seat.

He shut the door as quietly and firmly as he could, careful to lock it back up. As he had come, he carefully made his way back to the cabin through the darkness.

THIRTY-EIGHT

Colton had woken up at six A.M. as per usual. He was careful not to rouse Emma as he began his morning routine. He made his way to the nearest bathroom and washed his face off. He took a long hard look at himself in the mirror while he stood at the sink. The only face he had ever failed to read was his own.

Reading other people, to him, wasn't a habit. It wasn't a defense mechanism. It wasn't a game or a hobby. It was an addiction. He had a void within that he could only hope to fill with external awareness. If he could understand enough people through and through, maybe one day he might gain the insight to truly understand himself. To this day, though, no serious attempts at introspection had ever yielded any sudden revelations.

He dressed himself and proceeded to make his way to the kitchen in hopes of quenching his sudden thirst. To his dismay, he could find no orange juice in the refrigerator. Jeremy must have finished it off.

No matter, though. The day was young and Colton was ready to get a head start. He didn't know Emma's exact plans for him today, but he knew he could help her out by going into town and picking up the various items and foods he knew she needed for camp today. Of course, he could also get groceries, like orange juice, to restock the empty refrigerator.

He stuffed his wallet in the back pocket of his jeans and

grabbed his keys from the counter. He considered stopping to write Emma a note, but decided that he would rather surprise her when he returned.

He exited the cabin through the side door of the kitchen, careful not to slam it on his way out. As he stepped outside, he paused a moment to appreciate the brisk morning air. He took a deep breath before making his way to the Jeep.

He unlocked the door and swung it wide open, only to find a large manila envelope waiting for him on his seat. Immediately, he cast wild glances in all directions, expecting to find someone. Alas, he was alone.

He turned his gaze back on the envelope and stared at it blankly. His initial alarm had rapidly evolved into curiosity. He blinked several times, half-expecting it to disappear as a mere figment of his imagination. He eventually decided to reach for it with as steady a hand as his growing anticipation would allow. When at last his fingertips met the paper, a cold chill traversed his body.

He continued to stare at it in utter bewilderment before shooting several more nervous glances all around. Was this an attempt by either Jeremy or Emma to spook him? Tormented by both interest and anxiety, he broke the seal of the envelope with a final resolve.

Out slid a small stack of blank papers. Colton turned them over, only to discover they were actually professionally taken photographs. By his estimation, there were over two dozen.

Before he was able register what exactly he was looking at, his eyes focused on the single familiar aspect of the first photograph: the Hindu Kush mountain range towering in the distant background of a barren landscape that he had looked upon day after day for two straight years. What intrigued him most, however, was the foreground: a gang of Taliban terrorists in the midst of laying waste to an oil refinery. He scrutinized the photo for a moment longer before flipping to the next.

Another snapshot of masked extremists leading a heavily explosive siege against an oil refinery — a different refinery than the one in the first photograph, though. With disturbed concern nearing fever pitch, Colton flipped to the next.

Again: the same theme, but a different refinery. In fact, as he rapidly shuffled through the next seven photos, each showed a similar situation: hooded terrorists blowing up refinery after refinery. Some were at night, others in broad daylight. The eleventh photo deviated slightly, however.

This shot revealed yet another attack, though a new character had been introduced: a young, well-armed, bald Caucasian man dressed in all black — a mercenary fighting for the enemy, by Colton's eye.

The next photo deviated further. The mercenary wasn't merely a gun-for-hire, but also an arms-dealer, evidently. He appeared to be delivering a large cache of weapons to the terrorists. The next few photos further documented this implication.

The next photo zoomed in on the mercenary's features. Colton studied him carefully. A three-inch scar traversed the left side of the man's forehead and temple. Green eyes like watchful sentinels sat quietly beneath sable, tapering eyebrows. Beyond the emerald irises, though, there was nothing. The man had the most blank, empty, void eyes of anyone Colton had ever looked upon. Then he had a sudden realization that made his breath catch in his throat; he had seen this man only a week ago deep in the forests of Acadia.

While his skin crawled and a shadowy chill settled over him, Colton now saw something else in the photo that his overwhelmed eyes had failed to notice upon first glance: the date in the bottom-left corner. This photo had been taken the 22nd of August 2002, exactly one month before the day his father went missing. He backtracked through the stack of photos he had already looked through to examine their respective dates. The earliest dated back as far as March 13th of 2001.

Spurred on by intensified trepidation, Colton flipped forward to the next photograph. What he saw next caused him to drop the photos and the manila envelope to the ground altogether. He steadied himself by putting a hand against the doorframe of his Jeep to keep from collapsing.

He took a few moments to calm himself. He didn't believe it. He stooped to gather the photographs from the ground. He tidied them back up and took a deep breath. With great reluctance, he began flipping through them once more.

Alas, it had been no illusion after all. In a photo dated the 16th of May 2004, sitting comfortably in the back seat of a car being driven by the green-eyed mercenary was none other than Harvey Payton himself.

The remaining ten photos were equally incriminating. The mercenary and Harvey Payton had known each other for a long time; the dates of these snapshots spanned from 1995 through 2006.

After he had seen enough, Colton slid the photos back into the manila envelope and tossed it all onto the passenger seat of his car. He climbed into the driver's seat and ignited the engine. He slammed his door shut and gripped the wheel tightly. He pursed his lips and closed his eyes. His mind raced. His heart raced even quicker.

Emma.

As quick as the thought of her entered his mind, he shut it out. This brief chapter of his life had ended. He had come to an impasse. Rather than try to reason with it, better he turn around and find a different path to take. This road led nowhere.

The early stages of tragedy had already begun, but he wouldn't stick around long enough to let hope weave its seductive lies. He had to escape while he still had the chance. He would consider no alternative. He would offer no goodbyes. No apologies. He would allow no pleading. No resolving. The damage had been done.

He should feel hatred. He wanted to feel hatred. He believed that if he could hate then it would mean he actually cared enough about something worth hating. But he couldn't. He had learned long ago that apathy was the best defense against pain. He wondered now, though, if it might not be better sometimes to feel pain rather than nothing at all. Nevertheless, it was too late for him. Numb was his chosen way of life, and it was time to spin on.

THIRTY-NINE

The rays of the morning sun peeked through the blinds to wake Emma from her peaceful slumber. Necessarily so, though; the light of dawn was a sure way of waking her up on time each morning as long as she stayed in the cabin. This way, she couldn't get away with hitting a snooze button — as she was prone to doing under normal circumstances.

She turned over to realize that, for the second day in a row, Colton was once again not to be found beside her. He was a natural early-riser, she figured. He couldn't help but get a jumpstart on his days. Recently, Emma had become something of an early-riser, too, though not entirely by choice. Regardless, she wondered what he was up to this time. By now, he could be anywhere, doing anything. She doubted he was making breakfast — she had noticed last night that they were on a severe shortage of food.

After she had readied herself for the day, she made her way out into the kitchen. Still no sign of Colton, though. She peered through the blinds of the window and discovered that his Jeep was not parked outside. Had he gone into town to buy some groceries?

As the thought crossed her mind, she suddenly sensed someone else's presence. Perhaps, unlikely as it seemed, Colton's own uncanny sixth sense had rubbed off on her a little. Regardless, she spun around to sight Jeremy standing in the door-less doorway that connected the kitchen to the meager living room. He simply stood there, arms outstretched, gripping either side of the trim of the threshold. He looked simultaneously exhausted and deeply concerned.

"Jeremy," Emma breathed. She hadn't spoken to or even seen him in days. "What's wrong?"

"Colton's gone," he replied flatly.

"What do you mean he's *gone*?" Emma asked, bewildered, but also terrified at his words, somehow already knowing what he meant.

He shook his head slightly, but kept his eyes focused on her. "He's gone. And he's not coming back."

Emma closed her eyes in agitation. "*What*?" she shook her head with her eyes still tightly shut, as if this was all merely a bad dream and she was still asleep. "Why would he leave? How do you know? Did he talk to you this morning?"

Jeremy remained silent for an uncomfortably long time, keeping his eyes trained on hers the whole while. When he finally responded, he didn't answer any of her questions. "I need you to drive me into town."

"What?" Emma asked fiercely, growing angry. "Why?"

"Because Colton is in danger, and I need to find him before trouble does. But I can't do that without some method of transportation. So, please, Emma, drive me into town."

A deluge of questions rapidly flooded Emma's mind, but only one came out. "Who *are* you?"

Another long pause ensued before he voiced an ambiguous answer. "Someone who Colton needs more than ever, even though he may not know it."

Emma didn't know what to say. She didn't know how to

comprehend what was happening. She didn't know what to do. At last, some part of her found the courage to ask: "What kind of trouble is he in?"

As was customary by now, Jeremy didn't respond immediately. He took his time, carefully calculating the best possible response — in his view, of course. The 'best possible response' didn't entail satisfying any bit of Emma's ever-growing curiosity. "The kind of trouble that might actually kill him."

The way he said it made Emma's skin crawl. As disturbing as the answer was alone, it also implied that he somehow knew that Colton thought he was beyond death's reaches. How, though? Clearly, Jeremy was not the man he had led them to believe he was. The question once again invaded her mind: Who was he, then?

"I can't stress enough to you how crucial it is for Colton's safety that you take me into town, Emma," Jeremy reminded when she didn't respond for several moments.

"And what will you do then, Jeremy?" she fought back. "Last I checked you weren't in any condition to go saving any lives. Last I checked you couldn't even walk without a limp. Last I checked—"

"Emma," he interrupted, still as level, calm, and exhausted as he had been when the conversation began. "It's not about me. It's not about you. It's about Colton. If you have any feelings for the man at all, then you'll do your part to help him."

"Why should I trust anything you're saying? Or not saying, rather? I don't even know who you are. Maybe it's you he's running from," Emma accused. Though she knew it was a hopeless stab in the dark, she nevertheless felt the urge to lash out.

He didn't bother defending himself. He knew he didn't need to. "Could you live with yourself if something happened to Colton and you knew that you could have done something to possibly prevent it?"

The thought struck her, paralyzing her with dread. She realized that if there was the slightest possibility that Colton was in a very real kind of danger, she knew that she ultimately had no choice. She shouldn't waste any more time avoiding the inevitable.

"Okay," she finally conceded. If she had expected his expression to lighten at all by her approval, she was met with disappointment; he bore the same exhausted, troubled look as before. "I'll take you. Now."

He reached behind the wall and grabbed a knapsack that he then swung over his shoulders. Emma narrowed her eyes, wondering where it had come from and what was inside. She wanted to question him about it, but what good would that do? None. Whatever was going on, he clearly wasn't interested in confiding with her about anything. If he wanted to keep his little bag of secrets all to himself, so be it. Emma only really needed to worry about one thing.

"Won't you tell me anything?" Emma asked as she ignited the engine of her white Audi sedan. "Don't I deserve to not be kept completely in the dark? I am helping, after all. And this, I sense, is the last time we'll be in each other's company."

Her words were met with another expected, long silence. It was so long, in fact, that Emma was beginning to think that he had decided to ignore her entirely without giving her any kind of response at all. Just when she decided to give up in frustrated resolve, though, he finally spoke.

"My encounter with Colton in Acadia the day he and I met, the day the three of us met each other... wasn't a random accident."

Emma's skin crawled as she pondered the possibilities of his implications. She drove on down the long gravel road that led away from the campground, gripping the steering while so tight her knuckles turned white. "You planned all of that? Meeting Colton? Having him find me at the cabin?"

Jeremy shook his head. "No. I only planned on meeting him. I didn't anticipate that he would jump from that cliff, though. I didn't anticipate plummeting to what was almost my death. Least of all, though, I didn't anticipate meeting you."

The way he said that led Emma to believe that he had known who she was before he had met her. How, though? She shook her head in agitation. Too many questions. Never enough answers. "Why were you trying to meet him?" she decided to ask.

Jeremy sighed and resumed his patterned silence. Moments later, though, he did respond. "It's complicated. I'd like to think you'd find out from him soon enough."

His answer, by design, gave her hope that seemed to distract her from its ambiguity.

"Once this is all over," he muttered under his breath.

"Once *what* is all over?" Emma asked, snapping back into her former curiosity.

At first, she thought his silence implied that he was designing another carefully crafted response. When five long minutes turned into ten, even longer minutes, though, she knew she had pushed the limit. He was done enlightening her — if he had done so at all. All he had really done was open up the doors to dozens more answerless questions. They continued their drive in silence.

When Emma at last arrived in town, Jeremy had her pull into and stop in a half-full parking lot. After she put her car in park, they sat in tension for another long moment.

She wanted to ask what came next; what she could do to help, but as she opened her mouth to speak, he spoke instead.

"Just carry on with your life as if you never met either of us. It'll be hard — I can only imagine. But in time, you'll hear from someone. That, I promise you. One way or another, for better or for worse, this will all make sense—"

"Eventually," she said, finishing his sentence. "Yeah, I get it. Thanks for looking out for him. Especially when I can't."

He nodded almost awkwardly in affirmation before moving to open his passenger door. When he was halfway out, Emma spoke again, halting him.

"Keep him safe," he heard her say. "Don't let anything bad happen to him. Bring him back to me in one piece."

Another pause followed, though it did not hold for quite as long as the others. "I will," he promised. "It's my job."

FORTY

Emma continued through the day as best she could. The kids must have sensed she wasn't entirely herself because they all seemed to behave even better than normal. It probably wasn't hard for them to sense it, though. After all, she was much less animated today than they had known her to be. She was far more hyper-concerned and overprotective now than she had been last week, when she had been free-spirited to let them explore at their own will.

In truth, she was scared. She was lonely. She was anxious. Hopeless and naïve as it was, she kept her cellphone close by her all day long, even though signal was sporadic at best and it wasn't likely she'd hear from Jeremy or Colton for days. Or maybe even weeks. Maybe never. How could she know? She could only wait helplessly and hope for the best.

Adding to her concern was Adam. Curiously, he had shown up this morning to once again be of service. She had made no attempt to speak with him, though. His sudden return seemed odd, but she was too preoccupied to question him about his recent whereabouts. He had made no move to talk to her, either. The two ultimately avoided each other as long as the kids were anywhere near. Emma had the feeling, though, that at the end of the day when everyone else was gone, he would make an effort to clear things up with her.

Thus, when five o'clock did roll around, it was with mixed

feelings that she said goodbye to the kids for the day; she was glad because it had been an ordeal to try to focus on them, but it was also with a heavy heart because now she was left alone with Adam. Without Colton here, she felt unprotected and uncomfortable.

When the last of the parents had left to pick up their children, Emma cast a subtle sideward glance to discover Adam silently standing several feet away with his hands in his pockets. Emma didn't know quite what to do, though she did know what would inevitably come next.

"Can we talk, Emma?" he finally asked.

Emma was still facing away from him, but she could imagine the pleading expression on his face. "Sure," she responded weakly.

"Would you like to go for a walk?"

No, I wouldn't. Not alone with you, she wanted to say with every fiber of her being. But she found herself saying the exact opposite entirely. "I'd love to."

So they set out at a slow pace down a trail into the forest. Neither looked the other in the eye and, for a long while, neither spoke. Adam finally let out a deep sigh.

"So, you're probably wondering where I've been this past week."

Emma's failure to respond affirmed his assumption.

"I shouldn't have left," he said, his voice trembling. "I'm just having a hard time with all of this."

All of this. These words, reminding her of Jeremy's own earlier, resounded through her mind. What *was* 'all of this?' She was growing tired of reeling helplessly in the dark.

"Yeah, well," she began. "I am, too. I have no idea what's going on around me. Everything's falling apart and I haven't the slightest clue as to why. You need to explain everything you know right now," Emma said firmly, finally releasing some of her pent-up agitation from the long day. She kicked a stick in her way for added effect.

Adam offered a quizzical look, but Emma didn't see it. He didn't know all that she was referring to. What had become of Colton and Jeremy, after all? Was this what had been troubling her all day? He pushed his questions aside for now; at the moment, it was more important to answer hers. "I have a few confessions to make."

Emma snorted in grim amusement. "I bet you do."

He ignored her bitterness and continued. "I'm not who you think I am, Emma."

She shook her head and rolled her eyes. "Of course you're not," she said with evident contempt in her tone. "No one is who they say they are."

"I'm not an adolescent white-collar thief here for community service," he began. "Well, I am a thief," he added. "But I've never been caught."

"Then *why* are you here?" Emma asked, stopping dead in her tracks. She was trying her best to repress losing all sanity.

Adam stopped walking, too, after taking a few more steps. He spun around to face her. "To meet you," he responded faintly.

Oh, one stranger that recently dropped in on my life actually planned on meeting me. That's very comforting, Emma thought to herself sarcastically. "Why?" she asked with a trembling voice.

"I recently came across a piece of information," Adam answered.

"What information?" Emma asked, unable to stand any more vague answers or secrets. If he didn't respond with a flat-out answer, she imagined she might simply walk off and drive home. Back to the Hamptons. At this point, she had had enough of this place. Only hurt had come from her stay here.

Adam had impressed himself thus far. His mercurial, awkward self had stepped aside to make way for clear, coherent thinking that he had not known for over a decade. No doubt, it was Emma's effect on him. Now was the time for him to reveal his hand to her at last — the reason why he had come. "I have information concerning your father," Adam answered after a contemplative silence. "Turns out... he also happens to be my father. You're my half-sister, Emma."

FORTY-ONE

13 JUNE, 2012

Half Dome. Yosemite. Colton had returned at last, after all these years. He had driven here straight from Maine, arriving earlier this evening. He had stopped along the way only to fill his gas tank. He had eaten nothing and had drunk only liters upon liters of water since his departure. He itched with a restlessness that he expected would not settle until after his ascent.

Though he could see lights and hear banter through the forest a distance away, he was alone enough here. Good. He didn't want anybody here to bother him. To watch him. Finally surrounded by the tranquility of nature, he decided he would at least try to shut his eyes to get some rest before his climb. He lay down on an appealing patch of moss and shut his eyes.

After hours of trying, though, he could only manage to fall half-asleep, too disturbed by thoughts of recent knowledge to ease into a peaceful slumber. When he finally gave up and rose from his natural bed, he guessed it was sometime around midnight.

He made the short walk to his tent and searched around the back for his climbing necessities: climbing shoes, a pouch of chalk, and a headlamp. A headlamp wasn't normally one of the few things he required for an ascent, but this ascent would be strikingly different than all the others — he would be climbing in the middle of the night.

To be extra careful, he put brand new batteries into the headlamp. He guzzled down another liter of water and tossed the empty canteen back into the tent. He slammed the rear door shut and locked everything up. He set his keys under the lip of his fender, just as he always did before going on an adventure. He slipped his shoes on and clipped the chalk pouch to a belt loop.

Once there, he flicked on his headlamp to get a better view of what exactly he was up against. He had never climbed Half Dome before. He was far beyond caring about a test-climb, though. He would rely on intuition and expertise alone to carry him up the face. Should he fail, his death would be no great loss to humanity. The world would simply spin on without him as it had after the deaths of so many who had already completed their journeys on this earth.

Here before him stood his greatest challenge with death yet: a shadow-cloaked, granite giant towering ominously above all of humanity, cruelly enforcing its grand indifference. What could Colton boast of in comparison to this archaic behemoth? It loomed above all of his storied scars. What could Colton fear of it? It rose above all of Colton's infinitesimally insignificant thoughts and emotions.

Here, he would graciously hand over to death itself its greatest opportunity to claim him once and for all. Then, in the end, he and his meager existence would fade away into oblivion.

Without further ado, he began his ascent.

FORTY-TWO

14 JUNE, 2012

Emma tapped her foot anxiously as she sat alone in the great library of her home in the Hamptons. A book that she had selected at random from the voluminous shelves lining the room sat open on her lap, though she hadn't read a word. She was far too distracted, angry, and confused to do anything but lose herself to her thoughts. She hadn't slept at all Monday or Tuesday night. Last night, entirely exhausted, she had managed to doze off for a couple hours. She had awoken abruptly sometime around four in the morning, though, from a nightmare.

Her skin crawled as the terribly vivid dream suddenly flooded her frightened consciousness. When a lone tear cascaded over the ledge of her distinguished cheekbone, she assured herself that Colton wasn't *actually* dead. He couldn't be. Not yet, at least. Jeremy still hadn't contacted her. He would, though, and he would tell her that Colton was safe and sound. Perhaps Colton himself would show up at her door one day and carry her off in his brawny arms without a word. Normally, the thought would have drawn a smile to her lips, but her recent temperament was a complete stranger to anything akin to happiness.

She cast her scattered mind into the clutches of more troubling thoughts. Her father... A liar. A cheater. A *murderer*. According to Adam, at least. She was here to find out for certain. She was here to confront her father once and for all. She was here… but her father wasn't. She had uprooted herself from her responsibilities in Maine to come home and storm in on her father, only to find out from Lance that Harvey was on a weeklong business trip of some sort. No matter, though. She would wait. She would have her opportunity… eventually.

A chill crept over her as she thought of what Adam had told her — how her father had been having an off-and-on affair with a 'colleague' throughout the 90s. How Adam had been born in secret in 1995. How he had been raised singlehandedly by his mother until Harvey murdered her in 1999.

Emma remembered how she had reacted to this news… or, rather, how she hadn't reacted. She had taken it as if it was a fantasy. Pure fiction. A bizarre dream. Then Adam had showed her a copy of the paternity test that verified almost all that he had told her and the terrible reality of the situation began to finally crash down on her head.

Though this news alone had very nearly destroyed Emma, the ensuing news that Adam's mother, a foreign woman by the name of Mona Luca Lane, had been mercilessly slaughtered by the hands of Emma's own father had caused Emma to promptly vomit and then pass out.

Even now she felt sick to her stomach after merely recalling the information. Adam had not disclosed any real proof about the alleged murder, but Emma, even in her disoriented, half-crazed state of mind, had been sharp enough to read that he was not lying to her. That didn't necessarily mean the claim was true, however.

Nevertheless, Emma found that she didn't naturally reject the notion of the murder. If her father possessed the audacity to cheat on her mother for a decade, who was she to fight for his innocence? She didn't know who he was anymore. Apparently, she had *never* known who he truly was. As sharp and intuitive and deductive as she had grown up to be, she had never recognized him for what he truly was.

Her own father: a two-faced monster. Her mother: a hollow slave. Her brother: a corrupt puppet. Her half-brother: living off whatever he could steal from the wealthy. Her lover: gone and possibly dead. Her life: a tragedy. Emma didn't fight the tears this time as they came to violently stream down her face.

And even after all of this tragedy, she had no one to confide in. Of course, she could never tell Lance or her mother. They would never believe her. Not without rock-solid proof. And she didn't have rock-solid proof. All she had was a story. But it was a *true* story, wasn't it? Wouldn't that count for something? Life, as it seemed, was too unfair to concern itself with truth, though.

No, her only choice, her only plan was to confront her father head-on. She expected he would likely deny everything outright and ask what kind of crazy things she had heard from that wild boy she was seeing.

All she could hope was that she would be able to unsettle him. For, if she saw even the slightest weakness, even the slightest chink in his armor of confidence, she would exploit it and destroy him. It sounded harsh — him being her father and all — but if everything that Adam had told her was true, it was more than deserved. Family by blood or not, Harvey Payton was no father of hers if the accusations bore truth. After all, Adam was family by blood, too, wasn't he? And how had the man who called himself her father treated him? He ignored Adam from the day he was born. He ignored Adam after killing the poor boy's mother. He ignored Adam when the boy took to the streets and learned the ways of a criminal life. He had ignored Adam's existence, and now he would pay for his ignorance and all of his other wicked transgressions, even if his own blood-daughter had to be the one to bring it all down on him.

FORTY-THREE

Colton sat utterly alone atop the edge of Half Dome. A lofty breeze rushed by, threatening to brush him over the ridge. He looked with hardened eyes off into the East as the first sign of the sun broke the horizon with a distinct flash. He didn't flinch as the first rays of light shot at his eyes. He watched as the shadow of the valley gradually succumbed to the sweeping radiance of the long-awaited daylight. The dark of the night had had its turn. The morning sun had returned to once again claim its former glory.

Colton wondered about the world. He wondered about his place in it. Excommunicated by society. Rejected by death. He was entirely unwanted by the universe.

Why are we here? The all-too-familiar question flashed through his mind from nowhere. This time, though, an answer resounded back.

To make a difference.

He narrowed his eyes, curious as to where from this response had come. From within — that much was obvious — but from where within?

He contemplated the sudden, unexpected answer. The answer that he had spent more than half his life doggedly searching for. The answer that had remained just out of reach despite his wildest endeavors. The answer that had not decided to reveal itself until now, after his life had once again been unjustly ripped out from underneath him.

Had he made a difference? This question was easy to answer. No, he hadn't. Whenever an opportunity presented itself, he fled in the face of hardship. He fled to pursue some misguided idea that he would divine his purpose in the midst of conquering death.

Yes, he had conquered death. He had conquered death over and over and over again. He was clearly at the reigns of his own life. Nothing dared take it over. But, in the end, what had he accomplished? What had he really done but escape his own destiny? Now, more than ever, he felt that not only did all of humanity have a purpose, but that he, too, owned a very specific destiny that had been set in place long ago by something he had now decided to simply call fate. How else could he account for all that happened? It was no accident. Rarely did he believe in the impossible, though this time he did — it was *impossible* that everything that had befallen him was random. Rather, as cruel as life had been to him, his purpose lay in the midst of it. And it was not yet too late to accept it.

All this time, he'd had it backwards. His purpose didn't lie on the road to death, it lie at the core of living his life. And his life couldn't be lived if he was too busy chasing oblivion. His life could only truly be lived if he made a meaningful difference in the world. And he could start by simply taking a single step in the right direction, because once he did, he would already be on the right path. And, in this life, the path is the destination.

Peace. The word from nowhere flashed through his mind. *Peace.* A concept that had been so unfamiliar and elusive his entire life, Colton had to remind himself what exactly it was. A fleeting concept that didn't even exist in memories of the past, but only in the past itself. *Peace.* A concept that somehow finally seemed attainable. But what did it even mean to him?

Emma.

Of course. A single step in the right direction, and it was very clear which direction was the right one. The only one that had given him a sense of hope.

Hope. His greatest enemy. And yet, his only chance at achieving meaning. Confiding in hope was the greatest risk he could take, but it was a risk worth taking. There was nothing more for him to lose. Too much had already slipped away from him. He wasn't about to sit by idly while his last chance at salvation slipped away, too.

He knew what he had to do, and he knew how to do it.

Just as the finality of his resolve settled over him, a sound from behind effectively broke the serene silence that had long-held his isolated world. He should have sensed someone approaching, but he had been far too absorbed in his own thoughts. He snapped his head around in an instant and, after sighting the newcomer, rose from the edge of the world.

"It would behoove you to mind your feet while you're sneaking around," Colton patronized. "It seems you've developed quite the disadvantageous habit of accidentally setting your prey on high alert."

For a brief moment, Vincent Gaffeur raised his dark eyebrows and looked lazily at his target. Afterwards, though, a lethal coldness washed over his façade. His predacious gaze shimmered with scorn.

PART III
THE TEMPEST

FORTY-FOUR

10 APRIL, 2009

Small flecks of pink and white adorned the blooming dogwoods. A particularly cold and dry winter had held a frigid grasp on quiet Franklin County, Virginia for as long as the patient sun had allowed. Spring had shown its first signs of life only two days ago.

Colton had also arrived two days ago, rolling into town in a white 1974 Jeep CJ7 that desperately needed a thorough wash. A turquoise, single-seat kayak sat fastened to the hardtop roof of the antique vehicle, and attached to the rear rested a weathered mountain bike. He had just driven straight from the Colorado Rockies, breaking once to nap a few hours at a campground in Missouri. After arriving in Franklin County later that night, he had checked in at a small motel that boasted a splendid waterfront view of Smith Mountain Lake. A full moon and a starry sky had illuminated the rippling water's tranquil surface that night, but Colton had stolen only a single cursory glance through his window before collapsing on the bed.

:-:

He had spent the following day handling last-minute arrangements for the service. He found a local tailor and paid to rent a formal black suit and shoes and such. A suit of his own was currently hung up in the closet of his dorm room in Connecticut, of course, but when he had left for Spring Break more than a week ago, he hadn't known he would be needing it.

After meeting with the tailor, he had made his way to the local florist and vaguely asked for a nice bouquet of orange and yellow flowers. He remembered picking tropical flowers with his mother years ago by the beaches of Guam...

He was twelve years old when his father was transferred to the Andersen Air Force Base in Yigo, Guam. Colton and his mother followed. They always followed. Andersen was the sixth place he had lived. Life during the two-year stay in Yigo was paradise. Almost every memory from those joyous years was a fond one. Alas, those happy days came to an end before long — as all good things do. Leaving Guam alone would have been difficult, but leaving only to be transferred to Afghanistan seemed like cruel punishment.

He was fourteen years old when his father was transferred to the Middle East. Again, Colton and his mother followed, albeit less enthusiastically this time. But they always followed. The Bagram Air Force Base in the Parvan Province of Afghanistan was the seventh place Colton had lived. The seventh country. The third continent. If life at Andersen had been paradise, life at Bagram was hell. They had dreadfully meager rations for food and, worst of all, they were in the middle of nowhere. All Colton could see beyond the base was dirt, the distant mountain range, and the occasional herd of goats. They had been stationed a fair distance away from any village, too, so he wouldn't be able to spend time with and learn from the locals during this stay. He and his mother kept a calendar on which they would cross off the passing days. One thing alone gave them hope while in Afghanistan: the day they were scheduled to be transferred out.

Slowly, very slowly, two years gradually became lost memories of the desert sands. The days began to blur together, and, if not for the calendar, Colton would have believed he was stuck reliving the same exact day over and over. One day, however, his life changed. That day was the only one he remembered in his entire stay at Bagram.

"Will you be able to pick them up this evening, sir?" the florist shop clerk — a hunched, elderly man with wispy white hair — had asked from behind the shop's counter to unknowingly interrupt Colton's flashback.

"Yes, sir," Colton had responded, struggling to return to reality. "How much?"

"Forty-eight dollars." The clerk lifted his head to meet Colton's icy blue eyes. "What's the occasion?"

"They're for my mom." Colton refrained from making eye contact while he counted out the exact change to hand over to the clerk.

"I hope she likes them."

"She would," Colton muttered, turning away. As he left the shop, his cellphone rang. He pulled it from his pocket, curious as to who might be calling. He didn't recognize the number, but answered nevertheless. "Colton Anders speaking."

"Mr. Anders! It's Allen Finch. You remember, the lawyer who called the other day?"

"Yes, sir. I do."

"Ah, of course, of course." Finch paused for a moment. "Anyway, we have business that needs to be tended to. You know, just some paperwork. I was wondering if you would be able to stop by my office some time within the next few days to go over a few things."

"I'm free now, actually."

"Oh, perfect! My office is across the street from the local movie theater. You'll find it without too much trouble, I'm sure. See you then."

Colton had begun to speak again before suddenly noticing that Finch had already hung up. As he searched his memory, he hazily remembered passing a movie theater while driving into town the night before.

:-:

"Well, hello!" a balding, round man in his early fifties exclaimed, rising from his seat behind a cluttered desk to greet the young man who had just entered his office. "I take it you're Mr. Anders?" He offered his hand.

"That'd be me." Colton summoned a forced smile while he shook the man's hand. The firm grip surprised him.

"Please, please, take a seat." Finch sat back down and motioned to the chair opposite him. "This shouldn't take long. I've got the papers right here already, you see? Okay, let's take a look. I've already gone over this once myself. Just allow me to peruse both wills once more before I let you know what you need to know."

Finch grabbed a set of thick glasses from the top of a stack of papers and set them upon his hooked nose. He spent the next few minutes humming and mumbling to himself as he read over the manuscripts. When he finished, he suddenly bolted upright and let out a heavy sigh. He tossed his reading glasses back onto his desk and pinched the bridge of his nose with his fingers, tightly shutting his eyes. "I apologize sincerely about all this, by the way. And I apologize again for not expressing my apologies sooner." Finch leaned back in his leather office chair and began speaking slower and more deliberately. "It really is a terrible phenomenon. Why these things happen, I can't even begin to understand."

When Colton didn't say anything, Finch hesitated, then continued. "Did they tell you what happened?"

Colton slightly shook his head without meeting the lawyer's

gaze.

"Would you like to know?"

Colton nodded faintly.

"Apparently..." Finch began, taking a heavy breath to calm his nerves. "Last month, their remains were found washed up on the shores of a small, riverside village in southern Uganda. When their bodies finally arrived back in the States several days ago, autopsies revealed that they both died of bullet wounds. Your stepfather had a magazine's-load of thirty-nine millimeter rounds riddled throughout his chest. Your mother, who was determined to have died nine days after your stepfather, had a single fifty-one millimeter round lodged in her head." Finch paused. After a moment, he reopened his mouth, prepared to continue his dissertation of what the forensics report had read, but stopped himself before uttering another syllable to instead stare silently at the expression of the young man sitting opposite him. Pity stirred in his chest. Better to spare him the details that only led to more disturbing news, he decided. At least for now. "So... we believe the Lord's Resistance Army is behind their murders. Could you possibly enlighten me? Do you know what they were they doing in Uganda?"

Colton shrugged and shook his head. "Another philanthropic mission of Lenny's, I would assume." His eyes were cloudy.

Finch raised his thick eyebrows. "I see... Did he go on these 'missions' frequently?"

"I don't know what he's been up to with my mother the past few years." Colton closed his eyes as a long-harbored pain evidently threatened to suddenly overwhelm him. "But while I was still with them, we were always on the move..." he trailed off, staring past Finch with wide, empty blue eyes. "I've always been on the move." His gaze transcended beyond the confinement of the physical world.

"Well," Finch began uncomfortably, slouching in his chair and pretending to read the wills again. "Lenny left all of his money and possessions to your mother, and your mother left all of her money and possessions to you. So, connect the dots."

Colton didn't even blink in response. His face was blank — impossible to read.

"Essentially," Finch began, clasping his hands together. "That's everything that concerns you. I'll just need your signature and initials in a few places and the rest will be handled."

Colton's eyes glazed over again.

"It's not a small sum of money, Mr. Anders," Finch enticed, leaning forward and raising his eyebrows.

"I don't want it," Colton finally muttered in response.

Finch narrowed his eyes and furrowed his brow. "Mr. Anders," he began. "It's what they wanted. It's what your mother wanted. You wouldn't deny her only last will to you, the very last of her blood, would you?"

Colton sat in motionless silence for a few long moments before he suddenly sighed and gently nodded his head in agreement. Finch handed him a black fountain pen. He signed and initialed in the appropriate blanks. "What else?"

"That's it, Mr. Anders," Finch responded with an inauthentic smile. He promptly rose from his seat.

Colton remained sitting. A subtly perplexed look had crossed his features. He met Finch's gaze again. "No, that can't be all. There must be more. My mother... She..." he trailed off, at a loss for intelligible words. Finally, he found his tongue. "She didn't have *anything* to say to me?"

The lawyer said nothing.

Colton sat for several moments longer, waiting for what he

knew in the back of his mind would never come: a resolution.

Repressing his tempestuous emotions of frustration, fear, and despair, Colton rose from his seat and promptly left the office.

:-:

The day he had ultimately come for arrived at last. Colton stood alone at the rear of the gathered, watching as his mother and stepfather were lowered into the ground in their respective caskets. He stood there a long while — silent, passive, and meeting no one's stare. In his peripheral vision, he noticed Finch there, stealing glances in his direction every thirty seconds. The others, however, mostly ignored him. He assumed they were all here for Lenny. No one knew his mother, after all. She was a ghost. No friends and no family, save for Colton. And now, Colton, too, was dreadfully alone. Now, he, too, was a ghost.

After the service had ended and all others had gone, Colton drifted up to his mother's headstone and laid the bouquet of orange and yellow flowers on the fresh burial plot. He collapsed to his shaking knees, burying his face in one palm while resting the other on his dead mother's granite memorial. Beneath their impassive shell, his lost emotions boiled beyond control. Without restraint, he spilled the remainder of any tears that lie in the shadowy reserves of his soul.

:-:

He returned to Yale University two days later. He sat through his morning Philosophy discussion but couldn't focus. No spoken word even registered in his clouded mind. When class was over and the professor questioned him about why he had taken an extended Spring Break and missed the last three days of class, he offered a brief and insincere apology before departing. None of that mattered now, he reasoned. He didn't belong here anymore.

He retrieved his belongings from his dorm room, careful not to run into his roommate, and left once and for all. No goodbyes and no apologies. He was done here. Once again, he would start over.

Adam Lane could see for miles and miles. He watched as the waves fought ferociously, each trying to transcend the other. The violent swells spat sprays of salt to lick the briny air. The savage surges roared in fervent frustration. Mighty and mysterious as the boundless ocean was, it ultimately knew that, despite any of its desperate attempts, it would forever remain constrained to its earthly prison.

He stood atop a large boulder as he raised his arms in empathetic salute to the somber existence of the sweeping sea. A high wind rushed along his skin.

He retrieved a small bag of diamonds from his pockets and emptied them onto his outstretched hand. He lifted them before his eyes and inspected them one last time. He had stolen them a few months ago upon learning about his family and had planned on offering them to Emma. Now, though, the thought disgusted him. Here in his hand lie the very embodiment of worldly vice. Here lie the weakness of humanity. Here lie the epitome of hatred, greed, and violence.

With a generous hand, he cast out the gems into the depths of the desirous ocean. He watched as the amorphous sea sent out its salty fingers to claim them, swallow them whole, and sweep them safely beneath the very boulder he now stood upon.

Emma was safe. No longer could the lies of avarice torment

her. She bore his distant love, and he would forever tightly cling to the trace of kinship that she had left with him.

Adam turned his back on the sea and brushed his wispy black hair out of his eyes, seeing the world anew — as if for the first time.

Here, under this rock, suffocated by the depths of the sea, lie the pain of his past. With a content sigh and a heart free of burden, he stepped off the boulder, marking the beginning of the rest of his life.

FORTY-SIX

Colton shifted his footing and gradually began to move away from the ridge behind him. "I'm surprised... No guns?"

Vincent edged nearer.

Colton lifted his chin and opened his mouth as understanding suddenly dawned on him. "Ah," he breathed. "Better if you throw me off this cliff, right? Everyone will assume I fell." He nodded his head. "Good plan." As the words left his mouth, the assassin closed the gap between them in a flash and launched himself at Colton.

Colton was prepared, though, and tried to redirect Vincent off the edge of the cliff. Vincent must have expected such a reaction, though, because at the last second he accounted for Colton' shift in movement and sidestepped, lowering his right shoulder and burying it just beneath the center of Colton's ribcage.

The blow knocked the wind out of Colton. He staggered backwards, teetering on the rim of Half Dome. He struggled to catch his breath, but only had a split second to re-orient himself before he saw Vincent's foot flying towards his face. Still unable to breathe, he took a graze of the kick against his right ear as he narrowly bent out of the way.

His ear rang. He staggered again, losing control of his balance. As Vincent retracted his leg, Colton took half a moment to regain what he could of his bearings. A sudden rush of adrenaline sent a blast of air back into his lungs, and he took as deep a breath as the moment would allow. Before Vincent could shift his footing to attack again, Colton took the opportunity to take a leap away from the ridge. But Vincent didn't need to shift his footing, as it turned out; he spun around and sent another kick at Colton, this one aimed at the same ear that he had just grazed.

With his peripheral vision, Colton sensed the attack before it could land and ducked in quick response. He fell towards the ground and rolled towards Vincent. As he rolled up underneath his assailant's outstretched leg, Vincent redirected his leg in mid-kick to swing it down straight at Colton as he lay on the ground.

Before the kick could strike him, Colton sent an elbow at the back of the knee of Vincent's planted leg, causing him to buckle on the spot. When the other leg crashed down, it wasn't with near as much force. Colton had raised his forearms to catch the residual impact of his opponent's downward swing.

Before Vincent could tear his leg away from Colton's grasp, Colton wrapped an arm around the assassin's leg and swung a flexible kick of his own up just beneath the mercenary's right shoulder blade.

The kick landed, but it was either too weak or Vincent had too much protective muscle on his back for the attack to be effective.

Noticing his failure, Colton rolled away before the assassin could retaliate. As the mercenary came over him once again, Colton did a backwards somersault to roll himself back up onto his feet. Vincent had timed his next attack perfectly, though, tackling Colton the moment he was standing.

The next thing he knew, the morning sky overwhelmed his field of vision. He could feel the assassin's thick forearm wrapped tightly around his neck. The panic settled in quickly, and trained instinct replaced controlled thought. He subconsciously recalled a self-defense move he had learned from training with his father years ago. With as much strength as he could muster, he broke himself free and rolled away. Though his lungs still screamed for air, he had only a split second to catch his breath before Vincent was upon him again.

He grabbed a fist-sized rock to defend himself with, but the mercenary grabbed his arm in mid-swing and pinned it to the ground. With his free hand, he took hold of the back of Vincent's bald head and slammed his forehead into the Earth. While he had the opportunity, he reclaimed the rock and prepared to bash it into Vincent's skull.

It only took a brief instant for hesitation to paralyze him, though, and it only took that brief instant for Vincent to regain his bearings. Before Colton could act, Vincent seized the chance to send him flying backwards with a strong kick to the chest.

Colton fought to dig his fingers into the earth to keep from sliding over the edge of the peak. When he had stopped skidding, he stood up and spun around to face his enemy, only to be met with a brutal knuckle to his cheekbone.

Even after the painful blow, though, he thought ahead to what he expected his assailant to do next: a kick square in his back to send him flying over the edge of Half Dome. As the punch spun him around, he stumbled as swiftly as he could in efforts to get out of the way.

He couldn't move quickly enough, though, and the force of the kick sent him hurtling over the ridge. As he surged forward, he swung his arm around to grab the ankle of the leg Vincent had kicked him with. Alas, Vincent's balance faltered. They were headed to their dooms together.

Colton, looking skyward, sent one last reach towards the rim of the peak as he began his descent, but to no avail. His fingers merely brushed against the ancient granite.

Vincent, caught completely unaware, tried to grab hold of a

rock on the ledge as gravity began to claim him, but his fingers never found hold.

Without a word, he plummeted face-first down all two thousand feet of Half Dome to meet death. He closed his eyes. He held his breath. Crushing impact.

FORTY-SEVEN

Jeremy had reached the zenith of Half Dome only to watch helplessly as Vincent Gaffeur kicked Colton over the ridge. Alarmed, the cripple moved faster than he even thought he could and hurled himself at the ledge as both assassin and victim began to fall. He dove forward, arms outstretched, hoping he could grab Colton's desperate arm in time.

Jeremy blindly found a hand to catch and suddenly felt the full weight of gravity pull at his arm. He grinded his toes and the fingers of his free hand against the stone to keep himself from hurtling face-first over the edge. He heard a distinct *pop*, signaling that his shoulder had likely been ripped from its socket. He fought back at the pain and focused on maintaining his grasp on whoever he had saved. He gritted his teeth, using all of his strength to maintain his precarious position.

The stress alleviated all of the sudden when he saw a hand reach over the ridge and grab hold of a small outcrop on the ledge. He hoped desperately that those sinewy fingers belonged to Colton, rather than Vincent.

"Your timing is impeccable," Jeremy heard a familiar voice grunt.

A wry smile crawled across his lips. "I'm just here to return the favor. You save my life, I save yours, right?"

Colton closed his eyes and shook his head as he recognized

Jeremy's voice. He was wholly unable to believe that this man was his savior, and even more unable to believe that he had been saved at all. "What are you doing here?"

"Just happened to be roaming the area."

"Right." Colton snorted, unconvinced. "Go ahead and let go of my hand. I've got a good enough hold with my other for the moment. I can pull myself up."

"Careful," Jeremy cautioned, slowly loosening his grasp on Colton's fibrous fingers. He rolled away from the edge and watched as Colton heaved himself up and over the ridge. They shared a sigh of relief.

Colton nodded his head, breathing deeply. "Thanks. I honestly thought for a moment that I wasn't going to make it out of that one."

"Colton Anders narrowly escapes death, yet again," Jeremy said loudly, falling on his back to the ground.

"After we let the moment pass," Colton breathed. "I'm going to bombard you with questions."

"And I'll gladly answer what I can," Jeremy returned. "If you promise me one thing."

"Yeah?"

"This time, don't jump."

Colton raised his eyebrows in a look of slight amusement. "No worries," he promised, looking over to the sun. It had barely peaked over the distant Eastern mountains. It was bizarre for him to think that only moments ago he had been completely alone, meditating peacefully on the edge of the world. Now, Harvey's mercenary was dead, Colton had a new experience to put at the very top of his list of near-death experiences, and, of all people, Jeremy Wilde had come to save him.

Jeremy breathed deeply as well. He sat up and jammed his shoulder back into place. He grimaced.

Colton studied him for a moment. "You're the one who put the photos in my Jeep, aren't you?"

"I am," Jeremy affirmed, kneading his quadricep with his fingers.

"And you followed me here," Colton said as more of a statement than a question.

Jeremy nodded. "Just like he did," he said, pointing a hooked finger in the direction of the cliff base. "It was a tough hike up the mountain. I would have gotten here faster if it weren't for my blasted leg. I hope no one else is after you; both my arms are ultimately useless at this point."

Colton stared at his comrade with narrowed eyes. The man had been through his share of physical ordeals. How was he even still functioning after that fall? "Who are you?" Colton asked. "And how are you connected to all of this?"

Jeremy sighed and stopped massaging his leg momentarily. "My identity is... complicated. My connection with Harvey Payton and your deceased stepfather is even more complicated. All you need to know right now is that I'm not the mastermind behind all of this. I'm simply the envoy."

"You promised me answers."

"I did. And you'll get them. But it'd be better if you heard it all from someone other than me."

"Who, then?"

"My employer, of course."

"And who is your employer?"

"You've already met him," Jeremy answered. "Three years ago."

Colton shook his head, confused.

"I believe you know him as... Allen Finch."

Colton tried to be surprised, but, in truth, he wasn't. After everything, he didn't think anything could surprise him. Instead, he just stared out at the horizon. "Can you take me to him?" he finally asked.

Jeremy nodded. "Yes. He's waiting for you."

"Of course he is. This is all part of the plan, I assume."

"Not exactly," Jeremy said with a slight chuckle. "You'll understand soon enough."

"You're pretty confident no one else is after me?" Colton asked as he stood up. He flexed his arms and fingers and rolled his shoulders.

Jeremy shook his head. "I'm not sure about anything right now other than the fact that Vincent Gaffeur..." Jeremy paused to incline his head towards the cliff base. "Is dead. We're running out of time, though. We only have so long before Harvey figures out you've killed his prime mercenary. And when he does, we can be sure to expect unpleasant encounters with the rest of his goons."

"How long until you're ready to get out of here, then?"

"Well, whether I'm ready or not, we've got to be on our merry way. I'll just have to manage, won't I?"

Colton pursed his lips. "I guess so. Let's be off, then."

"Okay," Jeremy grunted, slowly rising to his feet. Colton offered a hand, but Jeremy refused it. "I have worse to get through than this."

"At least we're going downhill," Colton pointed out.

"At least you're *alive*," Jeremy countered, leading Colton to the path down the stone mountain.

"Of course I'm alive," Colton said matter-of-factly. "Did you ever doubt me?"

"Yes," Jeremy said bluntly. "You don't know who you're dealing with. You don't know who you just threw off that cliff."

"I didn't *throw* him off a cliff. It was a convenient accident."

This made Jeremy smirk. The kid wasn't so bad, after all. Dangerous and unnecessarily daring, maybe, but at least he could handle himself. As the thought came to mind, a distant shriek sounded from the base of the cliff. "Someone must have discovered the product of your 'convenient accident.'"

"Yeah, that's never a pleasant sight," Colton affirmed. "They'll probably think he jumped, or—" Colton stopped speaking at once and briefly halted in his step.

"Or what?" Jeremy asked, turning around. Suddenly, it dawned on him. "You don't think that..."

"The park rangers will scour the mountain looking for anyone who might have some knowledge of or be responsible for what happened? I think it's highly likely."

"What's protocol for them when something like this happens?" Jeremy asked nervously, following Colton as he started off at a brisk walk down the well-worn trail.

"I don't know," Colton answered. "This is a very popular hiking and climbing location, though. I'm sure they have some sort of efficient way of handling these things."

"This is your profession! How can you not know?"

"This is only the second time I've ever been here, Jeremy. And both times I haven't really stuck around long enough to meet people and figure out how things work. Just follow me. I'll get us out of this. Trust me."

For a long while, they walked in silence down the guided trail.

They run in to no one — something Colton finds suspicious; normally a plethora of adventurers would be enjoying a morning hike up Half Dome. Perhaps everyone was simply spooked. Or perhaps the rangers had shut it off and were setting up a perimeter around the base. Colton hoped for the former, but expected the latter. He kept his eyes trained for sign of movement and kept his ears tuned for any noise other than their own.

Nothing, though. Not yet, anyway.

When Colton began to pick up the subtle sounds of Jeremy's labored breathing, he realized that his companion must be fighting off incredible amounts of pain. "Why didn't you let us take you to the hospital?" Colton asked.

"Two reasons," Jeremy answered between breaths. "First, I had to keep a close watch on you. The late Vincent Gaffeur had a post set up in the woods just outside the cabin for an entire week; I didn't know if and when he was planning on making a move against you. I just knew I had to be there if and when he did."

The news that the bald man had been watching him this whole while disturbed Colton, but did not surprise him. Nevertheless, he asked his next question with a subdued, wary tone. "And the other reason?"

Jeremy remained silent for several moments before answering. "I couldn't risk any authorities recognizing me. I'm a wanted man, after all."

Colton raised his eyebrows, but still refused to be surprised. "Oh, yeah? What'd you do?"

"Nothing, really. It's not what you might think."

"I'm sure," Colton muttered skeptically.

"Finch will explain everything. No need to worry."

"Do I look worried to you?" Colton asked, casting an indifferent glance behind him to his counterpart.

Jeremy took one look at him before returning his gaze to the trail his tired feet tread upon. "No."

They hurried down the trail as fast as Jeremy could move. Several times, though, they had to stop and rest because of the gradually increasing pain in Jeremy's leg. Fortunately, however, they never came across any people. When they began to near the base of the mountain, Colton decided to diverge from the trail and loop around to where he had parked his Jeep. Jeremy followed to the best of his ability.

"So," Colton began, tossing a water bottle from his car to his companion. "What now?"

Jeremy caught the bottle with his less injured hand and guzzled more than half of its contents all at once. He let out a deep, refreshed sigh before answering Colton. "Sacramento. Finch will be waiting for you there."

"How will I know where to find him?"

"We'll find you. Just be ready."

"We?"

"I'm still watching over you. Just because Vincent's dead doesn't mean you're out of harm's way."

Colton grunted in affirmation before loading himself into the driver's seat of his Jeep. "I'll see you around, I guess." He ignited the engine. When Jeremy began to walk away, Colton called out to him. "Hey, hold up."

Jeremy stopped and spun around.

Colton stared at him for a moment with his piercing, deep blue eyes before speaking. "Thank you, Jeremy. I wouldn't be here if you wouldn't have been there."

"Yeah, and that would have really screwed things up. Get out of here." He waved him off lightheartedly and trudged along.

:-:

Almost three hours after leaving Yosemite, Colton arrived in the capital of California. This was the first time he had returned to his birthplace since his dad was transferred out in 1989.

Not knowing quite what to expect or be looking for, he drove around the city randomly for a while before deciding to pull into a parking lot downtown. He could see the tall white spire of the Capitol building not too far in the distance. Here he would wait for whatever sign Finch might send his way. He wondered if he was being watched right this instant. The idea that he had to relinquish a certain amount of control in this situation to people he did not entirely trust unsettled him. If there was ever an occasion that he would play along to someone else's whims, though, that time would be now — only so he could find out what exactly was going on.

After about ten minutes of patient waiting, he decided to turn his car off. As soon as he did, he heard a ringing from the passenger glove box. He widened his eyes, caught off guard, and then narrowed them in suspicion. He hadn't owned a cellphone in years. He wondered if Jeremy had snuck it into his Jeep last night... or perhaps even several days ago when he had planted the photos. Nevertheless, after several seconds of contemplation, he found the phone in the glove box and put it to his ear.

"Hello?"

"Mr. Anders," Colton heard a distantly familiar voice say through the other end of the line. "It's Allen Finch. You remember, the lawyer from a few years back?"

"Of course."

"Good," the man said slowly. "I have instructions for you. Are you listening?"

"Yes, sir."

"Of course. Listen carefully. From your current location, exit the parking lot and take a left onto Thirteenth Street. Follow Thirteenth for four blocks. That should lead you to Capitol Park. You'll recognize it when you see it. Head in there, and follow it all the way to the far right end until you reach the International World Peace Rose Garden. It's at the opposite end of the Capitol Building. It's impossible to miss. Take a stroll through there and you'll find me. Understood?"

"Got it."

"Perfect," Finch voiced. A silence hung on the line for a moment before he suddenly hung up the phone.

Colton stared at the cell blankly, not sure what exactly to do with it. He tossed it onto the seat beside him for the time being and re-ignited his Jeep's engine. He exited the parking lot and took a left onto Thirteenth as he was told. He followed it into Capitol Park and parallel-parked on the roadside. He exited, locked his car, and stashed his keys in his pocket as he took off towards the International World Peace Rose Garden.

When he arrived, he found Jeremy standing beside a man in a wheelchair. Jeremy watched Colton as he approached, but the man in the wheelchair was busy inspecting some roses.

"Ah, and here you are," the figure in the wheelchair spoke without looking up from the flower.

"Mr. Finch?" Colton asked, concerned. The jubilant man he had met three years ago was no more. He had transformed into a broken, somber-faced shell of the man he used to be.

The man slowly raised a trembling hand to Colton. Colton took it and shook it gently, unlike their first encounter when the attorney had surprised Colton with his firm grip.

Jeremy stood like a statue by Finch's side, watching their

surroundings carefully.

"Don't be alarmed, my boy," Finch said as pleasantly as he could. "Jeremy, why don't we take a stroll through the park?"

Colton walked alongside Finch's wheelchair as Jeremy pushed from behind. He wanted to ask what had become of the rambling, spasmodic, jovial man he had met three years ago, but he could not find the words. For several long moments, no one said anything.

"Where to start?" Finch finally asked with a light chuckle. "It's funny. I've been waiting for this moment for so long, and now that it's here, I don't know how to begin."

"Who are you? Who is Jeremy?" Colton didn't hesitate to ask as a multitude of questions suddenly seized his mind. "How did you two come across those photos? What are your connections with my stepfather and Harvey Payton?"

"Lenny, as you may have inferred by now, was not merely the eccentric, globe-traveling, millionaire philanthropist he might have led you to believe he was. I knew him long before he met your mother. He and I worked together. We were very close," Finch said slowly. He was in no rush to answer all of Colton's questions at once.

"Where did you two work?"

"The Central Intelligence Agency, of course," Finch answered as if it was obvious. "You couldn't put two and two together? I was Lenny's handler."

This news actually surprised Colton. He believed it, though. Far more inconceivable information had turned out to be true recently, after all.

"Yes," Finch continued. "We'd been onto Harvey Payton since the nineties. For years, we carefully constructed a case against him and his accomplices. So many complexities. So many implications. Treason. Murder. You name it. That case was the undertaking of a career. We nearly had him. It all fell apart in Afghanistan, though."

Colton flinched at this, remembering the hardship of the many dark days following his father's death.

"Your stepfather was on a mission to get photographs of the Taliban insurgents in the act of attacking the oil refineries. We already knew that Harvey was paying them off and supplying them with advanced weaponry," Finch explained. "We didn't know, though, that Harvey had accomplices on both sides of the war."

"In the military, too?" Colton asked with a raised eyebrow.

Finch nodded. "For some, he simply paid them off. Others required more creative forms of bribery. The most righteous didn't acquiesce until they were blackmailed. The end product? Harvey Payton created a vast network of 'friends,' consisting of very high-ranking officers in every branch of the United States Armed Forces, as well as the Central Intelligence Agency." He shook his head. "This network wasn't limited to overseas, though; plenty of domestic extortion, too. Homeland Security, NSA, FBI, Congress, the Senate. Even the Secret Service." The trembling man paused to recollect his thoughts. "The depth and breadth of the corruption... is unprecedented."

"*How*?" was all Colton managed to ask, completely floored by Finch's words.

"Harvey Payton," Finch began, pursing his lips before continuing. "Is a *brilliant* man. No one else could have pulled it off. It takes more than money and resources to do something of this scale. It takes slow, deliberate, methodical planning. None can match Harvey's level of cunning on matters such as these. The designated moles in the various branches of government and military were each very specifically selected by Harvey himself, and each man was assigned one very specific role. Together, they form an extremely secretive and extremely complex network."

"Imagine a spider," Jeremy spoke up. "And it spends years and years building a web of such intensity that it eventually completely covers the entire globe. And yet, somehow, no one ever even knew it was happening."

"Well," Finch began. "There were some conflicted parties involved in the network who, down the line, decided to opt out. Some tried to go quietly... others, not so. But even though no one man knew enough to do any real damage, a certain mercenary was given the task to ensure that not even the tiniest secrets were spilled."

"Vincent Gaffeur," Colton said, suddenly realizing the extent of the assassin's responsibilities.

"Harvey wouldn't allow a single soul to leave the web. Not alive," Jeremy said grimly. "Vincent was directly responsible for ending over eight-hundred lives. He was a career killer."

"There's no doubt that, from the very beginning, Harvey surrounded himself with the perfect people. Our entire mission to prove his crimes was sabotaged from the inside out. Years and years of evidence... all destroyed," Finch said in a whisper. His breathing was slow and labored. "When Lenny was detained in the Bagram Air Force Base the day after your father died, I realized Harvey wouldn't merely stop at destroying the evidence, but that he was wiping the slate completely clean. Anyone involved in my mission who may have held any remotely incriminating knowledge was ordered to be killed immediately. So, I fled as soon I heard of what happened to Lenny and faked my own death. I took on a new identity and tried to begin a new career. Lenny started over by fleeing with your mother," Finch recounted. "Harvey never did get his hands on any of your stepfather's photographs. No one but Lenny himself knew where that evidence had been hidden. Harvey's moved Heaven and Earth to try and find them..." Finch paused to take a steady breath. "But, so far, he's ultimately failed at that."

"Did he actually love her?" Colton asked, distraught. Despite all that he had just heard, knowing whether the character behind his mysterious stepfather even loved his mother concerned him most of all.

Finch turned his head to look up at Colton and offer a faint smile. "Yes," he answered softly. "Very much. He could have very easily run away on his own. He should have. I *pleaded* him not to drag you and your mother into his predicament, in fact, but he refused to listen. I'd never seen him so obstinate about anything before."

"And had he known that my father had *just* been killed?" Colton questioned, growing angry despite Finch upholding Lenny's honest intentions.

"He had indeed," Finch responded quietly. "And he recognized that your mother needed someone for support. She had been dependent on your father for so many years, she didn't know how to cope alone. If Lenny hadn't come along, your mother would have completely fallen apart. Who knows where you would be now if not for him?"

"I could have taken care of her," Colton growled, shaking his head. "I knew how to handle myself. I knew my mother. We would have been fine."

Finch remained silent for a long moment. "Do you know who shot down your father, Colton?" He spoke so quietly, even Colton had to strain his ears to hear him.

"The Taliban," Colton grunted bluntly.

An even more somber expression clouded his face. "No," the little man whispered. "The Taliban were not capable of such an attack at that time. They didn't have the weaponry in their arsenal." Finch paused to catch his breath. "The missile that shot down your father's plane was from another aircraft."

Colton froze, stopping dead in his tracks. Jeremy stopped pushing Finch forward.

"One of the officers who Harvey was paying off followed George Anders into the air when he mistakenly took a shift that wasn't his own. We have reason to believe that your father came across something he wasn't supposed to see — an impending Taliban attack on an oil refinery, perhaps. Whatever he saw, though, it gave the other officer reason to shoot him out of the sky."

Colton doubled over, clutching his knees with his veiny hands. He closed his eyes and shook his head. In that moment, all glory vanished in a vapory wisp; his father hadn't died a hero's death in active duty, after all. Rather, he was betrayed and shot down by his own brother in arms. And, underlying *everything*, Harvey Payton was responsible. Harvey Payton *murdered* his father. Would the pain ever end? He fell to the ground and stared off into the distance, captivated by a surreal daze.

"Would you like me to continue? Or have you had enough?" Finch asked gently.

Colton shook his head. "Finish."

Finch gulped. "Lenny," he continued after a brief hesitation. "Stole a couple hundred million dollars from Harvey a year before our mission imploded. It wasn't part of the plan. Completely off the record. I didn't even know about it until after his death. I only discovered it upon looking into his bank accounts to handle the paperwork that comes with death. Anyway, I did some digging on the matter and eventually learned that your stepfather wasn't acting alone. He had an accomplice in the heist..."

"Me," Jeremy said.

Finch nodded slowly in affirmation. "Jeremy was another field operative on the case against Harvey. He and Lenny worked alongside one another."

"Why?" Colton asked with a bewildered expression. "Why would you steal from a man like that? And how did you even manage to pull such a stunt off?"

"The details of the heist are confidential and complicated," Jeremy answered bluntly, sweeping his eyes over their perimeter once again. "*Why* did we do it? Because it didn't belong to him. It was blood money. Of course, it didn't belong to us, either. We planned to redistribute it to those who had been hurt by Harvey's actions — like you and your mother, for instance. Everything fell apart before we could carry out the rest of our plans, though. In the end, we both got caught. Harvey figured out it was us, somehow, but he dealt with us in different ways. I was burned by the CIA and branded a fugitive. He's even sent a few men to kill me over the years. Nothing too serious, though, considering what he's capable of. No, his focus was on Lenny. The man wanted his money back, after all, and it was all in Lenny's account."

"So the money I *inherited* was all stolen?" Colton asked in disbelief. He redirected his fiery gaze at Finch. "*You* encouraged me to take that... *blood* money. You knew! Were you trying to get me killed?"

"Calm down, Colton," Finch said conciliatorily. "Hear out the rest of your own history before you begin blaming and assuming. As Jeremy was saying, Harvey sent his men after Lenny and, consequently, your mother, too. Lenny proved to be tough prey to follow, though, and before too long Harvey pulled his goons off the job. You see... sometime during the hunt his men uncovered the existence of Lenny's photos, so Harvey decided to change his tactics."

"He decided to send the most experienced, lethal, calculating man he knew to accomplish a job that no one else could possibly do," Jeremy explained. "Vincent Gaffeur personally chased Lenny and your mother across the globe for three years."

"And then he killed them?" Colton assumed, still evidently bitter.

"No," Finch denied patiently. "Harvey would never have allowed Vincent to kill them until the photos were recovered. But then the unthinkable happened. We don't know what happened for sure, but our sources informed us that Lenny and your mother were murdered in Uganda during a rebel night raid. Harvey was absolutely furious. Vincent went on a rampant killing spree. The three of us here now are the only surviving loose ends."

"But Harvey doesn't know that," Jeremy added. "He thinks we're dead, too, which gives us a distinct advantage we haven't had up until now."

"Why hasn't he tried killing me until this morning?"

"Harvey's ruthlessness has an uncommon partner in patience. For quite some time, he's believed you to be the very *last* loose end. He thinks that, by sheer process of elimination, you've had the photos all along. He couldn't gather the knowledge he needed to gather if you were dead," Finch answered steadily. "When you met Emma, though, it would seem that all of our plans drastically shifted courses. At that point, he personally stepped in to act. So, after assessing the situation firsthand, he evidently came to the conclusion that now seemed to be the appropriate time to have you killed," Finch explained, keeping his slow, rhythmic tempo of speech. He chuckled faintly before continuing. "Little did he know that you would actually discover the very photos he'd been looking for all along the morning after meeting him. Leaving Maine when you did probably saved your life. It completely altered Vincent's plan of attack in your favor.

He underestimated you on Half Dome. His confidence killed him."

"What about the money, though?" Colton asked. "How was Harvey planning on getting his money back if I was dead?"

Finch shook his head. "Two hundred million dollars doesn't matter to a man like that anymore in a time like this. It's been years since the heist, and he's become increasingly obsessed with self-preservation over this past decade. He's more than willing to do whatever it takes to clear his name from any possible allegations, and those photos are awfully incriminating. To him, nothing is more important than removing all traces of them."

"What do those photos even imply? I'm not following."

"That's because you don't know how Harvey acquired all of his money," Finch said wearily. "He happens to own the only oil company based in the Middle East that has not sustained any attacks on its refineries. His company has profited billions. Understand that and consider those photos, few would call that a coincidence."

Colton's head spun as the understanding suddenly dawned on him. "That's one way to beat the competition."

"The implications go very, very deep. This isn't just corporate crime anymore... it's evolved into federal treason at nearly every tier of our government."

Colton didn't say anything. He merely sat on the ground beside Finch's wheelchair and plucked at a few blades of grass. "Why didn't you tell me all of this three years ago when I met you before the funeral? Why'd you draw this all out?"

"Because three years ago, you were emotionally compromised. This information would have pushed you over an edge from which there is no return."

"You don't know that," Colton spat caustically. "I would have wanted revenge... Almost as badly as I want it right now."

"Maybe," Finch said softly. "But revenge or no revenge, it would have caused irreparable damage. You were raw, Colton. Raw and vulnerable. It would have destroyed you."

Colton didn't argue. "So, why tell me at all? What do you need from me? You seem to have everything figured out already."

"Because," Jeremy began to answer. "Whether we liked it or not, you're involved in this. Keeping you in the dark would only have gotten you killed. Furthermore, we want you to have your revenge."

"What am I supposed to do?" Colton asked dubiously. "If we can't trust anyone, what solution is there?"

"We've been pursuing another lead," Finch answered. "It's taken some time."

"We're going to come at Harvey from two angles to back him into a corner he can't escape from," Jeremy added. "Right now, at this moment, he's more defenseless than ever... Vincent is dead. We know things Harvey doesn't. And he believes we're dead. We must strike now, though... while we still have the cover of the shadows."

"Care to enlighten me on the specifics?" Colton said with a resigned chuckle, tossing his hands up in the air.

"Harvey Payton has an illegitimate son," Finch answered. "When the boy's mother discovered records of Harvey's crimes in the Middle East, he silenced her by personally killing her on the spot. Got away with it, too. Never even went to trial."

Colton shook his head. "What chance do we actually have here?"

Finch and Jeremy exchanged weary, unsure glances. Jeremy shook his head and pursed his lips.

"Even our best angle is a long-shot," Finch began with a sigh. "We have a file of the paternity test. We have the photos. Law enforcement has records of the murder..."

"And that's it," Jeremy said bluntly. "That's all we've got. It hardly even scratches the surface of what's really going on... but it's better than nothing. If we do this right, it could open the flood gates and wash away Harvey's web of defenses."

"Who's the son?" Colton asked. "Where's he been all this time?"

"His name is Adam Lane," Finch answered. "After his mother was killed, he took to the streets and adopted the life of a criminal. After I met with you three years ago, I took it upon myself to find the boy in the Bronx. We spent some time together once I finally found him. I told him a little bit about who his father is. He deserved to know at least that much after everything he'd been through."

"A criminal?" Colton intrigued, brushing past all the other details. He narrowed his eyes in suspicion. "Describe him."

"Adam?" Finch asked. "Thin. Long, black hair. Pale in complexion. Remarkably intelligent — a genius, in fact, according to his IQ scores."

"I've met him," Colton responded without hesitation. "He was there. In Maine."

Finch and Jeremy both turned wide eyes upon Colton. Apparently, for a change, he knew something neither of them did.

"He was with Emma the day she and I met. He was volunteering at her camp for community service.

Finch cursed under his breath as he looked up at Jeremy. "Why wasn't I told about this?"

A wildly fearful expression fell over Jeremy's face as he

assumed the defensive. "I never saw him, sir."

"It's true," Colton spoke up. "Jeremy was too disoriented to recognize him when I took him to the cabin. Adam disappeared that evening. Never saw him after that."

"Do you think he's gone to Harvey?" Jeremy asked Finch.

Finch pursed his lips and pondered a moment, slowly tapping his index finger on one of his motionless legs. "No, I don't," he answered confidently. "This is my fault. I shouldn't have gone to him until this was all over. I only wanted him to know about his past before he went down a path he could never escape from. I never expected he would go to such lengths to find Emma."

"Why would he go to her rather than Harvey?" Jeremy asked.

"The basic human desire to find kinship," Colton offered with a shrug. "She's his half-sister. He's been pushed away and rejected his whole life. He's not the type to confront the root of a problem. He doesn't want to confront the man who's ignored his existence since the day of his birth, but he's tired of being unnecessarily lonely."

Finch nodded in assent. "Yes, and Emma must know about her father's affair now, too. She left Maine several days ago to return to her family's home in Water Mill."

"And she *is* willing to confront her father," Jeremy said as it dawned on him.

"And when she does..." Finch began warily.

"Harvey will get spooked and use his resources to destroy all evidence of the murder. After that, all we have are the photos. I don't know if they alone are enough to bring Harvey down. As incriminating as they seem, Harvey's lawyers could make Vincent the scapegoat. He's too dead to say otherwise, after all. I think they could find some way to weasel Harvey out of any charges," Colton added.

"And then we'll be finished, rather than Harvey," Jeremy concluded.

"Has she already done it?" Colton asked.

Finch shook his head, pinching the bridge of his nose with his plump fingers. "No. Harvey left for a business trip after he met you and Emma at the villa. He's still away. We have to act fast, though. It's your call, Colton."

"There's always another option," Jeremy muttered. All eyes turned to him. "Say the word and I'll put a bullet in his head. We can end this once and for all."

Colton weighed Jeremy's words in silence. The man singlehandedly responsible for tearing his family apart could be gone if only he wished it so. And yet... "No, death would be too forgiving," he dismissed, standing up at last. "We will not forgive, and will not forget. For the ones we have loved and for the ones we have lost, let us exact a vengeance worthy of those slain without mercy. Let him know his own cruelty. Let him suffer every degree of every wrong ever committed by his own hand. Let his malice turn inward until not the faintest trace of dignity remains. Let him hope for death. And let this shadow of hope... drive him mad."

FORTY-EIGHT

14 JUNE, 2012

Harvey Payton bid farewell to his golf partners for the evening and strolled up the entrance of the Ritz-Carlton Hotel of Half Moon Bay, San Francisco. The entranceway concierge gracefully swung the door open wide before Harvey could break stride. Harvey failed to look the man in the eye, but offered him a fifty-dollar bill from his pocket. The door attendant accepted most graciously.

The oak-bark soles of his leather shoes padded softly against the interior floor as he treaded towards the elevator. The elevator concierge greeted Harvey by name before setting them in motion towards Harvey's floor. He didn't ask Harvey about his golf match, though, so Harvey decided against tipping him.

He walked silently down the carpeted hall with a hand in his pocket. He came upon the door to his suite and slid his keycard to allow himself in. He flicked the lights on and strolled over to the windows of the main room. The cliff-top view of the Pacific was stunning. The evening sun had nearly finished its descent, casting a vermilion glow across the underside of the heavens.

He blinked blankly before turning his back on the view. As he spun around, a folder on the glass coffee table captured the attention of his gray eyes. Curious and suddenly not at ease, he studied it with a piercing gaze. He approached it slowly, as if at any moment the folder would come alive and violently spew its contents at him.

He stopped a foot away, hovering cautiously over whatever lay inside. With an apprehensive hand, he slowly lifted the cover of the folder. What he saw took his breath away.

He couldn't help collapsing on the couch behind him as he examined each photograph carefully. His heartbeat intensified. His skin crawled. His confidence shrank. His throat constricted. By the last photo, he couldn't breath. He came across a pale yellow sticky note at the rear of the folder. *Navio — 8 PM*, it read.

As Harvey's mind raced, he recalled the resort restaurant in the hotel named Navio.

In truth, he was more caught off guard than frightened. But the uncertainty of the situation unsettled him greatly, nonetheless. What was actually going on here? Had Vincent recovered the photos in the process of killing the boy? Harvey hadn't heard from his lead man in days...

In the back of his mind, though, he knew it couldn't be. This wasn't Vincent's style at all. Too indirect. Too suspenseful. Who could it be, then? And if this wasn't Vincent's doing, where was he and what *was* he doing?

Harvey nervously raised his arm to peer at his watch. Quarter past seven. He figured he might as well call Navio to make reservations. He hurriedly retrieved his cellphone from his golf pants' pocket and dialed the number he found in a nearby pamphlet.

"Thank you for calling the Ritz-Carlton Half Moon Bay Navio, would you like to make a reservation with us?" a voice answered on the other line after two rings.

"Yes," Harvey began hesitantly. "I would, please." His own words made him jolt. When was the last time he had said 'please?'

"May I ask your name, sir? And for when would you like your reservation?"

"My name is Harvey Payton. Reservation for eight o'clock tonight. If there are no available tables, I'm willing to pay—"

"Harvey Payton, you say?" the man interrupted. "Sir, it would appear in our system that you've already reserved a table for two tonight at eight."

Harvey's skin crawled. Someone had reserved a table under his name? "Right. Of course," he began in a trembling tone. "I must have forgotten. Forgive me. I'll be arriving soon."

"We look forward to your company, sir."

Harvey hung up and gently set his phone down on the glass surface of the coffee table. He stared off distantly with widened eyes into the invisible sum of his greatest fears. After all these years, after all the cover-ups, after all the money... The energy. The craft. The patience. And it came to this? This is how it would end? At the mercy of a nameless threat? He leaned forward to rest his elbows on his knees. He pressed the tips of his rigid fingers against one another as he oft did when deep in deliberation.

For the next half hour, he maintained this position, gradually succumbing to wave after wave of the wildest terrors that his uncontrollable imagination could conjure.

At ten till eight, Harvey cautiously raised himself upright. He departed his room and walked back down the long, carpeted hallway to the elevators.

"Back so soon, Mr. Payton?" the same elevator concierge as before asked curiously, perhaps eager to make small talk to earn a tip this time.

"Navio," Harvey said distantly. His eyes couldn't focus on anything. A misty daze had settled over him and refused to evaporate. The bright lights of the elevator disoriented him. When the steel doors opened, he stumbled out less than gracefully. The concierge said something to him, but the words didn't register coherently in his mind.

The next thing he knew, he was standing in the entranceway to the restaurant. An attendant was speaking to him. He reoriented himself best as he could. "Pardon?" he asked.

The attendant shot him a questioning glance before repeating himself. "Are you Mr. Payton?"

Harvey bobbed his head in affirmation.

"Follow me, sir," the attendant said, grabbing two menus and beginning to walk towards a square, two-seater table in the middle of the extravagant, high-ceilinged room.

Harvey seated himself and took the menu as it was handed to him, not fully registering where he was and what he was doing.

"Can I start you off with a beverage of your choice? Some wine? Champagne? Or would you like to wait for your guest to arrive, first?"

Guest. The word sent a chill down Harvey's spine. "I'll wait, thank you," he responded with a shake of his head. He dismissed the attendant with a wave of his hand.

Harvey opened up the menu and pretended to look over the meals but only managed to re-read the name of the first appetizer over and over again. He couldn't concentrate the slightest bit. Every few seconds he would flick his eyes upward to the analog clock hanging on the wall. His ten minutes of patience seemed like an eternity.

His eternity ended, though, at precisely eight o'clock. With his eyes still locked forward, he could sense a sauntering figure brush by him. Harvey's heartbeat quickened as the figure took a seat across from him. It took him a moment to recognize the face, and when he did, his heart abruptly stopped beating entirely.

So many words and thoughts came to mind, but he found himself physically incapable of speech. A softy, raspy groan was all that he could successfully voice.

The vindication of Colton Anders' knowing, azure eyes sapped the warmth from Harvey's being. The Payton patriarch felt hollow, save for the pure terror that huddled in the coldest corner of his soul.

No words Colton could conjure could respectfully justify the gravity of the moment, so he refrained from speaking for quite some time, content with merely gazing into the very soul of the man responsible for so much pain and destruction.

"Surprised to see me?" he finally asked.

"You're..." Harvey began to say. "You're alive."

"Sorry to disappoint."

"How?"

"Clearly, you underestimated me. Death can't take me, Mr. Payton."

"Vincent's dead, isn't he? And now you're here to kill me?"

Colton allowed a wry smile to curve across his thin lips as he slightly shook his head. "No," he answered bluntly.

"What do you want from me, then? What are you going to do?"

"What am *I* going to do? I'm afraid that's not the question you should be asking, Mr. Payton. The real question is: What are *you* going to do? I am, after all, allowing you the freedom to decide your own fate — something you never allowed me."

"Don't play 'God' to me, boy. Don't think you've already won," Harvey snapped abrasively.

Colton, remarkably unperturbed, held his unwavering gaze and maintained his empowering silence for a moment longer. "But I *have* already won, Mr. Payton. All that remains before us now is to decide in which manner you *lose*," he whispered, leaning closer to the table and raising his eyebrows.

Colton stared for several seconds longer as Harvey looked blankly into the distance. Then, Colton quietly dug through his messenger bag to reveal two sets of documents. One, Harvey recognized immediately: the photographs he had been in search of for more than a decade. He couldn't distinguish the other until further inspection. Colton gently laid them on the table and pushed them towards Harvey.

The photographs weren't much of a surprise, but the other set of documents were: a paternity test — the implications of which he had long since deliberately chosen to forget.

"You have two options," Colton said frankly. "Option one: I give these documents... a *very* high level of publicity. You rot away in a prison cell for the rest of your miserable life. Your money will be stripped from you. Your family will execrate your very existence. Society will defame you. Everything you have ever worked and fought and lied and killed for will not merely disappear, but turn against you in its entirety to utterly annihilate you... And you lose."

"And option two?" Harvey asked, unimpressed.

"I'm glad you asked," Colton began, casually waving away a waiter who had walked up to their table. "Option two: I keep these papers between you and I."

Harvey raised a curious eyebrow and leaned in closer to the table.

"You make every cent you have to your name appear in the bank account of your daughter so that she can then disperse it as she sees fit to its rightful recipients. Before she even knows of this, though, you'll already have disappeared without the slightest trace."

Harvey cast a sideward glance before settling his gaze back on his adversary.

"Your impromptu evanescence shocks the media. The bureaucrats on the board of your firm will squabble over ownership of your company and its assets. Conspiracies will arise concerning your whereabouts. Eventually, though, the public stops caring... Your family is deeply saddened because you've vanished without a goodbye, but mostly scared because you've left without a reason. Scared that you won't come back. But as the days go on, their fear turns to frustration, and before too long, their frustration mutates into a terrible hatred that consumes their slightest thought of you. This hatred is a blindingly bright but brief flame. It can't be sustained by a mere memory. When eventually your social identity becomes a shadow of a memory, your family, too, will finally forget you... Instead of rotting away in a prison cell the rest of your miserable life, you will wander some long-forgotten land with naught but the clothes on your back and the hairs on your head until dust and age finally break your body once and for all and your soul crumbles to obscurity. Until this anticlimactic demise, a chronic ache will plague your neck from constantly looking over your shoulder. You'll forget how to dream because you'll have to learn to sleep with one eye open. You'll find lonely solace in waking nightmares because, hellish as they are, at least they're an escape from reality. Time and time again, starvation will bring you to the brink of death without ever actually pushing you over the edge. Your malice manifested will have nothing to feed on but your own being until it, too, starves because it has finally hollowed you out to nothing but pure madness... How long do you think you can live like that? Now, logic would advise me against betting in favor of your odds, but some perhaps misguided intuition whispers seductively into my ear that you're just cunning enough to somehow live on, despite your wretched existence," Colton declared. "I can see your certain death, and though it ends far in the future, it begins now. It will be a long and terribly, terribly slow fall. You'll wish for a timely end, but pathetic fear will keep you from actually allowing yourself to die. You'll cling to your miserable life and some illusion of hope even though you'll know in the bottom of your empty, callous heart that yours is not a life worth living anymore. And though your name will be forgotten and you will lose everything without a trace of pride, I already know you'll accept these terms without objection." Colton paused to sear intensely into the swirling voids of Harvey's gray eyes. "Because a legacy lost to oblivion is better than the entirety of society knowing with utter certainty that the great Harvey Payton has been conquered at last."

FORTY-NINE

Harvey followed Colton out of the hotel without a word. He inhaled the crisp dusk air. An eastward breeze carried the scent of the briny Pacific. The summer darkness had nearly finished its descent upon the Western seaboard.

A family of four had gathered around a brick fire pit on an adjacent terrace. As Harvey strode in Colton's wake, he watched with a nostalgic eye as the children —a young boy and an even younger girl — roasted marshmallows over the open flames. Harvey flicked a disapproving gaze over the mother who was occupied with reading a book and wholly unaware of her little girl leaning in a little too close to the fire. The father, too, was tuned out, pausing his business on his laptop to cast a surreptitious glance at another woman.

"Give me your phone," Colton muttered from a few steps ahead.

Harvey's eyes hardened upon averting his gaze, but he complied without complaint. As they turned a corner, he heard a pained shout from far behind, followed by one of fear. Then, wailing.

When they arrived at a windowless navy van, he was ushered through the open side door. A cloth sack ripe with the stink of sweat and dried blood was promptly slid over his head by someone already sitting in the driver's seat. He crinkled his nose in disgust and held his breath. He could see nothing, but he kept his gray eyes open nonetheless. He didn't fight when they bound his wrists. He smiled smugly at the effort.

He was seated on what seemed to be a bench in the rear of the vehicle with his back resting against the interior wall. He rolled his shoulders. He was comfortable in his soft lavender polo, though he couldn't enjoy the same feeling of authority he so enjoyed when wearing his million-dollar suit. He hung his head low and waited patiently. He heard the side door opposite him slam shut. He listened to the van engine sputter to life. His filthy world of blackness was set in motion.

His captors said nothing — much to his disappointment. So much to be said, and yet no words dared interfere with the gravity of the moment.

As they rode along in silence, Harvey counted the minutes beneath his breath.

Before too long, he could pick up the all-too-distinctive noise of traffic outside his lonely world of confinement.

Upon counting to the twentieth minute, he slid himself over to the end of his bench closest to the rear of the van. He prodded around blindly with his fingers until he found a thick steel cable that diagonally attached the bench to the wall of the vehicle. He clutched it firmly with both hands.

Minutes later, the van took a hard right. He would have likely fallen off his seat if not for his hold on the cable. He listened as the tires screeched unpleasantly, grinding against the asphalt. He heard his captors grumbling to each other, though he could not make out their words. He could hear the engine working harder as his world began moving faster and faster. He gripped the cable as tightly as he could.

It was time.

A crippling force collided hard with the front right side of the van. A shockwave forced Harvey backwards into the wall that was rapidly falling away behind him. His world turned upside down. And again. And again. Utter silence. He passed into a void.

His mind grasped hopelessly at memories. Eventually, one fell into the clutches of his subconscious.

He found himself in his office — not his current office, but rather one that he had occupied thirteen years ago. He found someone else in his office, too — someone who had been snooping through his paperwork while he had been out. She was surprised to see him return so soon.

"What are you doing, my dear?" Harvey whispered from the doorway, his tone tinged with malevolent tenderness. When she shrank at the sight of him, he edged nearer.

She cast frightened eyes upon him and clutched a set of paper-clipped documents. "What is this?" she asked him, terrified, wounded, angry, and confused. Her unbridled emotions made her French accent more evident than usual. "Ghost companies? Shell accounts? Smuggling? Fraud?"

"They're nothing, Mona," he reached out to her as he closed the distance between them. "Put them down. Come here, my love."

"Under your order, funds from the company — *our* company — found their way to the accounts of people overseas. Bad people. Terrorists. That's not *nothing*, Harvey."

He did not refute her accusations. When he approached her, she did not cower away. He met her fiery gaze. They stared into each other's eyes for a long while.

Eventually, her expression softened. Her lips quivered. Tears welled up in her brown eyes. With a pained gasp, she raised a trembling finger to his face to tenderly caress the stubble on his cheek.

He took her hand in his. The thought of her touch pleased him. So soft. So smooth. So... delicate.

It seemed as though time froze for a long moment. A wordless calm came to replace the thick tension, but only briefly. He reached for her head in an instant.

She didn't have time to voice a yell before he slammed her face into his walnut desk. The blood gushed from her crushed nose first, staining the very papers she had held in her delicate fingers only moments ago. With a fistful of her sable hair, he raised her head from the wood before slamming it down even harder a second time. And then a third time. And then a fourth. And then once more.

When he had finished, he allowed her lifeless body to crumple at his feet. He ignored the cold stare of the corpse as he wiped his bloodied hands against his suit jacket. The stain would disappear, but the memory would not. It would not be a memory to forget; he had emerged victorious, after all. Yes, the blood would always remind him. The blood that had now seeped into the fibers of his suit. The blood that had now seeped into the fibers of his being.

His mind flashed. He blinked his eyes, awakening to the rubble in which he now found himself amid. The cloth sack must have fallen off his head, because he could now see his surroundings. As it all registered, the first thought that came to mind was the longing to be wearing his million-dollar suit now, at this moment of new conquest.

He found a jagged piece of metal protruding through the side of the van and heaved his body over to it. He was sore but uninjured, for the most part. He cut the zip-tie that bound his wrists. Now freed, he inspected the interior damage of the collision.

The lighting was very faint, but Harvey could see that the van was on its side. Two motionless figures sat buckled in their sideways seats at the front of the van. Blood from Colton's limp head dripped onto the body of his companion in the driver's seat. The shattered glass of what used to be the windshield and right passenger window were littered across the body of the driver.

Suddenly, the rear doors of the van were flung open. After a moment of allowing his eyes to adjust, Harvey could make out four masked figures standing before him.

"Street cameras," one of them grunted, tossing a matching ski mask at Harvey's feet.

Harvey bent down to pick up the mask, weary of putting something else over his head again. He did so anyway, despite his reservations, and stepped out of the van and onto the asphalt of the intersection. He looked around. They were underneath an abandoned overpass in what appeared to be the inner city of San Francisco. Only a cluster of vagabonds, mesmerized by what was going on, stood grouped together on the sidewalk.

"Check if they're alive," Harvey ordered. Two of his men ran around to the front side of the vehicle to retrieve the driver and passenger from the wreckage. Another handed him a handgun. He kept a watchful eye on his destitute observers.

"Driver's alive but unconscious," a voice called out a moment later.

"Passenger, too," another added.

"Good," Harvey said. "Take them."

FIFTY

16 JUNE, 2012

Emma threw her cellphone as hard as she could across the living room. It collided with a lamp, causing an unpleasant crash as the light hit the floor. Ceramic shards littered the family's treasured, 17th century Persian silk rug that covered almost the entirety of the massive room's mahogany floor. Emma's newly broken phone was scattered amongst the rubble.

She was beside herself with unprecedented fury. She stood utterly motionless save for the deep rise and fall of her chest as she looked upon what she had just done.

Her mother was having tea with neighborhood 'friends.' Lance was 'in a meeting.' None of her phone calls to her father were going through; she couldn't even reach his voice mail. She had heard nothing from Jeremy. She didn't know if Colton was alive. She was completely and hopelessly alone.

At this point, she teetered dangerously on the brim of absolute insanity. She had still not recovered in the slightest from the complete reversal her life had thrown at her. She had tried curbing her stress by painting, but the imagination of her mind's eye had run dry, making room only for a cloud of ambiguity and terrified anticipation that became increasingly dense with each passing day.

She suddenly collapsed, aiming to land on the daybed behind

her, but misjudged and landed hard on the Persian rug instead. She ignored the immense pain in her head that followed and quickly drifted into unconsciousness.

When she opened her eyes, a cloudless, cyan sky took up her entire field of vision. She blinked, orienting herself to the unfamiliar daylight. A funny sensation tickled her skin. She rolled her fingers, clutching at what felt like blades of grass. She swept her arms out at her sides as if they hadn't been used in years. The back of her hand brushed against a tall stalk of something jutting up from the grass. She grasped the stalk and plucked it from its roots. She brought it before her face and flicked her eyes away from the azure abyss to behold what she bore in her gentle fingers: a meadow rose.

She examined its features with a curious gaze. The vividly surreal shades of pink and violet surpassed the intensity of any other colors she had ever before looked upon. Rimmed with over two dozen petals, the welcoming flower appeared to reach out in every direction. Under the brilliantly radiant sun, the golden stamens tenderly swayed to and fro in the light breeze. She lifted the rose to her nose and inhaled its sweet scent.

Emma. The zephyr breathed her name over the distant hills and across the sea of viridescent green. She sat up carefully and listened to the whispering meadow. She found herself alone in a deep, lush valley surrounded by a ring of faraway mountains that pierced the firmament with their soaring peaks.

Emma. She turned her head at the sound of her name and noticed a lone tree in the distance. Its looming branches seemed to stretch for miles in the emptiness of the grassy valley. She noticed a lone figure, diminutive in comparison to the colossal trunk of the great tree it stood beside.

Emma. Her name lightly reverberated across the paddock once more. This time, it seemed to come directly from the tree. She rose to her feet and took a step towards the sweeping branches. She carried her vibrant flower at her side with a tender touch.

As she neared the tree, the shadowy silhouette gradually elucidated into a man who stood with his back to her. His hands sat resolutely upon his hips. His long hair billowed in the light breeze. A sudden flash of movement alerted Emma, though the man remained standing stationary. She took notice of a smaller figure running around the man's knees. It was a young boy.

Euphoric, innocent laughter filled the void of the hollow valley. She could feel the forgotten sense of her own joy dance in the irises of her widened, anxious eyes. A light, hopeful smile played upon her attenuated lips.

All at once, though, the sound of laughter faded away. As Emma strode toward the tree, she watched as the boy looked towards her curiously. He was too small and too far away, though, for her to make out the details of his youthful face. She hurried her pace, but the tree remained distant. The boy remained unrecognizable. Even as she broke into an anxious run, she could get no nearer.

Hopelessly, she watched as the child drifted further and further out of sight. The man began to shrink in perspective as well. As he slowly half-turned his head to almost look at her, she could just barely catch the roughly hewn features of his jaw before he, too, was suddenly gone from her view. When he vanished, the sky flashed brightly, forcing Emma to shut her eyes. When she reopened them, she saw that the great tree had disappeared as well.

She lifted the meadow rose before her face to watch as the petals began to break off one by one. She observed curiously as they floated away from her, carried away by an eastward breeze, trailing whimsically through the aromatic air towards the faraway mountains.

She looked back at the meadow rose to see that one last petal still clung obstinately to the stalk. It fluttered unconfidently in the light wind, threatening at any moment to break away from its foundation to follow its adventurous counterparts.

The breeze intensified and the petal wavered more uncontrollably than ever. Just as it appeared as if it would break off, Emma's world flashed again and then went black.

She opened her eyes. She blinked, dazed and confused. Then she saw him. At first, she couldn't summon the words to her mouth. The anger had momentarily ceased, though she could still feel the embers of rage lightly burning in the bottom of her heart, threatening to alight in a blaze at the slightest provoking. She swallowed, struggling to find her voice. "Where is he?" she asked weakly, barely able to hear herself speak.

Harvey Payton, crouching down beside her, gently caressed her graceful cheek. He raised a gray eyebrow, pretending that he didn't understand.

"Colton," Emma said, her strength and anger returning. She sat up. Harvey retracted his hand, but did not otherwise move. "Where's Colton?"

At first, Emma could gather nothing from her father's empty gray stare. When he triumphantly smirked, though, a flash lit up his eyes with wordless stories. In an instant, she decided the worst of her fears had come to pass.

Sensing her sudden realization, Harvey twisted his sneering mouth open to compound the effect. "He's dead."

With those words, all traces of hope finally disappeared beyond the horizon of Emma's foreseeable future. A catastrophic, relentless darkness settled over her lonely world, very eager to consume her. She was tired, after all. So tired of being strong. Desperation seized her in her weakness.

And so it wasn't a thought that her desperate fury had suddenly given rise to, but an impulse. In an instant, she yielded to her swelling rage and did all that she felt she still had the power to do: harden her expression and wrap her wiry fingers around her father's throat.

ACKNOWLEDGEMENTS

All my life I've been a creator, viscerally shifting from one medium of creation to the other. From art, to music, to Legos, websites, and now my first novel, I've always had a relentless supply of inspiration and resources at my fingertips, and I have my parents alone to thank for that. Through constant encouragement and unceasing, genuine interest, they have meticulously crafted me into the storyteller I am today, and to say that I will be forever grateful is a dramatic understatement. Of course, I never could have even gotten off the ground with *Chasing Oblivion* if not for Claire Chewning, who not only inspired me to finally put pen to paper, but kept me at it without allowing me to lose interest and meander onto my next project prematurely – as I am hopelessly guilty of doing. But I would not have the love I have for a good story today if not for my second grade teacher, who I will always lovingly call Ms. A, and I would not have the deep appreciation I have for literature today if not for the English teacher I had at the end of my primary school career – Mr. Fallon. I believe there is nothing more engrossing, soul-gripping, motivating, or haunting than a story with a message, and I would have no story or message to tell if not for these exceptional educators and role models. And finally, for being the gracious individuals to first read my story and critique my craft, I thank friends old and new alike: Will Evans, Hannah Palmerton, Samuel Gerstemeier, Brent Shenton, and – last but never least – my crazy brother Cleyton.

AUTHOR'S NOTE

I remember I didn't take *Chasing Oblivion* seriously until after I was five chapters in. I vividly recall deciding for some reason that five chapters was the point of no return. If I could get that far, I could finish all fifty. I was a senior in high school when I crossed this five-chapter threshold, and I was starting out my first year of college when I finished the fiftieth. It took one more year to go back and polish everything up. Some will tell you that writing the beginning of a story is fun and that the hard part is keeping it going. Others will say that a good foundation is difficult to achieve, but it keeps everything else coming naturally. I say they're both right, and they're both wrong. Everything is hard. Nothing worth doing is easy. Little offers more potential and little is more intimidating than a blank sheet of paper. With a project such as this, I could only take it word by word. I decided where I was going while I was moving, and only looked back after the fact. It kept the anticipation and second thoughts to a minimum while I wrote. And looking back now, I can honestly say I didn't expect the story to end up where it ended up. I didn't intend to write a tragedy. But I'm very pleased with the result. I didn't set out writing this story with a sequel in mind, but at this point I've decided at least one more entry in the series is necessary. So rest assured that this is not the end, but only the beginning. And in the beginning, you may anticipate the end, but you can never know exactly what the end will bring.

ABOUT THE AUTHOR

   Evan Grinde is a twenty-year-old enthusiast of life whose
restlessness has driven him into the arms of everything from
fly-fishing to computer programming. Like the protagonist of
this novel, Evan also enjoys rock-climbing and getting lost
outside. Beyond fish, computers, rocks, and the outdoors,
Evan has two black belts in the martial arts and likes to tickle
the ivories of his family's piano. Evan's latest project has
initiated him as one of Virginia's youngest entrepreneurs.
Through his mission-aligned startup Evan hopes to set a new
standard for responsible business practices and tell the
stories of progressive nonprofits, startups, and fellow artists.
To learn more about Evan, his latest project, and news on the
release of his next novel, visit www.QuantumRush.com.

Made in the USA
Charleston, SC
30 January 2014